HUMANS, BOW DOWN

Also by James Patterson

A list of more titles by James Patterson
is printed at the back of this book

HUMANS, BOW DOWN

JAMES PATTERSON

& Emily Raymond
With Jill Dembowski
Illustrations by Alexander Ovchinnikov

CENTURY

1 3 5 7 9 10 8 6 4 2

Century
20 Vauxhall Bridge Road
London SW1V 2SA

Century is part of the Penguin Random House group of companies
whose addresses can be found at global.penguinrandomhouse.com.

Penguin
Random House
UK

First published by Century in 2017

www.penguin.co.uk

A CIP catalogue record for this book is available from the British Library.

ISBN 9781780895499
ISBN 9781780895505 (export edition)

Printed and bound by Clays Ltd, St Ives plc

Penguin Random House is committed to a sustainable future
for our business, our readers and our planet. This book is made
from Forest Stewardship Council® certified paper.

PART ONE

CHAPTER 1

BE WARNED. *YOU*. Yes, I'm talking to you. Reading a treasonous book or digital tract like this one is punishable by hanging. That's if you're one of the few left who even knows how to read.

Can you read, friend? I know, I know, it's a stupid question. Or maybe a test? Maybe a trap?

Listen very carefully. It's fair to say that there's not much hope anymore—not for you, and definitely not for a poor wretch from the Reserve like me.

The joke on the food lines at the Res is that they're measuring us all for body bags. But that's being way too cheery. It'll be mass graves at best.

I'm just saying...look around, and what do *you* see?

Trash piled high as a Colorado snowdrift in January, smelling like mid-July in Bangkok, or Los Angeles, or Paris. A jagged junk heap of broken pallets and busted-up furniture: baby cribs and cradles, smashed door frames, windows and mirrors. A greasy, toothless hag—the former Mrs. Cullen—who captures stray cats (one of them mine) and boils them in soup.

Welcome to the Reserve, where the wind whistling up the mountain feels cold even in the summer. Where the sky's the only clean thing there is.

There's nothing to do up here. There aren't any jobs, and there's no good soil to farm. It's like living in a giant, open-air, high-altitude prison.

Babies die in childbirth every day—some in the gutters, or in abandoned cars, or on filthy mattresses in dark and tiny rooms. The kids who do survive grow up hungry, bitter, and desperate. Most people croak before they're fifty, and if they don't, they wish they did.

There's a rumor blowing in the foul winds that the government's going to come out here and raze this mountain ghetto to the ground, exterminating every man, woman, and child.

I believe it. That's the truth, not just a filthy rumor. Actually, I know it's true. I know things that you don't. Be patient. I'm going to tell you everything, all the sordid details.

But try walking around with the weight of that knowledge on your shoulders: *Pretty soon, we'll all be dead. Exterminated. Annihilated. Massacred.*

And there's not a thing we can do about it but wait.

Maybe that's why I stole a motorcycle that night. Because what difference did it make?

Besides, I needed transportation. I was going to see my family, such as they are. Misfits. Jailbirds.

So power on, power up. Release the clutch slowly and gas it at the same time, easy, easy, not too much—now enjoy the ride!

I jerk forward, dizzy on gasoline fumes and hopped up on adrenaline, feeling the power of the bike rattling between my legs. I squeeze the clutch again, shift into second...and stall out.

My best friend in this hellhole's on a Yamaha up the road, a good fifty yards ahead. Even from here, I can hear him groan and laugh at me.

"Girl, you're on *fire.* You almost made it to second gear this time," Double Eight (I call him Dubs) yells over his shoulder.

I flip him off, then bend down to adjust my headlight, which is sagging toward the ground. Our motorcycles are boneyard specials: mismatched rusted parts held together by bolts and luck. We're *supposed* to be learning how to fix them in the Reserve Trade School.

Usually we just skip dumb-dumb school. But today... well, *today* we decided to steal the classroom materials.

But I've never driven anything more powerful than a bicycle before, because it's against the law.

I kick piles of trash out of the way, trying to clear a smoother path for take-off. Dubs circles back and glides to a stop next to me.

"You gotta relaaaax," he says. "Otherwise we're going to have to put the training wheels back on." Dubs grins like the lovable fool he is and revs the motor. "Ready or not, here goes nothing!" he yells.

Clutch, throttle, gas...

"The road to prison waits for no man," he crows, "or

5

woman." He peels away first, leaving a fat black streak on the pavement, a puff of dark smoke in the air. "Yeeeeehaw!"

There's Dubs for you. He could be the poster boy for everything the ruling Hu-Bots say is wrong with the human race. He looks like a born thug: dirty, scarred, missing about six teeth. His jokes are crude. And he's about as wild and crazy as they come.

It wasn't *my* idea to steal the bikes, is what I'm saying.

"Loosen up, Six," I say to myself. We all just go by the first few numbers of our IDs, since they're a bitch to remember. Once upon a time, I had a real name. No one calls me by it anymore.

Power on, power up. Clutch, shift, gas, clutch, shift...
You're going to see your family today. Yahoo!

I hear the choking cough of the engine and I tense, but then I ease up and give that baby a little more gas. The bike bucks beneath me and roars to life, and suddenly I'm riding.

Second gear, then a smooth upshift to third. Fourth.

The wind whistles in my ears and brings actual tears to my eyes. The slums of the Reserve start to recede in my rearview.

The bike's a Yamaha R6, a dinosaur compared with what they've got in the City—what used to be Denver, Colorado. But pushing 90, 120, 130, miles an hour down a winding mountain road, it feels like flying. And if it means I end up in prison or as smear on the highway, at least I'll have had this moment.

I'll know what it felt like to be alive.

At least, for one bright and shining morning, I'll be able to say I was free.

CHAPTER 2

AT THE EDGE of the mountain, just before the highway dips down and splinters into the smaller streets of the City, I skid to a stop next to Dubs.

Below us, the buildings shine and the lights glitter tantalizingly. I take a deep breath. Here — unlike on the Reserve — the air's warm and clean.

"We're gonna be early," Dubs says.

I nod — I know. We've got places to go and my family to see, but I don't want to think about that yet. Instead I think, *What if we could live* here, *instead of high up on the mountain, in a stew of human filth? What would life be like in this city?*

The Hu-Bots would never let that happen, of course. They think we're hopeless savages. And, with our sunburned skin and our holey, dirty clothes — well, we look the part. I drag my fingers through my hair, but that can only take a girl so far.

"Whaddya say?" Dubs asks. "Wanna go stink the place up?"

I rev the engine. "Yeah," I say. "Let's get us some trouble."

We roll into the City—not Denver now, never Denver anymore, because lowly *humans* named it that—and ditch the bikes on a back street before a robot cop can bust us for illegal operation and theft of a motor vehicle.

And to think: we humans *created* this world. We designed and built it all—including the robots that nearly destroyed us and want to finish the job soon.

On foot, we head toward the city center. Dubs gnaws on a bug bar, offers me a bite. "Some delicious, nutritious insect protein for you?" he asks.

"No, thanks." Our rations include a half dozen bars a week, but I don't eat food made from cricket flour unless I'm truly desperate.

Everything's so perfect in the City that it's creepy. You might call it *inhuman*.

As Dubs and I approach downtown, we start to hear it: the white noise, the hum of a city whose residents run on electric current. *The Bot buzz:* it makes the hairs on the back of my neck stand at attention.

Today the low drone seems more ominous than usual. Like maybe, if I listen hard enough, I'll be able to make out whispered words, something like *Diehumansdie*.

I shake my head. I've got to stop thinking these morbid, depressing-as-hell thoughts.

Dubs breaks a branch off a tree and begins whacking the heads off rose bushes dotting a church lawn. Through a stained-glass window, I can see rows of Hu-Bots, their heads bowed, reciting the prayers of my ancestors.

Now that's something I'll never understand. My people used to pray to the gods they believed made them: *Our Father, who art in Heaven,* etc. But *we made the Bots.*

First we built regular Bots, with limited, programmable powers of reason. They could cook, clean, babysit, I guess. Simple, functionary stuff.

But that wasn't enough for us. We wanted robots that could think for themselves. That were smarter, stronger, faster than we were. So we created the Hu-Bots.

And that was our fatal mistake.

Dubs bats a bright-pink rose so hard, it crashes against the window of the church. He lifts his arms up to the sky. "*We built you! I* am your god!" he bellows.

"Dubs!" I hiss. "Don't."

Thankfully, the "parishioners" are too devout to avert

their eyes from the pulpit. That's another thing I don't think I'll ever understand: the Hu-Bots *loathe* humans, and yet they imitate pretty much everything about our culture.

"I just don't like this place," I say. But what I mean is: *We don't belong here, and I hate that.* Everywhere I look, I see the remnants of human creativity, of our ingenuity, of our past.

If only I could do something—*anything*—to make it different.

We round the corner and enter a busy avenue lined with expensive boutiques and five-star restaurants. Very glitzy.

Even if Dubs and I had a plateful of money, we couldn't go into these places. They're *Bot only.*

I grit my teeth as we pass a crowded bistro and the smell of seared meat rolls out the open door. I don't care about being able to buy fancy clothes, but I'd kill to eat a *steak* sometime. I know I've had one before, but I can't remember what it tastes like.

Tall, willowy Hu-Bots and shorter, stockier Bots stream by us on the sidewalk as we stand there, *drooling.* The Hu-Bots are all elegantly dressed, and their faces are too perfect looking—like high-end mannequins given the breath of life. With their large, clear eyes, high cheekbones, and flawlessly smooth bioskin, they look distantly related to each other.

Which, in a way, they are. I mean, synthetic polymer skeletons do all come from the same factory, right?

I peer through the steak house window. A Hu-Bot—a blue-eyed, silver-haired female sporting the metallic choker worn by all Hu-Bots—delicately chews her meat.

"I mean, she—it—doesn't even *need* that protein," Dubs moans.

He's right. Sometime in the past few years, Hu-Bots engineered themselves to eat, simply for pleasure. (And yeah, that means they crap, too. I don't understand the biomechanical details, and I don't want to.) They make themselves out to be superior because their emotions aren't messy and "savage," like ours, but it's apparently totally civilized for them to cram their gullets with lobster, pizza, and milk shakes just because they taste good.

Meanwhile we humans, who do *not* run on batteries or

electric current or nanotechnology, survive on bug bars and mildewed bread and the gristly bones of wild turkeys.

"Maybe we should just go over to HCF," I say, "where we belong."

In the shadow of the gilt and glitter of the promenade is the HCF, or Human Charging Facility. It's the only part of the City where we humans can actually enter a restaurant. Even the *Reformed* humans—the ones who live in the City and serve our robot masters—have to do their business in this biological ghetto.

It's cramped and grungy over there, with big, ugly signs for H-RR (restrooms), H-L (lodging), and H-E (eats).

I keep staring at that juicy T-bone. "We're going to go there with *what money?*" I pat my empty pockets.

"*Humans!*" I jump at the sudden electronic call of a Bot-cop. It's hard not to be jittery when you're basically breaking a law just by breathing.

CHAPTER 3

"HUMANS!" IT SAYS again. It sounds like *hoo-mons*. "Papers."

The Bot-cop is rolling toward us, holding out a gloved, robotic hand. What an ass. A hard-ass, right?

Papers are the key to the kingdom, a pass to get around the City. My papers list the nine-digit number I was assigned—easier than names for the Bots to track—and identify me as a Reserver, and no, I don't have them on me. Why carry around something that identifies me as the lowest of the low?

Dubs finally wrenches his eyes away from the steak and turns to me. "Got yours?" he whispers.

"What do you think?" I mutter. "You?"

He grins. "Oh jeez, I used mine as toilet paper."

And *that's* all that needs to be said. *Time to get scarce.*

We run toward the market, which is always crawling with

the Reformers—essentially human slaves—doing the weekly shopping for their robot overlords. Maybe we'll be able to blend in, but I doubt it.

At the corner, Dubs and I split and run in opposite directions. It takes the Bot-cop a second to pick a target. When it looks like he's going for Dubs, I slow a little.

"Yo, Sparky," I taunt the Bot—because Dubs might be a year older, but I'm a whole lot faster.

The Bot-cop hesitates again. Then it switches course and motors after me. I dive into the crowd of Reformed humans, shoving my way past the dead-eyed workers of the City. I hunch my shoulders and turn my gait into a meek little shuffle, and suddenly the Bot can't pick me out of the crowd.

The human slaves shoot me uneasy looks; *they* know I'm not one of them, and they don't want to touch me. Honestly, I can't totally blame them.

When I'm pretty sure I've lost the Bot-cops, I straighten up, weave through the stalls, and let out a loud, reckless whistle. Dubs doesn't whistle back, but he's got to be around here somewhere.

Then, in the distance, I hear the trumpeting blare of horns. I can't hold back a shiver.

I clamp my mouth shut as the caravan rounds the corner. Ten black stretch limos inch forward slowly, ominously, their paint gleaming and their chrome blindingly bright. A rumor ripples through the crowd like a cold breeze: it's MosesKhan, commander of the police and army. That pig.

When the limos stop in the center of the market square,

CHAPTER 4

A HUSH FALLS over the crowd. There's always a pause when a Hu-Bot gives that order, a heavy, dangerous, messed-up silence. Following the order means humiliation. It's beyond wrong—it's an abomination. I want to cry out to all my fellow humans: *Grab a brick from the street and pick it up. Don't bow down—FIGHT!*

But I'm no leader. I'm a Rezzie loser, and a *girl* at that. No one's going to listen to me, right?

"HUMANS, BOW DOWN!"

I hear the rustle of clothing as people start to bend. My teeth are clenched, my fists balled at my sides, but if I stand much longer, there's going to be a scene.

Not that Hu-Bots engage in such viciousness—they're *evolved!* That's what they program the Bot-cops for, and the market is now crawling with those dutiful, murderous little workers.

I finally drop down, one leg at a time, and join my species on the cobblestones. The white brick digs into my skin through the thin fabric of my pants. But I'm glad it hurts. It *should* hurt to grovel.

The Bot brigade surges forward to crack down on "dissenters"—in this case, a frail, white-haired woman who can't seem to bend her knees. You don't see many old-timers these days, maybe because their hearts aren't strong enough to be repeatedly broken. She's thin and trembling. Something about her makes me think of my own mother.

Maybe it's the faded red purse she's clutching to her chest. My mom had a purse like that. I think so.

The loudspeaker voice chants, **"BOW DOWN, BOW DOWN, BOW DOWN,"** in an increasingly urgent loop. The woman is struggling desperately, trying to bend her old bones down to the bricks.

I stare at the ground when I hear the first crack of their billy clubs. I hear her cry out. Bile rises in my throat.

The Bots aren't advanced enough to understand pain — or mercy. They're just rotely following orders. That's what makes it maddening.

But what about the Hu-Bots in those shiny cars? The so-called intelligent machines, supposedly more ethical, moral, and sane? *That's* who's giving the cold-blooded orders.

Each time I hear the old woman moan, the white bricks blur in my vision. *Don't let this happen, Six!* I tell myself I can tackle a Bot. Or throw myself between the old woman and the clubs. But fear holds me back, holds me down.

I am ... so fucking ashamed of myself.

It's him! The door to the first limo opens, and the Hu-Bot commander emerges. MosesKhan is close to seven feet tall, with eyes cold and black as outer space.

Those arrogant, merciless eyes sweep the crowd, and everyone bows so low, their tonsils practically rub the pavement.

"*Humans.*" He spits out a comment. "In the posture that befits their base nature." Then, with one last withering look at the prostrate crowd, MosesKhan climbs back into his limousine.

When I finally rise, I find I've bitten almost all the way through my lip. The last of the limos is pulling away. The elderly woman lies motionless on the cobblestones. Her legs are twisted beneath her. Purple bruises have appeared on her arms and face. She's weeping.

I hold my hand out to her, and when she reaches for it, her grip is firm and leathery.

"What are you doing?" It's Dubs, appearing out of nowhere.

"Something," I say.

He shakes his head. "Something idiotic."

"My purth...," the woman lisps through swollen lips. She spits a mouthful of blood—and a busted incisor. "Has my paperth."

"We'll find it," I assure her, sweeping the ground with my eyes.

"Thank you, dear," she whispers. "You're brave."

I cringe, knowing how much of a coward I am.

"Yo, Sixie," Dubs says. "Time to split." He points, and I see that the Bot-cop who hassled us earlier is back—along with two of his buddies.

I hesitate over the poor old woman, but Dubs grabs the collar of my shirt in one of his meaty fists. "Come on, I'm not letting you get us killed. Not today. Maybe next time." He shoots a glance at the old woman. "Sorry, lady."

CHAPTER 5

WE'RE RUNNING AT top speed down the narrow back alleys behind trendsetting restaurants and dress shops. Not just to get away from the Bots, but because we've got to make it across the City in less than ten minutes.

Now comes the *real* reason I stole the bike. The real reason we're here. It's the last Tuesday of the month: *viewing day at the city prison.*

By the time we get to the quadrant, it's 3:56. Late. The street in front of the Plexiglas gate is already teeming with desperate humans.

"No way we'll make it all the way up there," I say. *"Damn it."*

Dubs squints at me like, *Is that a challenge?*

The next thing I know, he's got his elbows out, head down, and we're plowing through the crowd. He's like a steamroller on legs—and me, I just hold on, rushing along for the ride.

We make it up to the front with half a minute to spare. The crowd is rowdy, anxious, pushing into us. Most of them are Reformed, but I spot a few Rezzies. They're the ones with the crazed eyes and the missing teeth.

A surge in the crowd smashes me against the Plexiglas. It's slick with other people's sweat.

"Back off," Dubs shouts at the crowd. "Don't touch me, dude!" He balls his fists like he's going to start swinging. He might just do that.

But right then the gong sounds, and we, along with the rest of the humans, turn to face the front.

At four o'clock on the dot, the prisoners come into the square. Clockwork, sick clockwork.

Everyone is trying to get the best view possible, trying to find their family members. Skinny arms wave frantically. Desperate voices cry out prisoners' numbers.

Suddenly, I glimpse my sister, and it's like a punch to the guts. Martha's cheeks are hollow. She seems to have shrunk inches just from last month. She's in the second row, maybe ten feet to my right. When our eyes lock, hers crinkle at the corners, a look of joy that hurts so bad, I almost have to turn away.

I don't see my brother yet — *It's harder when the other person isn't looking for you.*

"*There.*" Dubs nudges me. Apart from his cracked-up dad, his whole family died in the war. He's just here for moral support.

There. But is that really him? Every time I come here, my brother looks older. His hair's going gray; his lips and skin match it. He's how old — twenty-seven? Twenty-eight, at most?

The loudspeaker crackles. "CONSPIRACY, CURFEW VIOLATION, MOTOR VEHICLE OPERATION, THEFT..."

These are the visiting rights: the "privilege" to stare at our loved ones for thirty minutes while their so-called crimes are read aloud. We listen to the lies and witness how they've suffered. It's a silent trial, and they are convicted again and again.

"...LACK OF PROPER IDENTIFICATION PAPERS, TRUANCY, ASSAULT..."

The prisoners stand still in their red jumpsuits. Red, to remind us of the blood that flowed in the streets during the three days of the Great War.

Three days—that was all it took to almost completely wipe out our species.

My brother's eyes move over the crowd. "Hey!" I shout, useless as it is. He knows I'm here—I've come every month for six years—but his eyes skip right over my face.

The half hour goes so fast—and I can't let it end like this. Not today. Today, after all this time, he's going to see me.

"HEY!" I yell, louder this time.

"Hey!" Dubs echoes beside me. He cups his hands. *"Fifteen!"*

It's 4:27. The Bot guards are shifting, getting ready to pull the plug on this miserable sideshow.

"Goddammit, Ricky, *look at me!*" I slam my fist against the glass.

My sister puts her hand up. To stop me, or to gesture to my brother, or to wave hello. I don't know. It doesn't matter. She *moves*, and the Bots charge her.

"Nooo!" I shriek, even as the first Bot-cop slugs her across the face. Martha crumples to one side, but her fall is stopped by another cop's fist.

My screams ring out over the crowd as my sister slumps to the ground. I'm pounding on the glass.

One of the Bot-cops starts dragging her away, toward a windowless white building. *Where are they taking her? What's going to happen?* I'm still slamming my body against the viewing window, and so is Dubs. I'm bellowing with rage.

That's when my brother finally looks at me.

My face is crumpled with emotion, but his is stony. Ricky's eyes are hard and filled with hate. *I don't understand*

24

it, and it just about cracks my heart open. My brother—Fifteen—*Ricky*—shakes his head once, slowly, before the doors close him back inside. I can read his lips. *Fuck you, traitor.*

Just like that, my family is gone again. I feel like crying—but I don't cry. Not ever.

CHAPTER 6

"SIXIE, C'MON GIRL, we've got to get out of here!"

For once, Dubs is talking sense. He knows I could pound on this unforgiving Plexiglas until sundown. Or worse: I could get up and jump the next Bot-cop we see, just as a matter of principle, just because I *want* a beating.

"Come on, you gotta run," he says, holding out his hand, hauling me up, "run like you just stole an old lady's pocketbook!"

I wipe my nose and face. There's an ache in my stomach that's more than hunger. It's fear and desperation. My brother looked like he wanted to kill me, and my sister — being pummeled and hauled away. There's nothing I can do to stop any of this.

"Hey, let's go get some food," Dubs says. He can always shift gears like that.

"We don't have any money, remember?"

He shrugs. "Hold that thought, pretty lady. That might not be the case anymore."

I shoot him a look, but his eyes skitter away. Whatever he's up to, he's not sharing it.

We take the back streets away from the prison. Even here, everything gleams. There's no litter, no graffiti—no sign of life. Just sterile buildings, mirrored windows, and that low, Bot drone.

I run my hand along the glass face of an apartment complex and smile grimly at the greasy streak I leave behind. My human stain.

"Or we could catch a flick," Dubs says, too casually.

I give him a sidelong look. The only *flicks* shown anymore are the Killer Films. I don't know if I can handle one of those right now. The last time I saw a Killer, I bit my tongue to a pulp, damn near ground my molars to nubs.

I say, "Depends."

"On whether or not you're a little baby?" he fires back.

I have to laugh—but I slug him one in the arm, too. He doesn't even notice.

I know Dubs needs me to rein him in sometimes, and this might be one of those moments. The problem is, I'm on the edge myself now.

And if there's one thing on the edge—it's Killer Films. I mean, the Hu-Bot Freedom Brigade created them *specifically* to torture humans. Now they can't keep us away. We live for high risk.

"Depends whether you're buyin'," I answer. I know there's no way he's got money.

But here he is, fishing crisp bills out of his pocket. Dubs shakes his head. "You don't want to know," he says.

That's when I put it together. Yeah, I saw him toss that old woman's red purse when he thought I wasn't looking—not that there would have been cash in it. But, as the old woman said, there were *papers*. And Dubs must have taken them, sold them outside the prison.

I get a tight feeling in my chest. It bothers me a lot. But who am I to judge? In a world like ours, you do what you have to do. Sometimes that means stealing from the weak. And sometimes it means watching a movie designed to shock and possibly kill you.

"I'm in," I say. "Let's go die a little."

CHAPTER 7

WHEN DUBS YANKS open the theater door, the stench that wafts out nearly brings me to my knees. It's the smell of sweat and primal fear. I'm regretting this decision already.

But Dubs doesn't even seem to notice the stink—and neither does the rest of the audience: vacant-eyed glue junkies, skinny Reserver wretches, even well-dressed but miserable Reformers.

Yeah, I feel sorry for all of us. I slide into a seat next to my friend. And then I see something that stuns me: *Hu-Bots are in the audience, too.*

The lights dim, and everybody leans forward in their seats. What's coming next is not to be believed.

The movie opens on a plane hijacking, and if this were my first Killer Film, I'd think the vertigo I was experiencing was from the movie itself—the camera twisting and lurching as people tumble out of the tailless jet. But I know my body's reacting to the low-frequency sound spliced in— audio that humans can't hear but can *definitely* feel.

The nausea comes in almost gentle waves, but it builds until it crashes over me like a tsunami. I put my head down between my knees and retch—but my stomach's so empty, there's nothing there.

But when the seven-hertz sound stops and the nausea subsides, that's when the strobes come, flashing so bright and fast that each flare is like a knife. There's a car chase on-screen, but I can barely make out the action. This is much worse than I remember, coming in faster intervals and at a higher wattage, until I feel like I've been nailed to my chair.

But I can't look away.

Really. I physically cannot blink my eyelids or turn my head. My gaze is mercilessly drawn forward—by mind control or magnets or magic, I don't know.

Music comes crashing through the speakers now, a grinding, raging chorus. It's some death-metal band's anthem, looped and distorted and layered. My heart pounds like it's going to burst. I can feel every cell in my body throbbing in some mind-blowing mix of pain and pleasure.

It's the most intense experience I've had in my life. I'm scared and euphoric and sobbing and convulsing, and I know that the only thing I want in this entire world is to stare at this screen forever.

I'm seeing double now, and my ears feel like they're ready to burst. The blood flows fast and hot through my veins. I can't think. All I can do is stare.

And stare and stare and *stare* and—

My gaze is torn from the screen when I'm knocked

sideways by a crushing weight. It's Dubs, and he's off his rocker. His eyes roll back in his head, his tongue's lolling out, and he's flopping against me.

The seizures have started. He might die on me. Right here, right now.

Avoiding his flailing arms, I shove the bandanna he always wears into his mouth. His muscles immediately relax. For a second I breathe a sigh of relief. Then I realize he's passed out.

"Dubs! Wake up!" I manage to slide out from under him, gasping for breath. When I stand, I almost lose my balance again. My arms and legs don't seem to understand the signals from my brain.

And it's only going to get worse. We have to get the hell out of here. *Now.*

But how do I get Dubs out?

The people in the row behind me start yelling. I'm blocking their view. I look at them, pleading. "I need help!"

The guy nearest me snorts. Then he starts a chant that gets taken up all around the theater. "Die! Die! Die!" they chant.

I grit my teeth—I should have guessed that would happen. I turn back to Dubs and shake him hard, harder, as hard as I can. I slap his face, but his mouth falls open, slack.

Is he already dead? Did my best friend just die on me?

"Come on, Dubs, wake up!" I yell. "Wake up! Wake the hell up!"

I'm gasping for air. There's a strange, electric whirring in the air, and my whole body starts to hum. My skin begins to burn, and I feel like I'm being cooked from the inside out.

I think that—*but it's so hard to form thoughts.*

I think—

I think we might die here. Me and Dubs.

Then a shriek rips through the air. The film junkies turn toward the back of the theater.

Suddenly there's silence. The movie sound goes off as the projector switches reels.

Dubs has been one-upped: someone else actually *died.* In the back row, a girl no older than I am—fifteen or sixteen— lies spread-eagled across three seats. Her face is turned toward me. Her lifeless eyes stare straight into mine. Her mouth is frozen in a smile. Everyone around her is *clapping*— like she's just given the performance of her life.

Which, in a way, she has.

I slap Dubs one more time, a crazy-hard backhand across the cheek that's either going to wake him up or knock out half his teeth. The movie blares back on, and a huge on-screen explosion thunders through the room, and, whether it's from the triple-digit decibels or my beating, I don't know, but Dubs's eyes click open. I've never been so glad to see some-body's eyes.

"We have to go," I yell, "right now!"

He blinks for another second, then lurches to his feet, leans heavily on my shoulder, mumbles a groggy "Start running."

We're making a choice—to live.

CHAPTER 8

"WHAT ARE YOU, *Reformed?* Get in the car," Dubs snarls. He wipes his nose with the back of his hand, smearing blood all over his cheek. His breath comes in harsh, wheezing gasps, and his eyes look crazy, like big black pinwheels.

I say, "Whoa—" And I stop there, because I can hardly believe what he's done this time.

Still shaking from his seizure and pretty much looking like he got run over by a Bot tank, he's nevertheless managed to wedge himself into the driver's seat of an absolutely *beautiful* T-top Corvette parked around the corner from the theater.

He slaps the passenger seat—hard. *"Get in,"* he commands.

Now, I don't want to get on Dubs's bad side, but this seems crazy, even for him. For one, this is a Hu-Bot car, parked in full view of a dozen street cams. For another, he's in *no* shape to drive.

"Do you even know how many years in prison you're

looking at?" I shout. "Twenty, minimum. Judge takes one look at your ugly mug: *thirty.*"

Dubs works up a loogie and hawks it out the car window. It lands near my feet—*charming.* "You were fine with taking the Yamaha this morning," he points out.

"Those were *shop bikes!* No one gives a damn about crimes on the Reserve."

"You gotta feel this leather, though," Dubs says, giving the cushions a loving caress. "These seats must be made out of . . . baby's skin."

"You're sick," I tell him, for what's probably the millionth time. "*And* you're insane."

"This car has a keyless start, and it was unlocked," Dubs points out. "It's basically begging us to steal it. *C'mon, Dubs and Sixie, steal me, pretty please.*"

I run my hand over the smooth, cool surface of the hood, where the metal comes to a point. It's a brand-new replica of a classic vintage model: brushed silver, gleaming, as streamlined as a bullet. This car is worth more than our *lives.*

"You scared, little Sixie?" he whispers.

"No," I say. "I'm *not.*"

Truth is, and crazy as it might sound, I'm angry. I mean, the arrogance and privilege of these glorified synthetics! They think their society is so *perfect,* so *pure,* that they don't even have to worry about auto theft.

Someone should really teach them a lesson one of these days.

Someone like us? Dubs and me?

At a time like right now?

I glance up to the nearest street cam, and I wonder if

35

I'm being videotaped this very minute. I consider flipping the camera off. Instead I just give it a stare, then a shrug.

Kinda fatalistic, like: *Hey, it's your own fault, Bots. You've beaten us down. You've made us your slaves. And now you're gonna wipe us all out? You really give Dubs and me no choice. We have to steal this Corvette. It's our fate.*

I yank open the passenger door and slide in. I turn to Dubs. "Gun it!" I yell.

Dubs gives a whoop and slams his heavy work boot down onto the accelerator.

A second or so later, the odometer's nearing sixty and

rising, and I'm practically pinned to the seat by the Gs. We're racing on the back streets, headed to the dark side of town, where the Bots don't go.

From there, it's just a few hundred yards to the open road. *Then, home again, home again.*

It feels like we're flying. Hell, this thing's so hot shit, it probably *can* fly.

Then a thunderous voice seems to split the air in two. *"Get out of the car,"* it roars.

CHAPTER 9

FREAKED, DUBS YANKS the steering wheel to the left, and we swerve across the road. We're headed for the ditch on the opposite side when he manages to swing us back to center.

The tires screech on the asphalt, and the back of the 'Vette fishtails. "What the—?" Dubs yells. "Who the—?"

I whip my head around, but this is just a two-seater—there's no one there behind us. But I'm still pretty messed up from the Killer Film, and Dubs obviously is, too.

"We're just hearing things," I say, not believing it myself.

"Sure," he says, nodding. "That's it." Then he gives a low whistle. "One-eighty. Can you believe how smooth this 'Vette is?"

"No shit," I say, settling back. I want to ride in this beautiful, human-made car forever. And why not? Why should we even go back to the Reserve? Nothing there but a bunch of epically screwed-up folks living lives of misery.

I'm wondering just how long me and Dubs could survive on the road—*when that voice starts up again.*

"Do you honestly think you're going to get away with this? You mindless, stinking meat bags."

It's coming from the *dashboard!*

"Hey," I say. "Now that's just rude."

When I lean forward, I can just make out a camera tucked right up against one of the vents, like a tiny eye watching us. Next to it is an even tinier speaker.

"I'd like to point out that we *are* getting away with it," Dubs says.

I grin, because he's right. Plus, it's a cool thing to say. There are no sirens in the distance, no flashing lights coming up behind us.

"For now," allows the voice. "But I must ask: how does it feel to be so genetically stupid that you actually believe you can get away with stealing a Hu-Bot car?"

"Honestly—it feels pretty frickin' good," says Dubs, leaning right and taking a turn way too fast.

The tires squeal again, and I grab on to the door handle so I don't go sliding off the seat. "Yeah, how's it feel to be stolen by genetically stupid humans? Must be embarrassing."

The voice is silent for a few seconds. "What *kind* of stupid human are you?" it asks next.

I scoff. Like I'm going to give out my Reserve number or something. The truth is, I don't know if this is just a computerized car, working off basic facial recognition software—or if there's a live Bot out there, on the other end of the camera, literally watching every screeching turn we take.

Either way, I'm *not* giving up my serial number. "What kind of Bot are you?" I challenge.

"I asked you first," says the voice.

"Oooohhh," I mock whomever or whatever it is, *"good one."*

The road gets a lot rougher as we wind our way up through the mountains, toward the Reserve. Dubs is tense, peering into the darkness. The robot voice senses it and starts heckling him.

"Hey, genius, how'd you learn to drive? I thought you were all idiots incapable of remembering your identification numbers. And, you there, slouched in the passenger seat. You could almost be pretty, if you weren't so filthy and flea bitten. Were you suckled by jackals, is that it? Fatboy and the Jackal?"

Dubs grits his teeth and drives faster, and I'm thinking, *Okay, this is the part where we turn into red smears on the highway. Or else plunge through the guardrail and tumble down the side of the mountain.* Either way, it feels like death is imminent. Death by fire? I don't like that image, not at all.

"Stop the car," I yell.

"Huh?" My friend shakes his shaggy head. "You're kidding?"

I grab the steering wheel. "Dammit, Dubs, I said stop the car!"

"There's nowhere to stop!"

I realize he's right: there's no shoulder on the side of the road, and the turns are so tight, we'd never see another car coming.

"Stupid humans want to die," the voice says, almost gleefully.

Ignoring it, I reach over and knock Dubs's foot off the gas.

"Brake," I yell, and for once he listens to me. The car shudders to a halt halfway up the mountain, and for a second or two, everything's silent.

"Die, die, die," intones the car. "Humans want to die."

But I start to laugh. "No, the humans want to *live!*" I holler, and with all my strength I push Dubs toward the door. "Your turn to ride shotgun!" I yell.

He shakes his head again. "No way, girl! You can't even drive a *moped.*"

I punch him as hard as I can on the biceps. "Like you didn't almost get us killed six times already today? Look, we're either going to die in this car tonight, or we're going to prison for the rest of our lives for taking it. Which means I'm going to do some damn *driving.*"

Dubs thinks about this for a second. "Fine," he grumbles. He squeezes out and jogs around to the passenger seat while I slide behind the wheel. The adrenaline's practically singing in my veins. *Here we go.*

The 'Vette's so responsive, it's like I have to only *think* about pressing the gas pedal and suddenly we're rocketing through the air. The tires hug the road as we whip around turn after turn, climbing higher and higher.

It's like driving my own damn roller coaster.

Dubs is hollering and pumping his fists, and even the computer voice is quiet—like maybe it's enjoying the thrill, too. I want to take this thing all the way to the summit, where there aren't even roads anymore.

But way too soon, we're back at the Reserve. We pull in under the forbidding metal gates, already coming down from the high.

"Home, sweet home," Dubs says, his voice oozing sarcasm.

The place is dead tonight. There's no one around except one shirtless guy up ahead. He's stumbling around in a circle, talking to himself. And then he falls down.

I slow the car. I figure I'll see if he needs help.

"Don't stop," Dubs says.

"Why not?" The guy's half-naked.

"It's my old man," Dubs answers. "He wouldn't stop for me."

I don't like it, but it's his father, so I do what Dubs says.

And as I accelerate, the voice from the dashboard says, "Now, that was barbaric, even for the two of you. That was cruel."

I smash my fist into the console, and the voice goes silent.

Dubs brightens. "Good one. Sixie?"

"Yeah?" I'm still feeling bad about Dubs's father.

"And thanks for getting me out of that movie."

I shrug. "Thanks for letting me drive."

CHAPTER 10

"THOSE APES NEVER knew what hit them," Detective AlSordi says, grinning like, well, an ape. He hands Detective MikkyBo a mug of coffee as he gives her the once-over, taking in her smooth, ivory bioskin, her graceful limbs, her chest.

MikkyBo straightens to her full height: six feet, four inches. Her clear blue eyes narrow at her Hu-Bot colleague. He's obviously testing her. What an imbecile.

"Blam!" he yells.

Involuntarily, she starts, spilling coffee on her brand-new uniform. She's annoyed at herself. And at him.

"That's how you've got to deal with the human scum," AlSordi tells her. "With swift, merciless force." He leans closer to her as he holds out a picture. "See?"

"Seems like overkill to me," she says carefully, looking at the photo he's showing her—a picture of a crater in the ground, surrounded by scattered bits of debris and severed human limbs.

She sees a half-burned sign in the corner of the picture, and she can make out the letters ESH FRU—*Fresh fruit*. The humans were hungry, and they had raided a fruit cart.

And for that crime, they'd been blown to bits? Was such a response necessary?

She can't help asking: "Why didn't you try to capture and imprison them?"

Detective AlSordi snorts at the suggestion. "I don't want to get too close to the fleshies. I heard they're riddled with disease."

He starts walking away down the hall. But then he turns back and leers at her. "By the way," he says, "welcome to the force." His eyes go straight to her chest and stay there. *What an ape,* she thinks.

She blots up the coffee spill and then returns to her desk, where the police scanner sits.

She wills it to flicker to life, signaling her first case as a detective.

When she hears the buzz, MikkyBo jerks toward the feed, her mind alert, her reflexes already engaged. But it's only an incoming call.

"Mikky," says a gruff voice from the receiver.

"NyBo, greetings," she responds. Then she can't help herself: "Guess what I did?" she whispers excitedly. "I got Theft, Auto."

A former military man, NyBo has programmed his daughter, MikkyBo, to follow in his footsteps. But, with the human race so easily defeated, war strategists usually ended up monitoring the City's Reformed human population. She chose to try for detective instead.

"Well done," her father says. But his voice sounds strange. She senses something's wrong.

"What is it?" she asks, just as the scanner begins blinking red and green. *My first case,* she thinks. She quickly skims the information—a Corvette has been stolen in Third Quadrant.

"It's KrisBo," he says ominously.

At the mention of her younger brother's name, MikkyBo's skin begins to prickle uncomfortably. "What's wrong now? Tell me. Quickly."

Her father grunts. "He's been running around with humans."

"What?" She says this too loudly, and several of her colleagues glance over at her. AlSordi glares, and she almost flips him off. "Why would KrisBo want to run with scum?" That's the catchphrase for it—*run with scum.*

"Many illegal humans have been coming into the City from the Reserve. They're in every district, impossible to ignore." On the other end of the line, NyBo spits derisively. "Like *vermin.*"

MikkyBo closes her eyes. Her brother has always had an "empathy glitch." Over the years, it's driven him to form inappropriate bonds with others, from their drone chauffeur to early-generation Hu-Bots whose systems were defective.

"Showing compassion for failing Bots—that I can almost understand. But hanging with filthy humans?" MikkyBo whispers. "*That* I don't get."

"Yes, humans are a conundrum, aren't they?"

But it isn't NyBo's voice answering her; it's MosesKhan's. Her boss's voice.

CHAPTER 11

MIKKYBO SEVERS THE connection with her father and jerks to her feet. "Commander," she says, saluting him.

The chief military officer does not salute back. For an instant, MosesKhan gazes at her with cold, dark eyes. Then he glances toward her scanner.

"Your first case is still untouched," he observes. "I would have thought you'd have closed that by now, Detective MikkyBo."

How does he even know her name? "Sir—" she begins.

But MosesKhan cuts her off. "Don't look so surprised, Detective. It is the commander's job to know the talent of everyone on his task force." His tone is light, but she hears reproach in it.

He takes a step forward, and Mikky has to stop herself from flinching. "It helps that, as one of the youngest detectives ever appointed, your talent exceeded that of the rest of your class," he says.

"I expect you to make good on that talent. Finishing first in your Academy class is one thing, but dealing with unpredictable humans is another matter."

"Yes," MikkyBo agrees. "I've been told that the humans from the Reserve have been particularly unruly."

MosesKhan's face resumes its scowl. "You heard no such thing," he says sharply. "The humans are completely under control. It's *your* job to make sure they stay that way." He juts his chin at the scanner. "I want every human persecuted to the fullest extent."

"Do you mean *prosecuted*?" MikkyBo asks carefully.

"I meant what I said." He levels his gaze at her. His voice has become icy. "Their time here is coming to a close."

MikkyBo starts. "But they aren't our *enemies*—"

MosesKhan interrupts with a barking laugh. "They aren't worthy of being our enemies," he says. "They are a pestilence"—he reaches out and touches her collar with the tip of his finger—"to be eradicated."

CHAPTER 12

AS THE COMMANDER stalks away, MikkyBo sits down. She can't take time to think about what the commander just said. Not now. She has to gather information about the case on her scanner. She has to do her job and do it brilliantly.

There are surveillance cameras positioned all over the City, and MikkyBo reviews every second of footage from the last twelve hours. Her brain digests hundreds of images as quickly as they flash by.

At the sight of two humans—one male, one female—congregating in the City after curfew, she pauses the feed.

She zooms in, identifying them as Reservers. Whereas Reformed humans are clean—for humans, anyway—and move along in a meek, respectable slouch, these two wear dirty clothes and walk with an insufferable swagger. The girl looks as if she spent last night in a trash can.

Both appear to be nearing their third decade. This piques MikkyBo's interest, since the remaining male humans should be put to work or jailed, according to Capital Center policy. There will clearly need to be more thorough sweeps of the Reserve population from now on. Mikky makes a mental note to add this to her report.

The girl is slender, with fine, delicate features fixed in a frown. She's desecrated the smooth skin of her arms with strange, inked markings. For a moment, she looks toward the camera, and her green eyes almost seem to meet MikkyBo's. The girl hesitates, and it's as if she's trying to send a message somehow—but it's in a silent, primitively human language that MikkyBo can't understand. Then she watches as the girl slips into the car—and drives away with the male.

MikkyBo sighs. *What a waste.* If humans could only control themselves, they might evolve. But these stupid kids? They won't have that chance. They'll either die in prison, or...

She hears MosesKhan's voice again: ... *be eradicated.*

A note flashes across the screen then—the Center has *flagged* the car theft.

MikkyBo squints in confusion at the scrolling letters. Why would the Center be interested in such a low-level crime? It doesn't make sense.

Maybe it's a mistake, she thinks—although Hu-Bots rarely make those. Then another, more unpleasant explanation occurs to her: maybe this is MosesKhan's way of warning her. Letting her know that he's watching what she does and how well she does it.

MikkyBo sits up straighter. She can feel herself getting worried, and irritated. Negative emotions have always troubled her, and being reminded that she's capable of them only aggravates her more.

She takes a deep breath and gazes at the white wall of her cube. She lets her mind float up like a bubble to find the Happiness. There it is—whipped and cloudlike, hovering just above her. Then it's smooth and sweet on her tongue. The taste of sugar and caramel overtakes her. Happiness.

When she's eaten an entire tub of imaginary butter pecan ice cream, she feels better. She can see things clearly once more.

I, like all Hu-Bots, am rational. Those two kids, like all humans, are irrational.

CHAPTER 13

I DROP DUBS off and leave the Corvette behind his place in B Housing. There're a few evergreen trees for cover. I don't know what we're going to do with the car. I guess we'll figure it out in the morning.

I live all the way over in X Housing, which is a mile farther across the scabbed earth of the Reserve. I pull up the worn collar of my shirt and shove my hands in my pockets, trying to keep warm as I stumble down the bumpy mud path home.

This is the only time I don't mind being on the Reserve: in the middle of the night. It's so dark in the mountains, you can't see the piles of garbage everywhere. It's cold enough that the flies stop buzzing.

I stop at the top of the hill before the turnoff to X Housing and look up at the stars. I wonder: Is there a place out there where I could be free? Where congregating with other humans isn't a crime? Where I might have a chance to fall in love?

The closest I've come to congregating is hanging around with Dubs; the closest I've gotten to love is the time I made out with him back when we were, what—thirteen and fourteen? We kissed and kissed—but then we burst out laughing.

A security chopper cuts across the horizon, and I duck down crumbling stairs, toward block X. I shake my head; I know salvation doesn't come from the starry sky.

I open the door to my tiny room, and when it clicks into place behind me, a voice says, "Reserve number 68675409M accounted for. Two hundred minutes past curfew. Penalty: fourteen days' hard labor."

"Screw you, machine head," I say as I sink onto my bed. "My whole *life* is hard labor."

My "solo sanctuary"—that's the Bots' term for it—is basically a prison cell with no lock. It's nine feet deep and six feet wide. My thin, narrow, lumpy bed is the only piece of furniture.

I've tried to decorate the place a little. Hanging on one wall is a jagged piece of an old mirror and an ancient, faded poster for a movie called *Aliens vs. Predator 2*. Whenever I look at it, I imagine Hu-Bots and other robots fighting each other to the death. It's a happy thought.

I don't have any family pictures because the drones leveled our house, but I salvaged a few photos of other people's families.

I also tacked up a crumpled old toothpaste ad showing a mom, a dad, a boy, and two girls. It could almost be my family, if the brother were scowling—and the two parents were corpses.

I lean back against moth-eaten pillows and look around at

scraps of other people's lives: a cracked blue china plate (the same pattern my mom had), postcards of Las Vegas (before it went up in smoke), and an old TAG Heuer watch (which would be worth something if it weren't mostly smashed).

Considering that everything I own was scavenged from the trash, I think I'm a pretty good decorator.

I'm still wired from the ride, so I take out the pipe Dubs gave me for my birthday and the baggie his cousin Trip slipped into my pocket the other day. I carefully pack the leaves into the bowl, light up, inhale.

My exhale is a cough. Trip specializes in the skunkiest

weed around, but when she's giving it to me for free, who's to complain?

I grab the last of my stash of chips. The snackies taste like cheese-flavored sawdust, unless I'm high—which I am.

I reach for the bowl on the shelf above my bed. Dubs would tease me for bothering with a bowl, especially a plastic one with cartoon elephants on it. But the only vivid memory I have of my mother is her telling me to use a dish "like a big girl." So in the privacy of my cell, *I'll be a big girl and use the damn bowl.*

As long as I'm thinking about my mom, I decide to take a little ride with the Q-comp. I can't remember very many details about my parents, but I have something better: *their* memories.

Or the digital copy of them, anyway. It's all here on the Q-comp.

Whole-brain emulation was just getting popular before the war, and my parents liked to be first where tech was concerned. But even digital memories don't last forever: thousands of mind-upload communities were wiped out when the Hu-Bots destroyed the Houston Cloud. I worry that someday, the Mountain Central Cloud will follow it.

Then I'll have nothing.

CHAPTER 14

I MAKE A neural connection and scan through the files. I haven't watched all my parents' memories, but I have certain ones I go back to. The day my mom taught me to toss a baseball is one of my favorites. I'm about three, and I look so clean and innocent and *happy* that I can't believe it. I mean, I'm wearing freaking *sandals*.

The memory is my dad's, actually, and through his perspective my mom looks so beautiful. She keeps batting her hair away from her face, and her eyes crinkle every time she looks at little-kid me. There's so much *life* in those eyes— how could the Bots have murdered my mom and dad?

It's too much. Or else the weed's worse than usual.

I don't know, but I feel tears coming, and I have to beat them back.

I mind scroll through my mom's memories, searching for something—*anything*—else.

I find one I've never seen before.

In it, I'm a baby bouncing on my mom's hip. But I sense this isn't a happy memory. We're deep in the mountain forest, and it's dark and cold. There's a high fence around us, patrolled by soldiers packing heat. My mom looks terrified. So do I. It's too much to watch right now.

I turn off the Q-comp abruptly, my body tingling all over.

I don't know what that memory was about, but I don't like it. Suddenly everything feels wrong. I glance down at my empty chips bowl and then over the shelf, where I keep the one thing of value I have.

The gun.

It's a semiautomatic I found on a dead rebel after the war. Even at eight, I knew that when you see a gun, you take it. I've kept it a secret, but I've never felt like I might have to use it.

Until tonight.

I can't go to prison. I won't. Never, ever.

I pick up the gun, turn it over in my hands. My palms are sweating, leaving greasy streaks on the metal. I start to pace the foot and a half of space between my bed and the walls.

How could I have thought that one thrill ride was worth being hunted down and maybe killed?

CHAPTER 15

I'M OUT BRIGHT and early the next morning because I never actually slept a wink.

I blazed through a pack of cigarettes instead — a month's stash for me and Dubs — thinking about my parents and life before the Great War. I kept wondering if it would have been better to die back then.

Happy thoughts, right?

I saved one last cigarette for the morning smoke with him. We usually meet near the trade school, so I cut through Dump Valley.

It's barely 8 a.m., but there must be a hundred kids scavenging through the giant mounds of trash. Dubs and I used to do the same thing, until we learned that if you search long enough for buried treasure, you'll find buried bodies instead, sometimes baby bodies.

I hurry up the slope until the path spits me out in Tent

City, which, believe it or not, smells even worse than the valley trash dump.

"Hey hey, Sixie!" Toothless Ten calls out from his moldy cardboard shack. "You pretty young thing. You got a fiver?"

I laugh. "Yeah, right. What for? Rotgut? Weed?"

Ten sucks his gums and glances toward the prossy straddling the fire hydrant. "Sometime a man needs a little love."

I follow his eyes. The girl is one of Two Twenty-One's sisters—they all have dark, coppery hair and full lips, sneering but sexy. She's younger than I am—maybe fourteen.

"Girl, you gotta get out of here," I call to her. "Go tell your brother to keep better track of you."

The girl rolls her eyes at me but doesn't move.

"She's closed for business," I tell Ten. Then I reach into my pocket and pull out a handful of change, which is all the money I've got. I walk over and put it in the girl's hand. "I bought you for the next three hours," I tell her. "Now git."

She knocks me in the shoulder as she stomps away. "You're hopeless," she says.

I'm hopeless? So much for doing the right thing, if that was the right thing. Maybe I am hopeless.

I spot Dubs on the far side of Tent City, fishing out beer bottles that have rolled into the gutter. Because of his dad's habit, he's never seen a bottle he doesn't want to smash. He grabs one and hurls it at J Housing. It explodes into shards of bright-green glass.

"Do you *have* to do that," I mutter, walking up, "every single morning?"

Dubs looks over at me, grinning. "No," he says. He tosses an empty fifth of vodka back and forth between his hands. "But I *want* to. Every single morning."

Then a bicycle horn toots, and we turn to see our shop teacher, Mr. Austere. He's riding straight toward us, up the path. Austere's his Reformed name, anyway, mockingly given by his Hu-Bot masters. He wears it like a badge of honor.

Idiot.

"You'd better not miss another class," he calls, puffing hard from pedaling. His face is beet red.

"And *you* better slow down," Dubs says. "You look like you're having a heart attack." He flashes a gap-toothed grin.

63

Austere huffs, and his face gets even redder. "When my time comes . . . you'll be the one carrying . . . me on your shoulders," he yells. "You two . . . are going to wind up . . . ditch diggers at the cemetery . . . Remember . . . You heard it here . . . first!"

"Better than fixing motorbikes I'm not allowed to ride," I say as he pedals away.

"I'd love to pitch dirt on his coffin," Dubs mutters. "That'd be fun."

A car horn sounds, and I freeze.

"Relax, girl," Dubs says. "It's just a couple of Bots."

"Bot-*cops*." Sweat beads on my forehead. *This is it,* I think. *They found the Corvette, and now they've found* us.

Dubs takes a long drag. "So? We're being good little citizens, remember? We're on our way to trade school."

The voice blares from the loudspeaker on the sedan's roof. **"HUMANS, BOW DOWN!"**

My face reddens, but I obey. I might've taken my time in the city square, but right now, in my own territory, I just want to get this over with as quickly as possible.

"Wow, Sixie," Dubs says from the ground next to me. "That's the fastest I've ever seen you get on your knees. Been practicing?"

"Silence, hoo-mans," a Bot-cop snaps.

The Bot-cop keeps us on the ground—like we're bad *dogs* or something—for a good two minutes, then glides off like nothing ever happened.

"Stupid Bots," Dubs yells after they're gone. He brushes dirt from the knees of his jeans. "Stupid goddamn Bots!" Then he turns and stomps away from the school.

"What are you doing?"

"What do you mean, what am I doing?" He squints back at me, the sun in his face. "I'm cutting class. Like we do most days."

I sigh and look out across the Reserve, scanning the horizon for more Bot-cops. "I just think we have to be careful. We need to get rid of that Corvette..."

"That's *exactly* what I'm talking about!" Dubs says, his good humor returning instantly. He claps me on the back and pushes me ahead down the path. "We'll use the many talents we've acquired in dumb-dumb school and work on an *actual car*. The better the shape it's in, the faster we can unload it. And, don't worry, Princess Paranoid, we'll dismantle that computer."

I think about that for a minute. Then I grin. "Let *me* do it, okay? I want to smash that thing with a hammer. I want to kill it."

CHAPTER 16

IN THE OLD Cultural District of what used to be Denver—inside one of the illegal "unseen" theaters—a beautiful woman struts across a dimly lit stage. Her eyelashes flutter like black butterflies, and her long, thin fingers are tipped with red polish.

When she stops center stage, she lifts a microphone from its stand, and a bright spotlight clicks on.

The audience of mostly perverse humans gasps.

And MikkyBo, hidden in the shadows at the back of the hall, gasps too.

Unlike Mikky, the crowd isn't surprised that the woman is, in fact, a man—decked out in a platinum-blond wig, a shimmering green dress, death-defying stilettos. No—they're noticing the one thing MikkyBo knew already: that the performer on this forbidden stage is a *Hu-Bot*.

And not just any Hu-Bot, but her brother, KrisBo.

Mikky had seen his name on a flyer for a "drag show." She hadn't known what that meant, but she does now.

KrisBo smiles, revealing perfect snow-white teeth, and the crowd murmurs in agitation as he waits for the music to start.

MikkyBo's fingers tighten on the arms of the seat. What happens next? Will the humans kneel reverently—or riot? One can never tell with *Homo sapiens*, and that's the problem.

The music swells—and KrisBo takes a deep breath and begins to sing.

The crowd hushes, but still the air feels charged and dangerous.

KrisBo is oblivious to everything. Pretty soon he's strutting across the stage, blowing kisses to the front row, twirling his pale-gold ringlets theatrically. His voice is breathy and seductive. He's a natural performer.

And he's winning the tough, jaded audience over. MikkyBo studies the sea of human heads, none of which comes higher than her shoulder. She sees that they're all bobbing to the beat.

"Work it, girl!" someone hollers. Loud cheers erupt from the front row.

For the first time in her life, MikkyBo has absolutely no idea what to think. Humans are moral degenerates and budding killers, every single one of them just waiting to bite the Bot hand that fed him.

So why are they cheering for her brother, blowing him kisses, even tossing money onto the stage?

Is it possible that they actually *like* him?

KrisBo shimmies his slim hips. He obviously likes *them*. They holler and clap and scream, and when his song ends, they yell for another.

And then the truly frightening realization dawns on her.

It isn't the humans she needs to protect her brother from right now—it's other Hu-Bots.

MikkyBo stands up. She vaults over the back two rows and rushes into the aisle. At the front of the theater, humans are standing, dancing, waving their arms around. She pushes through the sweat-soaked bodies and launches herself onto the stage.

Kris goes pale when he sees who it is. The music's still playing, but he's not singing anymore. "What are you doing here?" He steps backward, tripping over the train of his dress. The microphone screeches with feedback, and somewhere, someone shuts off the music.

For a moment, the whole room is silent. She grabs her brother's hand.

"KrisBo," she says firmly, "it's just a glitch. I've heard about other Hu-Bots losing control, but it's okay. We'll fix this."

KrisBo snatches his hand away from her. "You're such a *robot*, Mikky. Who runs your life? Do you know what that collar makes you?"

MikkyBo's hand goes to her throat.

"A dog on a leash." KrisBo spits out the words.

All right, that's quite enough. I am an Elite.

"Time to go, KrisBo." Mikky steps forward and, in one quick motion, presses her boot hard against the backs of her brother's knees. Already unbalanced by his heels, he crumples to the floor in a pile of glitter. Before he can scramble away, she picks Kris up and slings him over her shoulders.

The crowd begins to shout. They want more singing—or else they want *blood*. A bottle goes whizzing by her head, and then another. KrisBo is screaming, banging his fists against her back, but she barely notices. All she cares about is protecting her brother.

"Robot!" he yells at her. "Stupid, unfeeling robot!"

"No one can ever know about this," she whispers, not entirely sure if the words are for KrisBo or herself.

CHAPTER 17

OLD TIME ROCK 'n' roll music pumps out of jerry-rigged speakers, and a handful of stoned girls stutter step around on the packed-down dirt that's the Reserve version of a dance floor. A circle of guys sits on old milk crates, passes around a spliff the size of my middle finger.

This is what passes for a party in the Pits. But I'm in no party mood. I'm scared.

It's strictly against the law for humans to gather in groups larger than four, so little kids are stationed as lookouts. But the Bot-cops don't usually come to this part of the Reserve anymore. Neither do Dubs and I.

We're here to sell the stolen car, not reminisce about the bad old days. We worked on the 'Vette all last night, tuning, polishing, buffing that thing to shine like diamonds.

"I'll be sad to see her go," Dubs says. He's squished into the driver's seat, running his hand along the gleaming dash.

"I just want to get out of here in one piece." I glance over at the stick figure of a man leaning against a beat-up Dodge Charger. He's got an entourage of junkies and flunkies surrounding him. "Think he'll buy?"

"If anyone will, it's him," Dubs answers. "The dude *runs* the black market. And he's a race king. You know he's always looking for extra parts."

"Then let's do this," I say, opening the door. I can't help brushing my hand along the silver body of the Corvette. For all I know, it'll be stripped for parts by morning.

"Hey hey, Zee Twelve. What's been going on?" Dubs shouts a too-friendly greeting and extends his fingers out for a tap.

Zee Twelve sucks on his cigarette and leaves Dubs's hand hanging. So we just stand there, staring at his small, black eyes and pockmarked cheeks, waiting for him to answer. He exhales finally, blowing the smoke in Dubs's face.

"What's going on?" Zee repeats slowly. His voice is low and smooth, with an undercurrent of mockery. "Well, right now, *my friend,* I'm wondering what a couple of *trade-school slugs* think they're doing talking to me."

Us? Trade-school slugs? Now, that's hilarious. He might as well call me a cheerleader.

"You got any ammunition?" I blurt. "For a Colt M1911?"

"Ammo costs money, *little girl.*" Zee Twelve gives me the once-over, noting my holey jeans and patched-up coat. He throws the butt of his joint at my boots. "More than you've got."

"You might've noticed our ride," I say. I'm already sick of this skinny, meth-faced Rezzie thug. I gesture behind me at the Corvette, which practically shimmers in the middle of this dump. "It's for sale."

Zee Twelve smiles, revealing dull, gray metal teeth. "Betting men don't buy, friend," he tells me. "We *win*."

Perfect. He's not buying. He has no money. Which means we need to find another option before the Bot-cops find the 'Vette — and us.

Then Dubs opens his big mouth and says, "Fine. We'll race you for it. We win, you give us ammo — *all* the ammo you have."

Zee Twelve shakes his head, smirks, and says, "And when *I* win?"

Dubs crosses his scarred arms over his chest. "You get the Corvette."

My mouth falls open. Zee's a race king, and Dubs and I have driven a car exactly *once*.

I grab him by the arm and haul him toward the 'Vette, calling, "Excuse us," over my shoulder. Dubs, taken by surprise, stumbles.

"What's your problem?" he demands.

"What's *my* problem?" I hiss. "Why don't you just *give* him the car for being a goddamn nice guy, huh?"

Dubs shakes his head. "Sixie, it's a wager. That's how shit works." He shrugs. "Everybody knows that."

He looks at me like *I'm* the dumb one.

"That Charger's five hundred horsepower, max. I can freaking smell the radiator fluid, dude. That thing's a dog. It goes zero to sixty in about a month. Meanwhile, you and me have *this*." He pats the side of the Corvette.

He sounds so sure of himself. And I want to believe him.

I glance back toward Zee Twelve, who's slouched against that tin can of his. Maybe, just maybe, there's a way this could work. There are usually at least a hundred people at the races, and if the 'Vette does well, that's a hundred potential buyers.

Of course, if we lose, there are no bullets and nothing to barter with. But still.

Dubs can tell I'm changing my mind. "Yeahhhh, boyyyy," he crows, "I mean, girrrlll."

When we get back to the group, I stick out my hand to Zee Twelve. "We can beat your sorry Dodge any day of the week, not to mention any other shit piece of junk you can dig up," I say.

This time, Zee Twelve reaches for my hand. He yanks my arm close to him, so that we're standing eye-to-eye. "Tonight," he says, almost tenderly, and strokes the inside of my palm.

"Tonight." I nod, resisting the urge to shudder at his creepy touch.

"You're going to make her fly," Dubs says as we walk back to the Corvette.

I stop midstride. "Wait—*I'm* the one driving?"

He taps me on the sternum once, twice, three times. *"And don't you fucking lose."*

CHAPTER 18

SHE SHOULDN'T BE nervous or scared, but she is. That's how Mikky is built. She glances in her rearview mirror as she races up the steep highway, into the mountains. Six Bot-cop utility vehicles follow her—on the commander's orders. This is her show, her first, but something about it bothers her. There are too many Bot-cops.

When the stolen Corvette's identity interface signaled its location along the Reserve border, Mikky assured MosesKhan she could handle it on her own, with a Bot or two for backup. The commander insisted on six units.

Overkill. But why? Is it because he doesn't trust her?

She parks the car at the eastern edge of the Reserve and signals the Bot-cops to do the same. They'll go the rest of the way on foot. They're heavily armed—with Mercy 72s.

Too much firepower, she thinks.

The Mercy 72 is the "compassionate" weapon of choice

among the Hu-Bot Elite, because the bullet is designed to tar-get the victim's heart. Mikky's been told in training that it's quick and painless.

Is MosesKhan trying to protect her, trying to keep her safe in the Reserve?

"Detective," says a voice, cutting through the darkness. "Central Command has visual imaging. Coordinates are Z twenty-nine, X eighty-seven—"

The Bot-cops are lined up. Everyone's waiting for her command. That's better.

MikkyBo has to focus. She's got to retrieve this stolen car, which is apparently so important that a small army has been dispatched to retrieve it. A small army carrying Mercys.

Everything is going to be fine. Order has to be maintained. Do your job.

Mikky steps forward, and the Bot-cops fall in behind her. She's half a foot taller than any of them — the only Hu-Bot in the group. The one in charge.

She draws the Mercy 72 handgun from her belt and takes off the safety. But she can't help hoping she won't have to use it.

It doesn't occur to her that, just by thinking this, she is already a traitor.

CHAPTER 19

"NO WAY." DUBS is shaking his head. "This is bullshit. We've been hustled."

I'm in the Corvette, sitting at the starting line of the make-shift Pits track, watching Zee Twelve pull up alongside. But he's not driving the beat-up Charger we saw earlier.

Instead he's strapped into some lime-green Franken-Porsche with flames painted on the hood. It's about the ugliest coupe I've ever seen, but I can tell by the sound of the engine that it's got major kick.

"Your girl said she could beat any car," one of Zee's side-kicks reminds Dubs.

Guess how much I'm regretting *that* cocky moment?

"*Could,*" Dubs snarls with such fury that I think he might twist the Rezzie's head off. "But we *agreed* to race the Dodge." He stalks over to my window. "You can't beat him, Sixie," he says quietly.

"Gee, thanks for the pep talk, coach."

"That's a twin turbo. You can't win."

"Losers cannot win," the computer voice butts in, as if our earlier conversation had never stopped. "Losers lose."

"The fuck...?" Dubs and I both gasp. Didn't we destroy the console this morning? With sledgehammers?

"Your surprise is quite adorable to witness," it simpers.

I turn to Dubs. "We've got to get this race over with. And, no matter what happens, we're getting rid of this car."

The track's only three miles long—mostly a straight course, with a sharp curve on a steep downhill, a turn-around, and then the same course uphill.

Before I have time to think up some fake, bullshit strategy or send up a silent prayer to a god I don't believe in, the flag goes down.

I have the better position—inside for the first turn—but in my millisecond of hesitation, Zee shoots forward and veers inside. I floor the 'Vette, but I'm already behind. Just like that. Two seconds.

"Pathetic," the computer crows. "You brainless meat sack! You have no idea how to handle fine machinery, do you? Also, your hair looks terrible."

I grit my teeth, ignoring the sneering voice. Seconds later, we're nearing the halfway point. The Porsche is faster, but it has a hard time on the narrow turnaround.

I crank the wheel, whipping the Corvette into the one-eighty. I gain some ground—but not enough.

"Don't worry, though," the voice returns. "You'll get a fine education in prison. You'll learn to be obedient. To grovel. To keep quiet when you're tortured."

"I don't *grovel*," I retort. "I'm not anybody's *slave*."

"Slaves bow before their masters," the computer insists.

Perfect timing. I'm riding up on the Franken-Porsche's tail—closer, closer. I crank up the volume on the console.

"I'm my *own* master," I hiss.

The computer takes the bait, and the voice booms out of my speakers. **"HUMANS, BOW DOWN!"**

Zee Twelve slams on the brakes, just as I thought he would. I shoot forward, passing him before he realizes that it's not actually a raid.

I can see the finish line ahead. I grip the steering wheel even tighter and narrow my focus. Maybe I'm going to win this thing. Probably not, but maybe.

Then I feel a hard slam against the side of the Corvette, and my head snaps forward. Major frickin' pain. For a second, I'm blind. There's blood in my mouth, and I think I just cracked a tooth.

I realize for the first time that the car might not be the only thing I lose tonight. I might lose my life.

Zee rams me again, then pulls away for another strike. When he cranks the wheel to rev up for the grand slam, I hit the brakes. He careens sideways.

The flags are up ahead, the sidelines packed with people, and the two cars are dead even. OK, maybe I'm half a length behind.

An awful roar builds. Zee Twelve has shifted the Porsche into some kind of freaking *rocket* gear. He shoots past me in a blur of blue flames.

"You stupid girl, you lost!" the computer voice shouts.

"Enjoy it," I spit at the console. "Tomorrow you're going to be hacked down and sold for parts."

"What?" a different voice—probably that of the Hu-Bot who owns the car—cuts in. "I don't care what MosesKhan says. Hack into the slipstream!"

Oh shit, I think as the gas pedal locks and the steering wheel tightens. I have zero control now. Worse, we're heading straight for the edge of a cliff. *So this is how it ends.*

There's nothing to do but hold on. The Corvette surges forward as the Hu-Bot hacker uses the last of its juice and rides up on Zee Twelve's bumper. The 'Vette swerves right, and hard left, and smashes into Zee's back right wheel.

The Porsche spins out, and I shoot forward. I smash my forehead on the steering wheel. Dizzy and whiplashed, I struggle upright—just as the Corvette screeches to a halt six inches from thin air, the edge of the cliff, death.

But Rezzies are running at me, cheering that I won. I don't even know how it happened, but it doesn't matter. I watch the scrawny little gangster Zee stumble out of his wrecked car.

Moments later, his boys start loading boxes and boxes of

ammo into the Corvette's trunk. I take the pistol from the glove box and load her up.

Dubs hustles over and pounds me on the back.

"Still a loser," the computer voice interjects. "Always a loser."

"Always trapped in a dashboard," I snort.

Trip, Dubs's cousin, comes speeding toward us. She throws her arms around my neck, and I stagger backward, off balance. Wild-eyed, wild-haired Trip is usually a little too nutty for me—but tonight I just laugh and hug her back.

And then we're all cackling and high-fiving each other, and for the first time in about forever I feel almost *happy*.

That's when shouts shatter the night air. "BOTS!"

I look up—and see robot cops swarming toward us. They've cut off the road, and they're also all over the opposite slope. A chopper noisily whirs overhead.

Then I see the leader—a Hu-Bot—and she has a Mercy 72 cocked and ready. Ready for what?

CHAPTER 20

"RUN!" I SHOUT to Dubs, who's standing there, as dumb-founded as I am.

But run *where?* The Bots have encircled us—so there's nowhere to go but over the cliff. And, last I checked, none of us can fly.

The Rezzies are screaming, trying to hide behind rocks and cars and shadows. They're just kids.

I feel Trip's hand in mine and hear her panicked voice in my ear. "I'm scared, Six."

There's a steep rock wall near the cliff's edge, and for a second I've got this crazy idea that we can scramble *up* it to safety. But it's twelve vertical feet up. Even if I didn't get shot, Trip and Dubs would never make it—and I'm not leaving them behind.

The Bots' high-power flashlights slice through the twilight.

"Ohmygodohmygodohmygod." Trip's hyperventilating. Her

sharp nails are digging into my palm. I resist the urge to shake her off. She's a kid—and she's afraid.

Their Mercy 72s are drawn, but they're not firing. *Yet.* Slowly, the Bots drive us toward the edge of the cliff, like we're sheep.

The Bot-cops don't register our panic, our shrieks. They don't understand fear. And, even if they did, sympathy's not in their job description.

"We gotta charge 'em," I yell to Zee over the noise. I'd rather take a bullet than fall a thousand feet. Hell, if I'm going to die tonight, I want to die fighting.

"Halt, humans," cries a metallic voice.

But we *don't* halt. Dubs has come up beside me, and he's got his head down like a bull. We're actually pushing back, gaining a little ground. I expect the bullets to start any second. All it takes is one Hu-Bot command.

Then a shrill whistle sounds, and the Bot-cops halt in their tracks. That's when I see her.

The Hu-Bot angel of death, striding forward. And she is definitely *not* ugly. No, the robo-chick in charge of this madness must be six and a half feet tall. She's dressed head to toe in black, with a face so beautiful, it almost hurts to look at it. She's an Elite.

"What the—" Dubs starts to say. His eyes are about popping out of his head. He takes a step forward, like he's considering flinging himself into her arms, even if it means he'll take a bullet to the heart.

I grab his sleeve, and he turns around, his eyes crazy with fear. The Hu-Bot has spotted the 'Vette, and she's about to spot us—she's hustling on those long, muscular legs, her gaze sweeping the crowd.

But then the Capital Center helicopter suddenly drops low, stopping only a couple dozen yards over our heads. The wind is so strong, it tears up my eyes; the deafening thunder of its blades shakes my body.

But, no matter how loud the chopper is, I can still hear on the loudspeaker: "HUMANS, BOW DOWN!"

We can barely move, let alone bow, so the crowd topples forward in a lopsided wave. Hands go up. We're surrendering. Everybody. What other choice do we have?

When I stand again, I see the Bot-cops taking a few steps *back,* which fills me with a surge of hope—until they start lowering their guns. And now they look like they're taking aim…

Oh, shit no.

Yellow flashes spark from the gun muzzles. The screaming is deafening now. They're firing into a bunch of kids— kids who've already surrendered! Who haven't done anything wrong in the first place except try to have a little fun!

Better to be a moving target, so I sprint low toward the Corvette. Bullets ricochet all around me. Dubs is only a few steps behind.

Then I remember Trip. I whip around and almost wish I hadn't. Trip's still on her knees, madly trying to press her hands against the bloody hole in her friend's stomach, as if she could stuff the kid's entrails back inside.

"She's gone!" I yell. "You have to come with me."

I yank Trip to her feet and hold her head down as we race toward the car. The chopper's firing at us now.

Trip's still screaming about God—and who knows? Maybe God really *does* exist, because somehow we make it to the 'Vette without being shot.

I shove Trip hard into the backseat, behind Dubs. I slide into the driver's seat. I've got one hand on the steering wheel and one on the gun.

I floor it, peeling out in a spray of gravel, the back of the 'Vette swerving like it might not be able to keep up. Bullets are slamming into the car.

We're almost out of there, almost free of the carnage— but then I swerve toward the Hu-Bot goddess. *She* is in charge, and *she* ordered the massacre.

She's turning around now, yelling orders to the Bots, but,

between the gunfire and the chopper, it's impossible to know what she's saying.

Not that it matters. She's not paying attention to any humans. Not even the one slowing the 'Vette to a crawl... positioning a gun... squinting above the barrel... taking careful, deadly aim. *Humans, bow down, my ass.*

CHAPTER 21

"I SAID, *HOLD your fire!*" MikkyBo roars.

But her team doesn't follow her order. She doesn't understand what's going on, or how to stop this. The Bot-cops keep shooting, their bullets ripping into the teenagers. The screaming pierces MikkyBo's ears, and the chopper swings its giant spotlight around in circles, illuminating every terrified human face.

She watches a kid stumble and fall to the dirt—in his eyes a look of confusion as blood leaks out of a wound in his chest.

She continues to scream the order to stop firing. Finally, she knocks one of her own cops down. Then another.

"Listen to me! I'm a Hu-Bot detective!"

No one listens to her orders.

More gunfire lights up the sky, the bullets slamming into bodies. MikkyBo looks up, sees that the Tactical Force helicopter is spraying bullets, too.

"Stop firing now! Stop this madness!"

It's impossible to know what to do in the chaos of a shoot-out. The Bots, transformed into killing machines. The helicopter, raining down death.

MikkyBo touches her choker lightly, but only for a split second. She thinks she knows how to make this right. She takes aim at the nearest rogue Bot. Takes a deep breath. One, two—

She's hit! Someone shot her!

MikkyBo's right leg collapses beneath her, and she lands hard on both knees. Her nerves are flooded with pain. She has to grit her teeth to keep from crying out.

Then she sees the stolen Corvette, the tattooed girl, wild-eyed behind the wheel. In the passenger seat, her loutish friend. *These* were the two she was after from the start. And the girl just shot her!

She howls in rage. *None* of this would've happened if it hadn't been for them. All of this bloodshed.

She struggles to her feet and charges the car. She ignores the excruciating pain. But the girl guns the engine. She shot a Hu-Bot detective—punishable by death—and now she's getting away? That's not happening.

Shifting course, MikkyBo races toward her own vehicle. "Offender on the move!" she yells. The Bots still fail to respond. She doesn't care about them anymore. The only thing she can do is go after those two—the instigators, the original car thieves.

Reaching her car, she yells into the console, "Renegade Bots shooting bystanders! Unknown number of casualties! Emergency assistance needed! Now!"

But there's no answer to her message. Only silence.

And that's when MikkyBo understands what she should have known from the moment the Bots began firing.

I want every human persecuted to the fullest extent, her commander had said.

This wasn't a mistake. It was premeditated murder.

CHAPTER 22

WE'RE FLYING DOWN the highway now, the android death squad miles behind us but the sound of bullets still ringing in my ears. Trip's shaking and shivering in the backseat, curled up against the door like she's still trying to dodge bullets. Dubs keeps reaching back to reassure her, but he looks pretty freaked out, too.

It's only because I'm driving that I'm not losing it myself. I've had plenty of experience with death—kids starving, old timers OD'ing—but I'm going to relive the bloodbath in nightmares for years.

Assuming I live that long.

"Did you see what they did to Eff Seventeen?" Trip gasps. "Blew her face off! I saw it, man. That wasn't a Mercy gun."

Dubs speaks in a crackling whisper. "It was worse than a Killer Film."

"Don't talk about it, okay?" I'm gripping the steering

wheel so tight, my knuckles are bone white. "It's over. We got away. We've got to worry about ourselves now. They're going to come for us."

"They already are, you sorry sack of guts," says you-know-who.

Dubs drives his fist into the console again. This machine won't die.

"Aggression is indication of a failure to evolve," the know-it-all voice remarks.

Trip sits up in the backseat, her red curls all messy, her face pale. "Where are we going?"

I realize she's never been off the Reserve before.

"Wherever you're headed, whatever stupid decision you make, you're being tracked," the computer promises.

"Dubs, you've got to stop that stupid voice," I say.

But he's not paying attention. He's twisted around in his seat, peering into the darkness, where two pinpricks of light are growing larger.

"They're coming after us."

"Coming fast," Trip says, panic rising.

"Come on, Sixie!" Dubs yells as the flashes of red light up the inside of the 'Vette. "Go, go! They want us dead."

Like I need to be told! But, racer or not, this car doesn't stand a chance next to a police cruiser—I've seen those things go from 0 to 160 in less than four seconds. We've got only one option.

"Ammo's in the glove box. Reload."

He scrambles to do it, cursing. Trip's making little cries of fear in the backseat. She sounds like a little trapped fox.

The cruiser pulls up next to us. I can see the dark-haired

Hu-Bot waving a Mercy pistol in her right hand. Which means that her aim doesn't even matter: one shot, and my heart explodes like a supernova.

But she's not *pointing* it at me. She's *waving* it, like she's trying to get us to—

"Pull over?" Dubs yells. "Is she joking?"

Like we're going to stop—so we can get sent to prison for life? Or eat a bullet from a Bot-cop? No way that's happening.

I swerve away, accelerating. As long as I'm breathing, I'm *driving*.

This time, when the Hu-Bot pursues, Dubs fires a round. It careens off the cruiser, doesn't even chip the paint.

"That surprised her!" he crows. "You should see the look on her face!"

What, did she think that shot in her leg was an *accident?* Maybe the Hu-Bot's not as smart as she thinks she is. *Or maybe I'm the dumb one?*

Dubs squeezes off another round, but it doesn't faze her. Her voice blares through powerful speakers mounted on the bumper. "You are in violation! Pull. Over. Don't make me kill you. That's the next step of protocol."

"Do it, you stupid Hu-Bitch," Dubs hollers. He shoots again. This time the bullet cracks the windshield. Score one for the good guys.

"Humans! Stop! Please! You will be—" the Hu-Bot begins, but Dubs cuts her off with another shot, and she skids away.

For a moment, everything goes quiet. Trip's not whimpering. Dubs isn't cursing. There's nothing but the sound of our engine and the rushing wind. Maybe we scared her off. Did she actually say *please?*

Then I hear Dubs say, "Oh *shit*." Trip screams like the little girl she is.

A split second later, I feel the impact. A thundering crash rattles my brain. The Hu-Bot rams us, just as Zee did—but harder, much harder.

Time slows down. Trip's piercing scream seems to last for an hour.

The world's spinning around us. Then we're airborne. Flipping over and over, and *this is it*—

CHAPTER 23

MIKKYBO WATCHES THE Corvette launch into the air, spinning horribly out of control, and then slam back down to the ground, rolling over four times before landing on its roof. It slides, squealing, another fifty yards—then comes to a stop at the edge of a hay field.

Smoke rolls out of the mangled pile of steel and shattered glass. For a second, MikkyBo is frozen in her seat. Her body, unaccustomed to so many intense feelings at once, is malfunctioning. Her heart's gone haywire. She can't feel her hands. There's a ringing in her ears. She feels almost *human*. It's terrible. Unacceptable.

Shaking all over, she manages to open the cruiser's door. But before she can climb out, she leans over and vomits all over the highway.

She knows she shouldn't care, but she does: three more kids are dead now. It's all her fault.

Slowly she stands — her leg is healing itself — makes her way across the highway toward the gruesome wreck. Flames are licking at the edges of the hood now. The whole thing might blow. Looks like it.

MikkyBo has the Mercy out, but there's no way she's going to need it. No way anyone could have survived. That kid who shot her? She's nothing but a bloody pulp behind what's left of the steering wheel.

MikkyBo knows she must call in the accident, but she doesn't — not yet. She needs to see for herself...

The twisted bits of metal. Glittering shards of glass. Smoking engine. The blood on the road. The wrecked, empty interior of the Corvette.

She stands tall — shocked. *Empty? What the* — ?

She looks wildly around in the darkness, and that's when she sees them. They're halfway across the field. Limping, stumbling, helping one another. Wounded — who knows how badly.

Thank God, she thinks, relief flooding her body like a drug. And she knows something else — *I shouldn't be feeling this way.*

Two girls and one enormous boy, heading for the wilderness as the night gets deeper, and much colder.

Catching them would almost be a kindness. Better prison than a night in the black woods. Out there, they'll suffer from their wounds and from the cold. Hypothermia will set in. And what about the predators — bears and wolves and cougars, their numbers back up after the decimation of the human population? No, those three will never survive. *Their only hope...me.*

Capital Center vehicles are approaching.

"What the hell is this?" she mumbles under her breath. How did they get out here so fast? *Because they knew a massacre was coming?*

They circle around her, penning her in. They idle for a minute—just long enough for her heart rate to spike again.

You're an Elite Hu-Bot, she tells herself. *Trust yourself. Trust your instincts. You're a detective.*

Then—the worst shock yet. Commander MosesKhan steps from one of the cars. His face is dark with anger.

Your instincts are wrong. All wrong. MosesKhan set you up.

CHAPTER 24

"COMMANDER," MIKKYBO SAYS quickly, saluting, trying to pretend she's calm. "Did you get my report on the renegade Bots?"

She hopes that if she focuses on what she did *right*, there's a chance she'll avoid reprimand and humiliation.

MosesKhan glares at the smoldering Corvette. "Tell me, Detective, how is it that you could not accomplish such a *simple* mission—even with an army at your fingertips?"

"They were not under my control," MikkyBo says. "That was what I was trying—"

"Of course they weren't," the commander interrupts in an angry tone. "They were under *mine*."

His?

"The Bots were firing on unarmed citizens," she says.

"You mean the Bot troops were assisting you," the commander corrects. "They were narrowing the field of humans so you could complete your mission." He pauses. "Except that you *did not do so.*"

MikkyBo feels sick—and angry. MosesKhan ordered the slaughter of dozens of young humans because he feared she wouldn't succeed on her own? That simply isn't logical. Hu-Bots don't fail.

"Sir, surely I would have apprehended—"

The commander cuts her off again. "So you're admitting that you are ill-equipped to deal with unpredictability? That is distressing, since humans are the most unpredictable of creatures."

MikkyBo stands taller. She wants to throttle the commander, a ridiculous urge. "Sir, had I known—"

"Silence!" MosesKhan roars in her face. "It is not my job to explain things to you. You were to apprehend two criminals—"

"There were three, sir," MikkyBo interjects. *She* can play the interrupting game, too.

MosesKhan's eyes flash as he walks in a slow circle around her. He's too close. His breath is cold on her neck. "Three humans in one car...that you were unable to overtake in your cruiser?"

"I was able to overtake them. But then there was an accident, and..." She stops.

"And what?" MosesKhan leans forward to hear.

"They ran," she says, cowed now. "Into the woods."

"You're telling me that three *injured* humans escaped an *Elite* detective?"

"I did confiscate the car," Mikky points out, as the Corvette belches up a small fireball.

"The car is of no consequence!" MosesKhan says, his cheeks turning a brilliant shade of plum.

MikkyBo is in agony now—but she makes herself ask: "What *was* the point of the mission, sir? Help me understand."

The commander looks around at his entourage. Then invites her inside his car. The door shuts with a quiet, ominous *click*.

"The point... was to find *her*," MosesKhan says, "the car thief. The girl. Six, as she is called."

"Who is Six?" Mikky presses.

"She's human scum. But with a quantum computer in her possession."

"She has a Q-comp?" Mikky asks, disbelieving. She knows how dangerous they can be—which is why all of them in human possession have been confiscated. Every one. So how could that Rezzie girl have a Q-comp? It doesn't seem possible, doesn't make any sense. Strains credulity.

"The girl, Six, possesses information that is both highly dangerous and highly valuable." The commander stares into his detective's eyes. "She has the key to a memory bank of information that could give the human race a dangerous advantage. She is the grandchild of a human hero. And you, MikkyBo, you let her slip right through your fingers."

CHAPTER 25

"SIX, HOW MUCH farther?" Trip cries out.

We trudge deeper into the woods, toward the icy heart of this steep, towering mountain. All around us, shadows bend and shift, and the evergreen trees seem to tremble in the cold.

I shake my head, but everything still looks blurry and strange. Either I got a concussion in the crash, or else I'm in major shock that we're actually alive.

Not that we're in great shape now. Dubs is limping, and so is Trip. She's bleeding something awful, weeping quietly. She cracked her head, and her ankle might be broken. He's got a black eye and a big gash on his arm, and he lost another tooth. And me? Well...

"You're leaving a helpful trail of blood, Sixie," Dubs points out.

The cut on my leg, the one I wrapped with an old tube

sock, is still dripping. "Great—so if the Bots don't find us, the wolves will."

Trip gives a small, whimpering cry at the thought.

"Don't worry, cuz," Dubs says. "I'll protect you from everything."

But we all know that's an impossible promise.

No one says anything else, and we slog along in silence for a while. It's getting colder, and pretty soon my teeth are chattering. But since I'm also hoofing it uphill, I'm freezing and sweating simultaneously—which sucks, and is also terrifying.

When we finally get to a place that isn't too steep or too exposed or too snowbound, we stop to assess our situation. A quick look around tells me this much: it's even worse than I thought.

Trip can hardly put any weight on her ankle. My right eye has begun to swell shut. Dubs is leaking blood all over himself. We don't know where we are. We have no food, or water, or blankets. It's night, and it's already below freezing.

"Well," Dubs says, wiping a red smear across his forehead, "this is a nice spot for a picnic! Whatcha got for us, Sixie?"

"I'd kill for a bug bar right about now," Trip whispers.

"I'll take a look around," I say quickly. "Maybe find some berries." I bend down and pick up a rock. "Or a raccoon!"

"Well, look who's suddenly a huntress," Dubs says. "Does extreme danger bring out the killer in you, Sixie?" He nudges me in the ribs.

"You want to help me?" I ask. "Or keep talking stupid shit like that?"

Dubs ducks his head apologetically. "Help," he says meekly, and bends to pick up his own rock.

I realize this is total madness—us pretending like any animal's going to come within fifty yards. I'm just creeping through the darkness, a jagged rock in my palm—because doing *something*'s better than doing nothing.

I'm so cold that prison's almost starting to sound good.

I stop and lean against a tree. I'm suddenly overwhelmed. Memories of the surprise attack wash over me in waves—the screaming, the terror, the slaughter. How quickly the Bot-cops turned themselves into a firing squad. And how the Hu-Bot in charge did nothing to stop it.

Maybe I should just lie down in the snow. I've heard that freezing to death isn't the worst way to go . . .

Then I see a flash of movement out of the corner of my eye, and before I even know what's happening, I've already flung the rock. I hear a *thud,* and the shadowy movement stops abruptly.

I hold my breath for a moment and then creep forward. My feet are making crunching noises on the frozen ground.

There, lying in the snow, half-hidden by the underbrush, is a rabbit.

It's not dead, though—it's stunned. Frightened. Its eyes blink madly; it doesn't want to die.

But this fierce need boils up in me, like nothing I've ever felt before, this desperate desire to escape this situation, because *I don't want to die, either*—so I take the rock again, and I bring it down on the poor thing's head.

The rabbit's hind legs kick out, spasming wildly. Then, in another moment, they go still. It's done. Dubs is standing over my shoulder.

"Wow. I didn't think you had it in you," he says.

I pick up the soft body, still warm, and I hand it to him. I feel terrible. "Skin it," I say.

"With my teeth?" he asks, but he looks like he'd be willing to try.

I reach into my jeans and pull out a rusty pocketknife. "Use this."

He gives me a funny look, like maybe he's realizing he doesn't know me as well as he thinks he does.

Trip builds a fire—and we roast that little bunny over it. It's gamy and fatty and stringy—and it might be the best thing I've ever tasted. I suck every last bit of grease from my fingers. That rabbit probably saved our lives, at least for now.

"Sixie," Dubs says sleepily, "you're a hunter *and* a chef. You'll make someone a nice little housewife someday."

I kick him in the shin. "Not *your* wife!" I say. "Not any-body's wife."

CHAPTER 26

HOURS LATER, I'M lying as close to the fire that Trip built as possible. We're under a rocky overhang, and we've made a wall of pine boughs to shelter us from the wind.

There's nothing to do but hope for sleep. Dubs and Trip seem to have found it easily enough, but the silence in the forest unsettles me. For one thing, I can't stop listening for the snap of branches or the crunch of a footstep—some tiny sound of approaching Bot doom.

I pull out the Q-comp.

I'm so glad I thought to snatch it from my room last night. Cloud activity and memory access have been illegal for years, and if I'm caught with this thing, I'll get another two decades in the slammer—but at this point, who's counting?

Anyway, the Q-comp is my legacy. I heard an insane rumor once that my grandfather, J. J. Coughlin, invented human brain emulation in the digital form. Well, maybe he invented the technology, and maybe he didn't: all that matters to me is that this little palm-sized gadget lets me see my parents again.

I don't hesitate when I connect to the cloud—I know right where I'm headed. Someplace *warm*.

I close my eyes, and I can feel the hot sun on my face. I'm gliding through the glassy turquoise water of a pool. *This is my dad's memory*. A June afternoon. I've relived the same scene a hundred times.

There's a tree covered with tiny yellow blossoms, and in the shade of it sits my mom, tanned and smiling in a red bathing suit, sunglasses perched on her head.

The air smells like fresh-cut grass and barbecue. Our neighbor, a big guy named Charlie Potts, is grilling hot dogs for the kids. It's my sixth birthday, right before the Great War. There's a giant cake with my name on it sitting on the dining room table.

A small blond girl teeters on the edge of a diving board. "Not the deep end, Sarah!" I say in my dad's voice.

The kid is me, but *this is my dad's memory*. I feel what he felt looking across that pool—fear, pride, and overwhelming love—as the kid starts bouncing on the end of the board, pigtails flying.

And then the kid—me—jumps. She seems to hang in the air for an instant, bathed in sunlight. Then she plunges into the water, making a huge splash, and Dad races toward her, ready to haul her up.

But she surfaces, slick as a dolphin, grinning and spitting water. "That was *awesome!*"

The water's cool and the air's warm, and I'm feeling all the emotions of father and daughter. And what kills me—what

just about *rips me open with longing*—is how happy we were. How carefree. How beautiful we were together. Our family.

We weren't hungry or frightened or lonely or desperate. We were just *happy,* and we believed we would get to keep on being happy.

How stupid we were. How naive.

I wake up shaking. I don't know if I accidentally broke the connection with the Q-comp or if I just drifted off, but when I open my eyes again, I still feel wet. It's not from a pool, obviously. It's the snow seeping through my clothes.

I feel like crying. The life we knew was so beautiful—why did the machines we created decide they had to destroy it?

And then, before I can stop them, more memories come. But these aren't from the Q-comp; these are my own.

Another perfect, sun-filled day. I was running down the street to the market, change jingling in my pocket. My mom told me that I could go buy an ice cream cone, and I was so *thrilled* that I paid no attention to the Bot cars rushing up my street. Nor did I register the distant pop of gunfire. I went to the grocery and picked out my flavors (strawberry and rocky road). I paid, then proudly strutted back to my house.

I was so deep in sugar heaven that I didn't notice that our front door was hanging by one hinge. I didn't notice the frightening silence inside my house—

No, I tell myself. *Stop!*

The first shots of the Great War? Seeing my first dead body at six years old, and thousands more after that day? It's everything I want to forget, *need* to forget.

I huddle closer to Dubs, whose snoring has woken Trip, too. Her eyes gleam at me in the half-light. "You all right?"

I shrug. "Sure. I'm good."

She reaches for my hand in the darkness. "Everything's going to be okay, Six."

But we both know she's lying.

CHAPTER 27

IT'S ALMOST MIDNIGHT by the time Detective MikkyBo arrives home. At least her leg has nearly healed itself. There's that. Riding the elevator up to her family's apartment in the government high-rise, she watches her reflection in the mirrored door. Her black hair is still smoothly tied back; her choker still glitters at her neck. But Mikky stares at herself as she'd look at a disturbing stranger.

Something inside her has shifted tonight. She feels neither proud nor certain nor Elite: instead, she's confused and scared. And she's sadder than she's ever been in her seven-year life span.

When she opens the door, her father glances up from his easy chair. "Ah, it's you, my MikkyBo!" he says warmly. "I was beginning to worry."

Mikky tries to find a smile. She hides the slightest limp. "You know you don't need to worry about me, Daddy."

"No, no, I don't. You've always been my perfect girl," NyBo

agrees with a nod and a smile. "Your brother, on the other hand ... your brother is going to be the end of me. He's wearing me down to nothing."

Mikky unbuckles her holster and sits at the kitchen table. She really doesn't know if she can handle another crisis today. "Daddy, I'm not your perfect girl tonight. Not even close to perfect."

NyBo looks startled by the despondent tone of her voice. He stands and hurries to her side. "You're shivering," he says, rubbing her arms. He holds the back of his hand against her forehead. "Your core temperature is too low."

"I was in the mountains. At the Reserve," she says. "Something happened there."

"What's wrong?" NyBo asks. "What happened?"

But she doesn't have a chance to answer. Her tiny tornado of a sister comes spinning into the room. She bounces into her big sister's lap.

"Kitty Kat," Mikky says, wrapping her arms around her, cuddling her. "You're getting big to be launching yourself at people like that. One of these days you're going to—"

" 'Cause bodily harm,' I know." Kat giggles. "Dad's always telling me that, too."

Suddenly Mikky starts shivering so hard that Kat is nearly knocked off her lap.

"Hey!" Kat huffs. But then she looks at MikkyBo, and her eyes widen. "What's wrong, Mikky?"

Mikky can't stop shaking. She's thinking about those dead kids—some of them no older than Kat. She clasps her hands together, then twists them so hard, she can almost feel her polymer bones cracking.

"Your sister is fine," NyBo says to Kat, but he sounds uncertain. "It's just that, uh, Mikky's slipstream is a little overloaded." He starts to usher his youngest child out of the room. "KatBo, you'd best get to bed. School in the morning."

When NyBo comes back from tucking Kat in, he sits across from Mikky. His dark eyes search her face as he takes her icy hands in his.

"Now," he says, "tell me what happened in the mountains."

By the time Mikky gets through the whole story, she's not shivering anymore. But she feels sick and empty—worse than she's ever felt except on the terrible day when her mother expired.

"The commander said it was necessary," she says hollowly. "But I think—it was a massacre. There was no just cause. We fired on those humans."

"Sometimes, the state must do hard things—for the greater good," NyBo says quietly. "You were raised to believe we live in a secure place, Mikky. And for Hu-citizens, that's how it should be. But you are Elite now, and so you are exposed to the complexities of politics and social order. Sometimes you may have to pretend all is well. Even when it might not be."

"Pretend?" Mikky narrows her eyes. Pretending goes against everything she's been taught by her mother and father. It goes against honesty, integrity, and good faith. "How can anyone trust me if I am pretending?" she asks. "And how can I trust myself?"

NyBo sighs. He is a perfect father, always. "In that case, you must do what you think is best. That was my way. But look where it got me. Decommissioned."

"I think I should report the human massacre," Mikky says.

NyBo purses his lips. "That could cost you your career as a detective. It's your decision, my dear, but make sure you think it through carefully. Very carefully. Then, Mikky, I urge you to do what you think is best."

CHAPTER 28

"DO WHAT YOU think is best."

That's what being Elite means, isn't it? That's what separates us from the humans? That's why I'm in such a state today, why I'm here putting my career and life in jeopardy.

"What's this?" MikkyBo's supervisor juts his chin toward the file Mikky has placed on his desk. He makes no move to pick it up. In fact, he stares at it like it's contaminated.

"It's my report on last night's incident at the Reserve," Mikky answers.

NoamSha is the complete opposite of the commander: a nervous man, unusually short for a Hu-Bot, and often as lazy as a human. Since he's always obsessive about "following protocol," Mikky thought he'd be pleased by her careful record keeping.

Yet his expression is sour, as if he's just eaten something rotten.

"You'll find a detailed account of the events," Mikky goes on, pushing the folder toward him.

She'd worked on it all night, replaying the horrors, wondering how she could have taken control earlier. How she could have stopped the killings. *But the commander, MosesKhan, said he was behind them.* So now what?

NoamSha finally reaches out and flips through the first few pages. "I've already been briefed," he says. "The commander informed me you nearly botched the mission."

Mikky is angry now, but she lowers her head meekly. It's best not to make NoamSha feel he's vulnerable to criticism from his superiors. "I take full responsibility for what happened," she assures him. "That's why I prepared this thorough report. I thought someone might want to review protocol, not to mention Bot communication. As well as any mistakes I may have made."

NoamSha snorts. "The *commander* has reviewed it."

Mikky takes a deep, calming breath. She'd like to take this sorry excuse for a Hu-Bot and shake him until his bolts come loose.

"Someone *else*, perhaps," she says carefully. "I know the premier wants to maximize human cooperation. I understand he takes the loss of life seriously. A raid on this scale, with so many casualties...I just think it should be looked into very carefully."

Her superior's eyes narrow. "You should do less thinking," he says quietly, "and more obeying." His pale hand slices through the air. "That's the end of it, Detective Bo," he says. "Go back to your desk. This matter is closed."

CHAPTER 29

AM I MAKING a huge, terrible mistake? I'm putting everything at risk, and for what—a few human lives?

Mikky accelerates up the winding mountain road, watching as the trees grow more stunted, the ground more brown and scabbed. She can hear the wind whistling through the rocky pass, and even inside her climate-controlled government-issue sedan, she shivers.

This is completely illogical. I almost feel like a human. *Why am I doing this?*

But as many times as she asks herself this question, Mik-kyBo always comes back to the same answer: *Because there's no one else who gives a damn about what happened.*

She knows that NoamSha will look at her report for no longer than the two seconds it takes him to carry it to the recycling bin. Which means that MikkyBo is on her own right now.

But it isn't until she enters the Reserve that she really understands what *on her own* means.

Mikky has to slow to a crawl to maneuver her cruiser on the muddy, pothole-riddled paths. She's heading toward what she thinks is the heart of the Reserve: a shoddy, garbage-strewn square with a headless, armless statue positioned right in the center of it.

The Great War destroyed even stone *humans,* Mikky thinks.

She grips the steering wheel tighter. At this speed, she can't look away from the humans the way she does in the city market. She can't ignore the pain and the poverty all around her: the cold, brutal concrete housing, the half-naked children picking through the trash, and the field of tents and lean-tos on the ridge that smells so bad, she retches as she drives.

It's terrible. It's heartbreaking. At the same time, she knows it's the humans' nature to be this way. Their *fault.* They lack the Hu-Bots' ingenuity and initiative. They let their impulses drive them into poverty and despair. They lie and fight and steal from cradle to grave; they live in filth and addiction.

All that any of these humans needed to do was agree to Reform, and then they'd enjoy a comfortable life in the City working for a caring Hu-Bot Keeper. And yet they refuse. They'd rather live like animals.

Something strikes the side of her car. MikkyBo inhales sharply, then looks out to see the dark, angry eyes of a young boy. As she watches, he throws his other shoe at her cruiser. It goes sailing over the hood. Someone jeers. Then there's another *thunk* as something else connects with a rear door.

She's a Hu-Bot in human territory—a Hu-Bot alone and vulnerable.

This is the dumbest thing she's ever done.

She tries to speed up a little, but the humans are coming out of buildings and crawling out of gutters. They're pressing themselves closer to her vehicle.

Mikky tells herself not to be afraid. She's here to help. Maybe she can make them understand that.

At the edge of the town square, she stops. The humans are crowded so close around her car now that Mikky couldn't go farther if she wanted to.

She takes a deep breath and then leaves the safety of her cruiser. She forces herself to smile in the cold, foul air.

"I'm here to help!" she calls.

Their response is silence. Then someone whistles at her, yells, "You can help me, Sexy Bot—I've got a problem down in my pants! You think you could work it out for me?" A wave of unpleasant laughter ripples through the crowd. Humans love their sense of irony, don't they? Hu-Bots have little use for irony.

MikkyBo pretends not to notice their insults. "I brought medicine. Bandages. Antiseptic."

The humans stare at her like she's speaking a foreign language. Her hand flutters up to her choker uncertainly. Then a middle-aged human—clean-shaven and dressed in clothing that is almost respectable—shoulders his way to the front of the crowd.

"What can we do for you, madam?" he asks, and Mikky immediately recognizes him as a Reformer. Perhaps he is a teacher at one of the Reserve schools—a thankless job, if there ever was one.

"I brought medicine," MikkyBo repeats. "For the wounded." She hesitates. "The massacre was an unfortunate occurrence and a breach in protocol. My goal today is to help the agitators and their families through this difficult time. Perhaps sponsor their transitions to Reformation . . ." She trails off.

The teacher is blinking at her. No one else says anything. And not a single human steps forward to accept her supplies.

What's wrong with these people? Are they too stupid to accept help when it's offered?

"I'm sure there's someone here who could use antibiotics," she goes on. "Or painkillers."

"You got any codeine?" someone shouts. "'Cause I snorted my stash last night. Whooee!"

MikkyBo frowns. This isn't how things are supposed to go at all!

"Listen," she yells, "if you are wounded or sick, please come forward. I can help you!"

But MikkyBo can feel the hostility in the air, crackling like electricity. She glances back at the cruiser, where she left the Mercy 72 tucked under the seat.

No. That's not what this is about. She's here to make peace. "I'm trying to help!" she shouts at them. "Don't you understand?"

"It's Hu-Bots who need to understand!" someone yells, and cheers go up in agreement.

A young boy's voice catcalls, "HU-BOTS, BOW DOWN!"

Mikky gasps. That is *sacrilege.*

Enough is enough.

"You're hopeless," she cries. Her voice booms over the crowd. The front row of people flinches. "Your whole species is hopeless!"

She drops the bag of supplies at the curb and yanks the car door open. But a human hand slams it back shut.

A male, probably twenty years old, leers at her. "I thought you were going to help me with my problem," he says, leaning in close to her neck. "Mmm, you smell as fine as a new car."

Angrily, she shoves him back. He stumbles. She manages to get back into her car and start the ignition.

The humans are hitting the roof, the windows, calling out obscene, cruel things.

To hell with humans. They're even worse than she thought. *How can KrisBo ever stand to be near them?*

But she's getting away. Sure, she's driving only about eight miles an hour, and her car's being pelted with rotten food, but it doesn't matter: she's safe.

And then she hears the choppers.

CHAPTER 30

"THEY'RE BACK!" SOMEONE screams, and the humans start dropping to the ground, covering their heads for protection. Others race for the safety of the tree line.

Mikky looks up to see the first of the helicopters zooming toward the Reserve. Seconds later, they swarm overhead like flies, nearly blotting out the gray sky. For a millisecond, she feels relief. They've come to protect her. But then, almost immediately, comes a terrible dread.

The scene at the Pits rises before her eyes: a girl's face exploding in red, the line of young men shuddering as bullets made them dance...

Mikky brakes and climbs out of the car, waving a white bandage like a flag of truce. *Don't kill them,* she begs silently. *Please, don't shoot.*

And, miraculously, they don't.

That's when Mikky realizes that they aren't the standard-issue police choppers that were used in the Pits raid. A Capital Center insignia is painted on their sides.

"Return to your housing blocks immediately," a voice shouts from a speaker. "The Reserve is now on lockdown."

The helicopters land in the square, kicking up wind so strong, it blows down a dozen tents. Soldiers tumble out—mostly Bots, with some Elite Hu-Bot ranks from the Center headquarters mixed in—and Mikky watches as the remaining humans rise and scatter.

When MosesKhan steps out of the last helicopter, Mikky swallows her dread.

She salutes him crisply. The commander ducks his tall frame under the still-spinning blade of the Center chopper and strides past her like she's invisible.

"Commander, I assure you the situation was not out of control. I realize I should not have been on grounds without an escort, sir, but—"

"The criminals have been apprehended?" he interrupts. "You've caught the girl—Six?"

She looks at him blankly.

MosesKhan stares down his narrow nose at her. "That is what you're doing here, isn't it, Detective? Looking for the car thieves? The girl?"

"Of course," MikkyBo says quickly. "I was looking for the car thieves. But I haven't yet—"

"You're alone?" he asks.

"Yes. As I said, I—"

"*I, I.* There is no *I*, Detective Bo," the commander seethes.

"Of course," MikkyBo agrees. "But, as we discussed, a human quantum computer is a direct threat to the Center. The girl has one—Six—"

"*Enough.*"

The commander never lets me finish a sentence, she thinks.

MosesKhan steps so close to MikkyBo that she can feel his breath on her forehead. "There is an independent streak in you, Detective Bo, that will not serve you well," he says quietly. "And a marked sympathy toward the human species that I find distressing." His mustache twitches. "The report you gave to NoamSha, for instance."

MikkyBo pales. That traitor—he did worse than recycle it! He gave it to the one person who shouldn't have seen it! "Sir—"

"The language was *emotional* for standard protocol," the commander says coolly. "Words like *innocent* and *murder,* when it's well known that humans are *guilty in their natural state.* There is a rumor that this misguided compassion for humankind runs in your family."

Mikky freezes. There it is. The threat. Has her worst family secret been discovered? Her brother?

"No," she says carefully, for she's terrible at lying. "That's incorrect."

"Excellent." He seems to believe her. "Because I might remind you that these are our enemies. Unlike their city brethren, these Reserve humans are *noncompliant.* Remember that next time you ask us not to shoot them."

Mikky gasps. She hadn't sent out that thought wave or opened a brain channel to him. *The commander had hacked into her encrypted slipstream.*

And she'd been thinking about KrisBo—which means that the commander has to know about him, too.

"If you'll excuse me," Mikky says, her voice shaky, *every-thing* shaky. "I have to go back to questioning the witnesses."

"I know you'll find those criminals, Detective," the commander says. "Everyone's counting on you, MikkyBo. *Especially* your family. I hope you won't disappoint us...Find Six, and all is forgiven."

CHAPTER 31

IF YOU THINK things couldn't go downhill from hypothermia and near starvation in the wilderness, well, I'm here to tell you you're dead wrong. They can go way, *way* down.

When we crept into the Reserve after two days of freezing and starving in the mountains, there was police tape blocking off X Housing, and the streets were crawling with Botcops. There wasn't a human in sight. They were all "sheltering in place," which was what the blaring speakers were ordering them to do. And, considering what happened the last time the Bots came to town, it would be suicidal not to follow directions.

But Dubs and I—we were *wanted*. And we couldn't get to our houses without being spotted and arrested, maybe shot.

Which was why, when a six-Bot brigade started to turn down our alley, we had to hide in the first place we saw: the three-foot crawl space under the back porch of Em Four's "restaurant"—a broken-down, illegal shack on the cliffside edge of the Reserve.

And so here we are. Above us is a rusted grate, through which Em's obviously been tossing food scraps, trash, and waste for decades. In other words, my friends and I are lying on a bed of moldy noodles, half-gnawed bones, and raw sewage.

I can barely breathe, and my eyes are watering from the stench. "When this is all over, Dubs, remind me to kill you," I whisper.

And he has the balls to look at me like I'm crazy. "It was your idea to come back, girl," he huffs.

"We were starving," Trip reminds her cousin.

"We were free!" Dubs insists stubbornly.

"No, we were on the run because of you and your stupid idea to steal a Hu-Bot Corvette!"

For the first time I realize how mad I am about Dubs getting us into this whole insane mess. And before I'm even aware I'm doing it, I've got a handful of rancid goo in my hand—and I *fling* it at him.

It splatters onto his forehead and drips down over one eye. The bad boy blinks at me, mouth agape, and for a second I think he's going to break his rule about hitting girls and straight-up sock me with one of his wrecking-ball fists.

Instead, his face cracks into a grin. "That's 'cause I live in the *present,* Sixie," he says, jabbing me in the ribs. "Who else can you count on to bring excitement into your life?"

Okay, I'm half smiling now—I can't help it. You gotta love a guy who can laugh off a sewage attack.

Then up above we hear a crash, followed by shouts

coming from the housing blocks across the street. I guess *shelter in place* is shorthand for "be interrogated and have the bejesus kicked out of you."

Is this all about us?

I hope it's not. But I'm pretty sure it is. So by the time I hear the next person screaming for mercy, I'm shaking with guilt and fear, and I half hope that one of my neighbors gives us up.

But no one knows where we are. Everyone I know and love is right here in this hellhole, and even *they* don't really know me. Sometimes I wonder if that's because I don't know myself, either. How can I, when my life — my history — was destroyed by bombs?

The Q-comp can give me back only so much of the past.

Trip's squeezing her eyes shut. "Make it stop," she whispers, reminding me what a little kid she is. "Make them go away."

Dubs sits up, nearly cracking his head on the floorboards. "Want me to try, little Trip? I could run out — draw their fire..."

"You don't mean that," I tell him.

He looks offended for a second, but then he nods. "You're right," he says. "I'm fine with dying in a hail of bullets, but not when I'm covered in shit. That's just undignified."

"Will you stop talking about dying, please?" I hiss. "No one's going to die today."

But right then, a light shines through the slats. There's a Bot-cop standing next to the back porch. He's playing a flashlight into our hiding place.

"Come out of there right now — or I'll shoot."

CHAPTER 32

WE FREEZE IN the light's beam.

I don't think the Bot-cop can see us, but he's obviously suspicious, which is never good. Has he heard us talking?

Turn around, I plead. *There's nothing in here. Turn. Around.*

Instead, he reaches down and, in one swift movement, yanks off three boards from the side of the porch. Forget the flashlight — now the daylight can almost reach us, even back here in the corner. The Bot starts to crouch down, and all I can see is the gun strapped across his chest. It's a Mercy.

And in a flash, my mind sees other things, too: the faces of the kids who were standing next to me two days ago, before they were mowed down by Bot bullets. And I spy a glimpse of my own possible death: killed by a low-functioning android while lying in garbage under a shack that sells rat meat.

I know death can come at any time, but that's just too depressing.

Without hesitating, I silently wriggle farther down into the garbage, burying my arms and legs, and even my *face,* into it. The soft, oozing sensation of sinking into rotting muck is so repulsive, it's a miracle that I don't vomit or pass out — or both.

I feel jiggly movement beside me as Dubs and Trip burrow down, too.

The human survival instinct — it's kind of a miracle, isn't it? We'd rather eat shit than die any day.

I tell myself that when the Bot-cop finds us, I'm going to

lunge for the gun. I'll count on Dubs to tear the Bot apart. Maybe Trip'll have time to make a run for it.

The cop pokes around on the edge of the sludge. If he had a heart, I'd say it wasn't in this particular duty. There's hope for us. After a few more minutes, he seems to give up. Turns away.

We wait a few more minutes to make sure this isn't a trick, a typical Bot-cop trap, but no other metal face peers into the opening. Finally, I poke my head up and nudge Trip and Dubs, next to me.

We're all gasping for air—all that organic matter breaking down into nitrogen will get you woozy—but I don't think any of us has ever looked happier than we do now, covered in filth.

Total human move, right?

Well hey, I've said it before, and I'll say it again: *At least I'm not a Bot.*

CHAPTER 33

WHEN THE BOT patrols have finally called it a night, we slink out from under the porch. At the Reserve black market, Trip barters her silver necklace for three hot showers and some new (used) clothes for all of us. Dubs buys food and blankets with the last of his cash.

Exile supplies.

Loaded up now, we make our way down the narrow path to the mountains. Ahead of us, the Pits bonfires burn. I hear drunken laughter and then the sound of a fight breaking out.

I can feel my footsteps slowing. Rezzies are loyal to one another, but if they know that Dubs and I are the cause of the Pits massacre, it's not going to be pretty.

Dubs nudges me in the ribs. "Pick it up, Sixie," he says. "You're walking slower than my grandma."

"Our grandma's dead," Trip reminds him.

"That's my point," Dubs says. Impatient, he shoulders past

me and starts high-fiving everyone around the main bonfire—like the other night never happened. Like we aren't standing on a killing field.

"Yo!" shouts Nine, a tall, black-haired kid who used to crush hard on Trip. "I thought you guys were gone for good." He tries to put his arm around Trip, but she shakes him off. "Zee Twelve said you got wasted by the Bots, but I said you got away."

Dubs nods. "Hell yeah, we did. We just came back to say adios," he says. "We're heading to the mountains again. Going to lie low for a while."

Zee Twelve limps out of the shadows. His leg's in a make-shift splint. "Lie low?" he repeats menacingly. "How come? Does it have anything to do with that 'Vette of yours?" He pokes his finger in my chest, hard. "The one the Bots wanted back *real bad?*"

Dubs wedges himself between us and holds his palms up. "We're just here to grab some stuff, Zee. Then we're out. The Bots won't bother you, okay? Because, yeah—they're after us."

Zee Twelve's eyes narrow. "You'd *better* get out of here," he says. "Because if the Bots don't get you, *I will.*" He spits on the ground at our feet, and then he turns and limps away.

"Aw, he's just pissed 'cause y'all wasted on him in the race," Nine says. "The Bots are after all of us, ain't they? One of these days this whole place is gonna go up in smoke…"

"That's why we have to fight!" shouts a girl with greasy red hair.

"You think so, Ell Two?" Nine says. "Heck, I'm ready." He karate chops the air. "Bring it on, skin jobs!"

"You been practicing kung fu?" Trip asks, giggling.

Nine grins at her. "My dad was Chinese. I don't need to

practice. It's in my blood." He chops the air again and almost loses his balance. I realize he's drunk.

The girl with red hair says, "You guys, we need *guns*."

I think of the Colt I've got stashed in my gear. That makes one pistol—against about a million.

But I know these kids aren't going to revolt. They're going to keep coming to the Pits to drink bathtub gin and huff paint. They couldn't fight if they wanted to.

And when it comes down to it, they *don't* want to.

But can I blame them? I don't want to fight, either, because that basically means suicide. But it seems like I don't have much of a choice.

I ask Nine, "How many kids did the Bots kill?"

He looks down at the ground. "Seventeen."

Seventeen kids who were just getting a few kicks watching a car race. Killed without mercy or regret. Or justice.

I clench my fists. "And you think you're going to fight back," I say bitterly. "Like last time?"

"We were ambushed after the race," the redheaded girl insists. "If we had been prepared—"

"I'm not talking about the other night," I tell her, my voice hard. "I'm talking about the war. Remember? It took *three days* for the Hu-Bots to wipe out almost our *entire species*."

"I'm not afraid," the redheaded girl says, crossing her arms over her chest defiantly.

"You should be," I snap. "We all should be."

Trip stares at me for a minute. She looks like she's shaking. "I think I'm going home," she says softly.

I nod. "Good idea," I say. "They're not after you."

Dubs watches her walk away. "Why'd you have to scare her off?" he asks.

"Because I don't need one more single drop of blood on my hands," I hiss. And then I grab my pack and head for the trees.

CHAPTER 34

MIKKY RUNS THROUGH the snowy woods, barely noticing the frigid cold. *The humans must be apprehended and brought to justice.* Her status as an Elite detective—and her family's well-being—are at stake.

Considering the weather and their injuries, the suspects can't have gotten far. MikkyBo uses her digitally enhanced night vision to sweep the area for footprints. Her lightweight polymer skeleton and high-capacity respiratory organs make the steep terrain easy.

But suddenly it occurs to her: she can track the humans with the Q-comp.

The Bots had sacked Suspect 1's solo sanctuary but found no trace of the quantum computer, which means the girl must have it with her. Since there are only a handful of Q-comps left, Mikky does a code scan for them via brain uplink. She finds several in the Center—where Hu-Bot ministers of culture mine human memory for study—but there's nothing anywhere near the Reserve.

Had the sense to shut it off, didn't you? she thinks, pushing her way through the underbrush. *Maybe you're not as simpleminded as you look.*

MikkyBo tries the cloud next. Accessing the Mountain Central Cloud via slipstream, she finds only one mind-upload bank still active. Judging by the zebibits of data, the bank is massive—whoever those humans were, they must have undergone whole-brain emulation instead of the more common selective scrap-streaming. It would be a nightmare to sort through, but Mikky doesn't have to. She can already see that a memory was accessed two nights ago.

Eureka.

After another quick code scan, she's staring at the coordinates of her suspects.

Mikky lets her internal GPS guide her, and within ten minutes, she's at ground zero: a small clearing surrounded by pine trees, with a rocky overhang that would have provided the humans with shelter from the elements. Snow dusting everything.

She nudges a mound of snow and uncovers the remnants of a fire. And there, not three feet away, hastily covered by branches, lies the quantum computer.

Mikky turns the Q-comp over in her hands. It's bulky and outdated—but, according to MosesKhan, this very device could compromise Hu-Bot society. If Mikky turns it in, maybe she can forget about the kids. Without the computer, they're no longer a threat.

Right?

It seems logical—but that wasn't MosesKhan's order. *Find the criminals. Deliver them to me. Dead or alive. Your family is counting on you.*

So where are the car thieves now? Mikky studies the snowy terrain, seeing no fresh prints but her own. But if they left the computer, she tells herself, they'll be back for it. She tucks the Q-comp into her vest and creeps back into the woods to wait.

They broke the law, she reminds herself. *They got people killed. They deserve to be punished. Don't they?*

It's the right *thing to do.*

Something in the back of her mind snags on that last part, but she pushes her doubts down, instead calling forth pleasant sensations while she waits. Mikky tries rocky road ice cream, and then peppermint, and then her old standby, butter pecan. Conjured on her tongue, they are wonderful and creamy—but, despite the rich sweetness, she tastes something bitter underneath.

CHAPTER 35

"BIG MAN, BUILD fire!" Dubs beats his chest and does his best caveman impression.

The tiniest bit of smoke curls up from the damp kindling. "You call that a fire?" I ask. I'd laugh if I weren't so damn cold.

"Patience, woman," he barks. He leans over and blows on the flames, feeding them bits of lint from his pockets. I toss in a few dry leaves and a handful of twigs, and pretty soon we've got ourselves an actual campfire.

It's risky to build one just a mile or two from the Reserve, but we're freezing. Hungry, too. I take out the small pot I "borrowed" from Toothless Ten (he won't miss it), the soup bone Dubs talked the former Mrs. Cullen into giving him, plus two carrots and a handful of mushy, sprouting potatoes we got at the black market.

"Wow, Sixie," Dubs says. "That looks almost *gourmet.*"

I snort. "Coming from a guy who lives on bug bars, that's not such a compliment." I scoop up handfuls of snow and throw them into the pot, then thaw my fingers over the flame while the "soup" heats up.

Dubs sighs happily. "You and me are outlaws now," he says. "Like Jesse James. Like Butch Cassidy and the Sundance Kid."

"Yeah, and remember how *those* guys ended up," I point out.

His brow furrows. "Dead?" he asks.

"Yeah, genius. Dead."

But he doesn't care a bit. "Hail of bullets, baby," he says, "and a blaze of glory. That's all I need."

And I don't say anything. Sure, he's my best friend — but I don't have to agree with him on that one.

Then Dubs looks at me, all serious for a minute. "I know it's not the best of circumstances or anything, but it's kinda nice, just you and me now. Hangin' out..." He stops. "Like, we don't have to say anything. We can just chill."

"I don't want to talk to you, either." I laugh, but then I, too, get serious. I look him right in the eye. "I wouldn't want to be in this mess with anyone else," I say. "You're my family."

I almost tell him I love him, but I know he wouldn't be able to take it. He's already blushing, lifting the lid off the pot and pouring the thin soup into our cups. He's normally as loud as a bull elephant, but give the guy a real emotion, and he clams right up.

"We should probably set up camp," he says later, after our bellies are warm, if not exactly full.

I stand up and brush the dirt from my jeans. "You can. I'll be back in a little while."

Dubs frowns. "Sixie, you're not going back for it. Not now. In the dark. Alone."

"Since when do you give a rat's ass about being careful?" I shove my hands in my pockets. I buried the Q-comp at our last camp because we thought we'd be back in a matter of hours. Now that my hunger's sated, it's all I can think about.

"Since I want to sleep, is when," he whines. "What's so important about it that we can't go tomorrow?"

"It's everything I have left of them," I say, more harshly than I mean to. "You *know* that."

And without another word, Dubs buttons his coat back up, kicks snow over the fire, and follows me on an hour-long hike down the mountain.

A little after midnight, we come upon the clearing, but as soon as we do, I stop dead in my tracks.

There are footprints everywhere.

I can feel the adrenaline spinning through my veins. I can't see much; the moon's still too low in the sky. When I try to listen, I can't hear anything but the pounding of my heart.

"I've got a bad feeling about this," I whisper.

But before I can say another word, Dubs is charging forward through the snow, barreling toward the place we buried the Q-comp.

"Dubs, no!" I yell.

Because the snow's falling fast, but the footprints are fresh.

Because we're in a clearing surrounded by trees.

Because we have no idea who's out there.

But Dubs, true to form, doesn't give a damn about any of that.

"We didn't come all the way back down here for that stupid computer to have it just be *gone*," he rages, rooting around in the brush and kicking snow everywhere.

I crouch behind a boulder, my eyes scanning the darkness for anything that might be heading for him. My fingers reach for the Colt and grip its cold handle. I'm searching every shadow, every crevice.

Except for the one right behind me.

CHAPTER 36

THERE'S NO TIME to struggle: it grabs me by the hair, yanking my head back; then a hand wraps around my neck. I twist and flail, but I'm caught like a bug in a net.

I don't even know what it is—human, Bot, freaking *Bigfoot*—but it's strong as hell. I claw madly at the gloved hands on my neck, but they tighten as my kicking feet are lifted off the ground.

I can't breathe.

Black spots cloud my vision as my oxygen level plummets. My brain sparks like fireworks. I feel a sudden, amazing rush—like the best high of my life. But I know what it means: my brain cells are starting to die.

I hear Dubs shout, "Let her go, you robotic asshole!" but it sounds like he's yelling from outer space.

Then he slams into us, and the Bot loses its grip—now it's holding me with only one hand. I start kicking, fighting like mad to get away, driving elbows and fists at anything I can reach.

The Bot pivots away from me, smooth as a dancer. I hear a pained grunt from Dubs as the Bot delivers a powerful blow with its other hand.

But my friend won't give up. He sounds that maniac roar of his—the one that sends anyone who knows him scurrying for cover. Then he charges. The Bot stumbles back at the impact.

The glove releases me, but it's not over.

I see a flash of black leather as the Bot delivers a lightning jab right to Dubs's nose. Blood spurts everywhere.

I'm still bent double, coughing, when Dubs collapses in a pile of red-splattered snow.

I glance up, my oxygen-deprived brain sputtering into gear like a boneyard bike. *I've got to get out of here.*

And that's when I realize it's *her.* The beautiful, black-haired Hu-Bot responsible for the Pits massacre.

For a moment we just stare at each other. I'm thinking: *You almost just killed me.* And: *But the other night you let us escape.*

I can't tell if I'm still spinning from lack of air, or what, but it almost seems like she's looking at me with *concern.* Like she's sorry she just crushed my windpipe and KO'd my friend.

Like she's about to let us go again.

But then she blinks and shakes her head like she needs to clear it. She narrows her glittering, unnatural eyes, and I understand what's about to happen.

So I do the only thing I can think of: I freaking *run.*

CHAPTER 37

I'M STUMBLING, SLIDING, and cursing my way through the icy woods, hoping against hope that the Hu-Bot experiences a spontaneous electrical failure.

Every frozen gulp of air makes my nose burn and my lungs seize. The muscles in my legs blaze in white-hot pain. Branches slap my face, and roots reach out to catch my ankles.

Behind me, I can hear footsteps. Even though I had a head start and I'm running for my life, the Hu-Bot psycho is gaining on me. She's probably not even running that hard. She's probably skipping along back there. Taunting me. Making me think I've got a chance of escape.

Which I don't.

Except...

Up ahead there's a choice to make: skirting along the base of a rocky cliff—or trying to climb right up it. I don't think

Hu-Bots were engineered to enjoy mountain climbing, so I figure going vertical is my one hope. I take a deep breath and start scrambling up.

For a short while, the Hu-Bot sticks close behind me, clambering over boulders like they're nothing but pebbles. Then the boulders start to thin out, and pretty soon there's just a sheer wall of cliff rising up. And this is what I've been looking for.

Humans have thousands of nerve endings in each finger; Hu-Bots have a fraction of that. If the Hu-Bot can't feel as well as I can—if her sense of touch isn't human sharp—then crawling up a cliff with tiny crevices for fingerholds is going to be a lot harder for her than she wants it to be.

And maybe I can finally gain some ground.

I wedge a hand into a crack and haul myself up, then find another hold and do it again. And again. And *again*. My arms are quickly exhausted, but I ignore the pain.

This is my last chance.

The Hu-Bot's still close behind me. We're spiraling as we climb, so by the time we're seventy-five feet up, we've come around to the other face of the cliff. There's a narrow river running along below us now, and I tell myself that this is good: that if I fall, it's better to hit water than boulders.

I point a quivering toe out to the left, find the foothold, then stretch out my left arm to grasp a tiny indent with two fingers, and then the rest of my body over to follow, balancing on a tiny platform for a few agonizing moments, until I'm ready to try to move again.

Now we're moving by inches—it's the world's slowest chase. My calves are in knots, my fingers bloody. Every step feels like it might be my last.

She's only a few feet below me now. *Why doesn't she just shoot me and get it over with?*

There's a tiny ledge right next to my right foot, and I can see her calculations. She's going to make a leap for it.

She pushes off the rock, launching herself toward me. Her hand hits the ledge, but she can't find a grip. Her fingers scrabble wildly. She clings to the cliff, balanced on a tiny outcropping on one foot. She flings her head up and looks at me.

"Help!" she calls.

Is she *joking?*

Does she really think I'm going to help her?

She's flailing now, losing her balance.

People say that Hu-Bots don't really have feelings. That they've just learned to fake them perfectly.

But when I look into those blue eyes, I see pure, undeniable terror.

She's screaming now, and the words are hard to decipher, but I think she's saying, "Oh God, oh God, please—"

I think of the Hu-Bots sitting in church pews carved by the humans that they later murdered, and my blood goes to ice. I lean down low, like I'm going to help her.

I say, "You have no god."

At that, her eyes open impossibly wide—and then she loses her grip and falls.

CHAPTER 38

DESPERATION AND DISBELIEF flood MikkyBo's mind. She reaches out, hands clawing at the empty air.

But you can't grab on to nothing. Gravity always wins.

Her hair billows up, and cold wind tears through her clothing as she spins downward. For the briefest of instants, it's almost like flying. Like a joy rush...

Then Mikky hits rock—and a sharp edge slices off her left arm clean at the elbow.

As Mikky's internal processors speed up, time seems to slow down. She stares at the space where her hand once was in shock. She knows it should hurt, but she's too shocked— too terrified—to feel the pain of it.

But what she feels next is worse than pain. It's something she's never experienced before. It's like being electrocuted over and over again. It feels like her entire being is nothing but one cosmic, silent scream of terror.

It is the exact opposite of a joy rush, and it *will not end.*

The wind catches her body, turning her around, and Mikky slams into the cliff again. She feels her leg twist at the knee, and her panic intensifies. Then comes another impact, and her head snaps at the neck.

Her head bobs like a yo-yo now, connected to her body by only by a thin flap of bioskin. She sees the river below, rushing up to meet her.

She is about to expire.

All her perfectly engineered processors can't begin to comprehend this thought. It's simply too horrific.

Crash.

MikkyBo lands on a rock in the middle of the river. Her body flops, but her head bounces. Then she's soaring up, back into the sky she fell from, watching her body slide off the rock and get dragged downstream, its three remaining limbs bobbing, its neck a ragged mess of tissue.

My head's come off, MikkyBo thinks, her mind numb with disbelief.

Then she slams back into the water. Water fills her nose and mouth. Her swirling hair brushes her cheeks. The rapids force her down.

She reaches for one last joy rush while her brain is still intact. She imagines chocolate-mint ice cream. She can almost taste it.

But before she does, there's a blinding light. A last gasp of electrical activity. Of consciousness. It's brighter than the sun. It lasts one beautiful, terrifying instant.

And then everything goes dark.

CHAPTER 39

TAKE THAT, YOU overbred can opener! I think, watching the Hu-Bot fall.

I'm feeling *great*—I'm safe!—until I realize she's rocketing down to earth with my Q-comp in her pocket, which means that my family's memories will be destroyed right along with her.

And then she screams, so high and scared. And next, her freaking arm gets torn off.

She's bouncing down the boulders like a giant doll. And, just like that, I'm not angry anymore. Suddenly I'm sick.

Because the thing is, even though Hu-Bots' insides are 3-D printed replicas of human insides and are made of tissue grown on lattices, I've seen enough real humans being blown up or ripped to shreds to know that the Hu-Bot looks as real as any of them on her way out.

It's *gruesome.*

I'm still clinging to the rock, my toes wedged in a crevice and my arms shaking, watching the whole horrible scene. And I can't help it—I start to think that maybe she wasn't just a dumb Hu-Bot, after all.

Maybe she resembled humans in other ways, too.

She tried to wave the Corvette to the side of the road, didn't she?

She never fired the Mercy.

She stood there after the crash and watched us limp away.

Which means that, in a way, she saved us—more than once. And what did I do for her? I laughed as she fell.

My stomach twists, and pretty soon I'm gasping for breath. But not from exertion—from tears.

I don't even understand what's happening. I've managed to keep a lid on my emotions for a *decade,* and now I'm freaking *crying* for someone who knocked out my friend, who tried to capture me, and who helped kill a bunch of my people.

Not even someone. Some*thing.* A mass of metal and plastic and God knows what else.

The Hu-Bot hits the river. Her *head* pops off like a champagne cork.

I stand there, shaking and sobbing, for another minute. And then I do the stupidest thing I could ever imagine anyone doing. It's so moronically insane, I can't even believe I'm capable of it.

But I am.

I pull my fingers from their crevice. I reach out to the air. And I jump after her.

156

CHAPTER 40

I'M SCREAMING.

Or at least I think I'm screaming. Every part of my body is sending screams to my brain, but all I can hear is the roar of the water.

By some miracle I survive the jump, but now the churning current is doing its damnedest to rip me to pieces, just as it did to the Hu-Bot when she fell.

Where's the Hu-Bot now?

The night's too dark, and the water's moving too fast; I can barely see anything. Just the white foam of the rapids, shoving me down. Just rocks in the riverbed, banging me bloody. I go under, and my larynx spasms as it closes to keep water out of my throat.

I kick hard off the bottom and thrust my head out of the river. Oxygen surges to my brain as I take in air in huge, grateful gulps.

I'm being carried downstream, faster and faster. I go under again, then resurface, gasping.

I grab on to a log wedged between two rocks, and for a moment, I can breathe. But then the log comes loose, and the water pulls me along as its roaring grows louder. The sound deepens, changes. And I know it without seeing it: downstream it's about to come to an end. Downstream it's about to become nothing but air.

Ahead of me is a waterfall.

The rapids drag me under again, tearing the log from my hands. I claw my way back to the surface, reaching out for something—anything—else to hold on to. Panic makes my feet slip. I'm breathing too hard, and I snort water into my nose. Desperate, I fling out my arms, pinwheeling them in some mad crawl stroke to keep myself from sliding over that edge.

My hand hits something solid, and I close my fist around whatever it is in a deathlike grip.

It's... an *arm*.

The Hu-Bot's arm—the one that's still connected to her torso. I guess the two of us are going to swirl down the great drain of life together.

Well, that's fitting, you moron. You got what you came for.

But the adrenaline's kicked back in, and I'm using reserves of strength I didn't know I had. I pull myself out of the frigid water. I claw my way up the Hu-Bot's body, using it as a bridge, and then hurl myself onto the shore.

My face lands on hard rocks, and I feel a cut open up on my cheek. But there's no pain—I'm too cold for it. My body's racked by gasps; my mouth spews out a fountain of water mixed with blood from the broken capillaries in my lungs.

Eventually the coughing stops, and I breathe in sweet air. I don't know if I've ever felt worse—or better.

It's got to be some kind of miracle that I'm not dead.

I know I can't stay here; I'll freeze to death. And I've got to find Dubs. But I can't move yet. I close my eyes, willing my heart to steady and my body to stop shaking.

After a few minutes, I open my eyes again.

And the Hu-Bot's staring back at me.

CHAPTER 41

I SHRIEK AND scramble backward before I realize what's happened: the Hu-Bot's head, separated from its body, has caught in an eddy near the shore. Her long black hair's snagged on a branch.

And I burst into tears. *Again.* I'm exhausted, freezing, alone. I don't know how I got into this mess, and I don't know how I'm going to get out. And those eyes just watch me, calm and blue.

I wave a hand in front of them: no response.

I reach down and pull the head out of the water. It's heavy, and there are leaves and twigs all tangled up in the thick, glossy hair. "I tried to save you," I tell it.

But that's not exactly true. I knew I couldn't save her even before I dove off that cliff.

I followed her down *because I didn't want her to die alone.* How messed up is *that?*

And so now here we are—a sopping-wet girl and a broken-down Hu-Bot—on the side of a Colorado river as dawn begins to break through the trees.

I scan the sky above me. Did the Hu-Bot send out a distress signal as she fell? Are the helicopters already on their way? How many years in prison do you get for destroying a Hu-Bot—a hundred? Or do they go all medieval on you and just impale you on a pike?

I need to find Dubs, and then we have to get back to our campsite, gather up our supplies, and start running.

It's because of you, I think, suddenly not feeling sorry for the dead Hu-Bot at all. *You couldn't just let us go once and for all. Cars get stolen every day, but you had to be a hotshot and bring in the full troops.*

The eyes are frozen open, and the mouth is caught in a scream—but, even so, the Hu-Bot looks perfect. Beautiful. Her damp skin, pale and smooth, her lips pink and full.

"Stop looking at me," I say, and I shove the head away from me. It rolls a few feet, knocks into a rock, and then comes to a stop. Facing me again. The deep blue eyes are still open, and I could swear they just twitched. Or *blinked?*

Can a Hu-Bot survive dismemberment and decapitation? That seems impossible.

I toe its cheek with my foot, studying the face for any signs of consciousness. Nothing. But the eyes... they seem to be watching me.

You're delirious, Six.

I need to get out of here—the cold is obviously making me crazy. I stand up, turning my back on the Hu-Bot face. Her body's on the shoreline, the feet still partway into the

161

water. I pick up a handful of stones, like I'm going to scatter them over her in some kind of half-assed burial. But then I remember: *the Q-comp.*

And I fling myself at her torso, my still-numb fingers ripping through her government-issue uniform. I find an interior pocket, protected by a zipper. I yank it open, and, amazingly, the Q-comp's still there.

I haul it out, my hopes surging—but it's as dead as you'd expect.

Now what?

Just leave, I think. But before I do, I need to do something else. I reach down and pull off the Hu-Bot's jacket and shirt. The material is so high-tech, it's almost dry already.

I try to avert my eyes from her skin, barely covered by thin undergarments. From the swell of her breasts. From the stump of her arm.

I slip out of my clothes and climb into hers. They're too big—she's six inches taller than I am, at least—but they're lightweight and warm.

Maybe I'm going to make it after all.

I stand over the pieces of her body for a minute, feeling light-headed and grateful. "Thanks, Hu-Bot," I say quietly, and I turn and take a few steps away.

But then, for some reason I can't fathom, I look back. And I see those blue, blue eyes watching me.

"You've got to be kidding me," I mutter to myself.

I stand there, uncertain, for way too long.

Then I gather up two long sticks and wind my wet clothes between them, making what looks like a little raft. I load the android parts onto it and start walking, dragging the whole thing behind me.

And if a giant Bot patrol finds me? Well, I've obviously gone so crazy that execution would be a kindness.

PART TWO

CHAPTER 42

NYBO PICKS HIS way through the trees, scanning the snow-covered ground for any trace of a footprint. It's been twenty-four hours since MikkyBo checked in with him—thirty-six hours since she left the house. His son, KrisBo, vanishes for days at a time, but Mikky has never been anything but perfectly responsible. This is how he knows, deep down, that something is wrong.

NyBo senses movement up ahead, behind a stand of pine trees. He rushes forward, relief flooding his systems: he's found his daughter, and now he will bring her home.

Bright lights suddenly glare down on him from overhead. Spotlights from churning Capital Center helicopters sweep through the dark forest.

The realization hits him like a punch to the face—it's not MikkyBo ahead. It's four android Bot-cops.

NyBo stops short, his fingers automatically reaching for

the Elite communication bracelet he used to wear. It would give him the details of their mission instantly. But there's no bracelet anymore. Not since he left the force.

He calls out to the lead Bot. "Do you have information on the location of Detective Bo?" he asks urgently. "You must be looking for her, too."

But they don't answer him. Instead, they reach for their pistols.

And point them at him.

"I am a Hu-Bot," NyBo snaps. "Your *superior*. Lower your weapons immediately."

The Bots shift slightly, but they don't lower their guns. NyBo stares at them in shock. In all his years on the force, he'd never seen a Bot disregard a Hu-Bot's command.

But Mikky said they'd disobeyed her that night in the Pits.

The Bots' unblinking eyes watch him without emotion. Their guns remain aimed at his thorax.

"I am a decorated officer in the Capital Center's Elite Force," NyBo barks. "You *will* stand down."

"A *former* officer, NyBo. Isn't that correct?"

NyBo whirls around. It is the commander, stalking toward him through the trees. Behind MosesKhan, another squad of Bot-cops combs through a clearing, kicking away the snow and shining their flashlights into rock crevices. NyBo watches as a Bot bends over, then straightens up with something that looks like a cooking pot.

"Commander!" NyBo says, saluting. "I assume you are searching for MikkyBo as well, and for that you have my deepest gratitude. Here are the coordinates that I've searched. Together, we can find her quickly, I'm sure of it."

His old military leader stares back at him coldly, his jaw set, and NyBo falters. His warning systems engage. A threat is in the air, as sharp as the icicles hanging from the tree limbs.

"Sir—" he begins.

The robo-dog at the commander's feet lowers its head and snarls. Without looking down, MosesKhan kicks it with his foot.

NyBo tries again. "Sir," he says, "Detective MikkyBo —"

"We are not looking for your daughter," MosesKhan says flatly.

"But . . ." NyBo stops himself. He had hacked into the Elite Force slipstream, and that was how he'd learned of the search party leaving the capital.

But if the Bots aren't looking for MikkyBo now, that must mean she's already been found?

"Of course, forgive me!" NyBo exclaims. "You have already

located her. Please accept my apologies for thinking I could aid you. I am so grateful." He smiles nervously. "I suppose she's already back at work and too busy to call!"

The commander does not return the smile. "MikkyBo's work with the Elite Force has concluded," he says.

NyBo's breath catches in his throat. "What do you mean?" he asks softly.

MosesKhan's eyes are dark and expressionless. "Your daughter has expired," he says. "Regretfully."

NyBo gasps. *No!*

"Her sensors went unexpectedly dark, I'm sorry to inform you," the commander says. He doesn't sound sorry at all.

NyBo shakes his head in disbelief. *Not Mikky. Not his daughter.*

"Don't look so upset," the commander scolds. "She served the capital as she was meant to. Even though your dedicated little MikkyBo botched her assignment, she still brought us to the car thief."

"The car thief?" NyBo hears himself ask. His processors, overwhelmed with grief, are running at half speed.

"J. J. Coughlin's granddaughter," the commander says. "It appears your detective skills are not as sharp as they once were. *Or perhaps you hacked into the wrong slipstream.*" The menace in his words is clear—but MosesKhan goes on. "The escaped war criminal's granddaughter was hiding out on that miserable Reserve all these years. Now that we've got her on the run, she's going to lead us right to J.J. himself!"

But all NyBo can focus on is the fact that his daughter is dead. With the wet snow seeping through his pants, the esteemed Sergeant NyBo, decorated military hero, begins to cry.

MosesKhan steps backward in disgust. "There is honor in death," he says. "But there is no honor in tears."

Tears are for humans, NyBo thinks. He wipes them from his face, but still they keep coming.

CHAPTER 43

SUNLIGHT FILTERS THROUGH the stained-glass windows of the church, decorating the pews with jewel-like spots of color. The room is filled with hundreds of Hu-Bots, all dressed in midnight blue, the official color of mourning.

NyBo stands behind the pulpit, his shoulders hunched in grief. His eyes scan the room for his son, but KrisBo is nowhere to be seen.

How could it be that *he*, former Elite sergeant NyBo, has lost a wife and *two children*? The pain of it is etched on his face. He almost wishes he would expire—right now.

His hands grip the worn wood of the pulpit as he begins the eulogy. "We're here today to celebrate my daughter Mikky," he says.

Then he notices MosesKhan standing near the back of the nave, his arms crossed over his chest. Next to him is

the premier, flanked by Bot guards. They don't look sympathetic — they look suspicious.

Of *him*.

NyBo understands instantly: they're not here to mourn
Mikky. They're here to make sure he doesn't say anything
critical of the Hu-Bot command.

He takes another deep breath. Then he starts to lie. "MikkyBo was a devoted servant of the Center," NyBo says wood-
enly. "A bright young Hu-Bot whose *only thought* was to serve
her leaders, to do her duty, and to be the best she could be in all
things. She loved her commanders and her fellow detectives,
and she was unconditionally committed to the Hu-Bot cause."

Then NyBo glances up at MosesKhan, whose nose is
wrinkled like he's smelling something foul.

Maybe, NyBo thinks, *he's caught a whiff of my bullshit.*

He remembers Mikky's tortured eyes when she told him
about the Pits bloodshed. She had started to doubt the wisdom of her superiors.

Was it that *doubt* that had gotten her killed?

But still NyBo goes on, talking about Mikky's belief in
order and uniformity and her deep faith in the wisdom of the
Hu-Bot Council. He talks until he sees MosesKhan look
bored and appeased. He talks until the premier nods in
agreement. *Yes, MikkyBo was a credit to the Hu-Bot race.*

He's almost done, but there's one more thing.

"Benevolent premier," NyBo says, addressing his leader
directly, "I have already lost one treasured child, but I must
beg you to look after another, who is also among the missing."

The Hu-Bots in the pews start to whisper, but NyBo
ignores them.

"Please," he says. "Save KristoffBo..."

Then, from the back of the church, comes a loud, strangled sob. NyBo starts, turns toward the door. And there, in the shadowy foyer, he sees his child.

"My son," NyBo breathes, his voice a mix of heartbreak and hope.

KrisBo steps forward, into the light. He's wearing a midnight-blue dress, with a black beaded shawl draped around his muscular shoulders. *"Daughter,"* he answers. "Your daughter."

Hundreds of Hu-Bots swivel around in their seats, and every last one of them gasps.

"The premier doesn't want to save me," Kris says—to NyBo, and to the whole congregation. "He wants to reprogram me. To wipe my existence clean. He doesn't want to save any of you, either."

The chaplain, waiting in the wings at the front of the church, steps forward and says, "Young man, if you'll just partake in the daily Recitation of Values with us..."

Ignoring him, Kris walks down the center aisle in his heels. "Let me tell you about MikkyBo," he cries. "Mikky believed in me. She believed in all of us, because she was taught that our race was merciful, and kind, and just."

There are a few murmurs of agreement from the pews, but KrisBo ignores them. He's crying openly now, makeup sliding down his face.

No, her *face,* NyBo thinks. But his mind can't process that.

"Mikky was ambitious. She was loyal. She did everything right. *So why is she dead?"* Kris asks, looking around. *"Why didn't the premier save her?"*

The room goes utterly silent. NyBo holds his breath.

The premier stands up, his cheeks white with anger. "It is not in my interest to save a glitchy Hu-Bot," he seethes. "What I seek is to *eliminate the glitches!*"

KrisBo flinches. NyBo rushes forward, positions himself between the premier and his son. "KrisBo does not have a glitch," he cries. "He's just grieving. Give him some time."

And then he pushes his sobbing son toward the wings.

He must keep him safe—for as long as he can.

CHAPTER 44

I THOUGHT I knew the way back to Dubs, but I was wrong.

After stumbling around for hours, dragging the Hu-Bot's body parts behind me like a little girl with a broken doll I can't bear to throw away, I finally have to stop. I find a small cave tucked into a high, stony ridge, and I go inside and *collapse*.

I know I need to build a fire and somehow find food — but all I can do right now is shiver. There's ice in my hair, and my teeth are chattering so hard, I'm afraid they're going to crack.

I curl up in a little ball in the corner, and somehow I manage to fall asleep.

But something wakes me in the middle of the night. A sound, a movement — a sense of threat. The cave is pitch-black and cold as a freezer. I stay as still as I can, listening with every cell in my body.

It's probably just bats flapping around, I tell myself, shivering. *Or maybe a fox or something prowling outside.*

I'm starting to drift off when the sound comes again.

"Hello?" says a voice.

I scramble backward in the dark, fear shooting through me. I smack my head against a rock so hard, the world goes white. A second later, though, everything's black again.

The something's not outside. The something's *in here.*

"Who's there?" I hiss. I reach into my pocket for a lighter, but my panicked fingers are too clumsy to light it.

No answer.

Everything's quiet for so long that I tell myself I was just dreaming. No one's here but me. Me and a couple of bats.

I give the lighter one last try, and now a small flame flickers on the cave's jagged walls. The light shines on the bones of a long-dead animal. And, of course, on the Hu-Bot parts— a head here, an arm there, the torso propped against the wall.

I'm spending the night in a *crypt*. Maybe by morning there'll be another dead body: mine.

I decide to build a fire near the cave entrance. Might as well die warm, right? I work slowly because I'm so weak, but there are plenty of twigs and dry leaves for kindling. In a few minutes I've got a nice little blaze going.

I turn to the Hu-Bot head. Its blue eyes are open and glassy. "Impressed with my fire-starting skills, aren't you?" I say. Then I toss a pebble at the Hu-Bot's forehead. "Of course you're not," I say. "You're dead."

It opens its mouth. "The—proper term—is *expired*."

CHAPTER 45

I JUMP SO high, I nearly crack my skull on the ceiling again. I grab a stick and hold it out like a sword. "Stay right there!" I yell.

The head blinks slowly. "Does it—look—like I can move?"

"I don't know! All I'm saying is: *don't*." I brandish the stick near her cheek.

She blinks again, her blue eyes almost black in the dimness. "Why did you save me?" she asks.

"I have no idea," I say. "How about a thank-you? How about a 'Gee, my microprocessors would be fish food if it weren't for you, pal'?" I throw the stick down in frustration. "I guess you're just really surprised, huh? Since you think we humans are just a bunch of wild animals." Then I make chittering noises and gnash my teeth at her. I probably look like a psychotic chipmunk.

The Hu-Bot frowns. "Don't tell me what I think, or how I think."

"Well, hello, *hypocrisy*," I sneer. "Like you skin jobs haven't been trying to control how we think for a decade!"

"It's for your own protection," the Hu-Bot replies calmly. "Your species shows extremely poor judgment."

And I can't help it—I start to laugh. Because I *must* have poor judgment: why else would I be huddled in a cave with a dismembered enemy android?

"Seriously," I say when I'm done guffawing. "Could my life get any worse?"

The android mutters something, and I turn toward the head. "What?" I demand.

The Hu-Bot sighs. "'There is nothing alive more agonized than man/of all that breathe and crawl across the earth,'" she repeats, louder this time. "It's from a book," she adds.

I roll my eyes. "Yeah, it's from *The Iliad*," I answer snidely. "And I don't know if you noticed, but I'm not a man."

Those blue eyes look at me in surprise. I'm a little shocked myself. It's not like I've got some enormous book collection back in X Housing. But I've read the ones I *do* have many times.

"I didn't think—" she begins.

But I don't let her finish. "And it was a *human*, an *animal like me,* who *wrote* that book. Think about that next time you tell us to bow down!"

The Hu-Bot looks at me with what seems like pity— which is ironic, because I'm not the one in several different pieces. "Why are you humans always so angry?" she asks.

I gape at her. "Gee, I don't know, Hu-Bot. Maybe because you killed my parents? Then made us your slaves? Or maybe I'm angry because you ruined my already hellish life over some rich android's car. Or because you and your goons snuck up on a bunch of unarmed Reserve kids and used them as target practice!"

"I didn't shoot anybody," the Hu-Bot cop says right away. "Honestly... I was as shocked as you were when the shooting started at the Pits."

"*Honestly.*" My harsh laugh echoes off the cave's walls. "Have a little bit more respect for my *limited* intelligence. Here's another bit of *The Iliad* for you. 'We men are wretched things, and the gods, who have no cares themselves, have woven sorrow into the very pattern of our lives.'"

"I'm not a god," the head whispers. "And I barely even feel like a Hu-Bot." She stares up at me pleadingly.

"No wonder," I scoff. "I mean, you're more like a pile of recycling."

"That's not what I meant. I meant in my mind. I'm like you. *A person.*"

"You're not a person!" I shout. "*I'm* a person—which is why I feel so shitty all the time. You wouldn't know what that's like, because you're a machine. A fake human made out of plastic and metal."

And I swear I see tears in her eyes.

I didn't even know they could cry. But that severed head can cry all night—I don't care. As far as I'm concerned, Hu-Bot tears are just another upgrade to trick us into trusting them.

The tears slide out of her eyes and make a small puddle on the rocky floor.

She really does look hurt. Sorry. Sad.

"Get over it," I mumble.

And then I turn away, because I feel weird watching her get so upset.

"I prefer to be silent now," the Hu-Bot cop says finally. Her voice is calm, but there's an almost undetectable quiver in it.

"Yeah, well, great, because I prefer for you to be silent," I snap. And then I throw my old shirt over her face to cover it up.

I should have left her by the river.

CHAPTER 46

"WHOA, LOOK WHO it is—it's *Sixie!*" The too-loud whisper hisses into my dreams, and my eyes snap open.

Dubs's flushed, round face is floating over me. I blink in confusion—is hunger making me see things?

But then Dubs slaps the sides of my face with his broad palms and cackles maniacally, and I know he's for real. He's got two black eyes—I guess the Hu-Bot punches took their toll—but otherwise he's looking just like himself: a little bit crazy.

"You have no idea how glad I am to see you," I gasp, sitting up.

"You'll be glad to see *this*." Dubs grins. He reaches into his pocket and pulls out a can of beer.

I think: *Beer? Really? How about* food? I decide not to offend him, though. "But I mean—I thought you might be dead."

"Yeah, I thought you might be, too." His face goes serious for a minute, then he takes a swig of beer.

I wonder where he found it—some abandoned hunter's camp? If so, that can's ten years old, at least. "How'd you find me?"

He grins again. "Persistence, little lady," he says. "I've been looking *everywhere*."

I rest my head for a second on his shoulder. "Thanks for not giving up on me."

His smile gets even wider, and I realize his eyes are all black and are pinwheeling around. "Are you—" I'm about to say *high*, but then Dubs holds a paper bag in front of my nose, and I smell the acrid scent of shoe glue.

"Want a sniff of Happy?" he asks.

My eyes dart to the Hu-Bot cop—I wonder if she's paying attention to this. If she's reflecting on our base human nature. But her eyes are closed, and her face is blank. "I'd rather have *food*."

Double Eight shakes his head, his lips pursed apologetically. "Didn't find any of that."

I put my hands over my empty belly. I can't even remember the last time I ate. I know that the fumes would kill my hunger for a while. That's why the poorest families in Tent City give glue to their kids when there's no food.

But it'd kill my senses, too, and I'm already weak enough.

Then Dubs lets out a low whistle. "What the hell is *this*?" he says. His eyes bug out in delight: he's finally noticed the Hu-Bot head.

"Look closer. I think you'll recognize her."

Dubs leans in. "Holy shit, it's the Hu-Bot bitch!" He picks up the head. "Well, hello, sweetheart!" Then he tosses it in the air and knocks it against the rocky ceiling. He giggles like a madman.

"Don't do that, you idiot," the Hu-Bot scolds.

Dubs drops her like a hot coal, and she lands facedown on the ground. "It talks?" he yelps.

"Yeah," I say flatly. "It talks."

He kicks it with his foot.

"Don't," I say—without even thinking.

Dubs turns to me. "Why not? You guys besties now? You been having heart-to-hearts in here?"

"Yeah, right," I snort.

"We're not friends," the Hu-Bot confirms.

"No, you sure as hell aren't!" Dubs yells. "Because Sixie's *my* friend, and she isn't gonna be besties with no talking tin can."

"Talking tin can?" the Hu-Bot sniffs. "My IQ is *twice* yours."

Dubs laughs. "Fat lot of good your IQ's gonna do when you need to walk somewhere."

The Hu-Bot's about to retort when a shout rings through the air. A shout coming from *outside*.

I freeze. "Dubs," I whisper. "Did you cover your tracks?"

He just stares at me with wide, spinning eyes. I guess that means no.

I motion to him to move farther back into the cave. I tell myself that maybe, just maybe, whoever's out there will just keep on walking.

And for a moment, it seems like the whole world is quiet. Safe. Peaceful.

But then it erupts in gunfire.

CHAPTER 47

CHAOS. AN EARDRUM-BURSTING volley of bullets.

I scramble backward and fling myself to the ground, pressing my body as tight as I can against the rocky wall.

Four Bot-cops fire from the mouth of the cave, their bullets opening craters in the stones. Dust and smoke fill the air.

I've made myself as small as possible, hiding behind the Hu-Bot's headless torso, but I know it's only a matter of time. Any second now, I'm going to feel one of those bullets ripping through my flesh.

Then Dubs, who was hunched down on the other side of the cave, stands up. Starts lumbering forward.

"What the hell are you doing?" I shout. "Get down!"

He advances on the Bots, barely flinching as the bullets fly. *How is it that he's not getting hit?* A rip appears in the arm of his coat, but he doesn't flinch.

I've got to bring him down, or else a bullet will. I jump to my feet and hurl myself toward my friend.

"Halt!" I hear the Hu-Bot head yell, but I don't know who she's talking to.

I'm shouting, too—swearing at Dubs, trying to get him down—but suddenly I can't get my breath. Suddenly it feels like a hand's squeezing my heart and a fire's been lit inside my stomach.

I double over, my hands clutching my guts. When I look down, I see blood. A lot of it, bright red and hot.

"I've been shot," I whisper.

Somehow, no matter how bad the circumstances, it's always a surprise to find out you're actually going to lose. Like, *really* lose.

I don't feel pain at first—not really. Just shock. Then the nausea comes, and I collapse. "Dubs, get *down!*" I yell from the ground.

"My gun!" the head is shouting.

"What gun?" Dubs yells, finally dropping low.

I can feel the pain now, sharp and terrible. I go fetal, curling up against my wound. I can see the Bots' dark silhouettes against the sky as they push forward through the narrow opening.

At least it'll all be over soon.

But now that Double Eight has been jerked out of his daze, he's *pissed.* He lunges toward the Hu-Bot's head, grabs it by the hair, and snarls, "Where's the gun?"

"My boot," the Hu-Bot says.

Dubs drops the head. He grabs the Mercy, cocking and

aiming it in one smooth motion. Then he faces the mouth of the cave, putting his body solidly between me and the Bots.

"No!" I try to prop myself up to stop him, but Dubs shoves me down.

"Come at me!" he roars at the Bots.

And they do come.

But Dubs doesn't back down. He drops the first one immediately with a neat hole to its metal forehead. The second takes a shot in the neck. Dubs lets out a psychotic war cry as he fires off round after round from the powerful Mercy. The

third and fourth Bot crouch down and keep shooting, but they're no match for Dubs's wild, human fury.

I can't bear to look anymore. I hide my face and wait for the shooting to stop.

When it does, I lift my head to see a pile of shredded metal bodies jamming the entrance. Four dead—excuse me, *expired*—Bots. And Dubs is still standing over me, breathing hard.

"You did it!" I whoop from the ground, and then wince, regretting it. "I guess that Mercy pistol can shoot to kill even if there's no heart to find, right, Dubs?"

But my friend doesn't answer. From behind, I see him sway a little.

"Dubs?"

Then I notice the holes in the back of his dark jacket.

The spatters of blood on the ground.

"Dubs!" I scream, and my best friend goes down.

CHAPTER 48

I DRAG MYSELF across the cave to where Dubs lies unmoving. A pool of blood darkens the dusty floor. It's growing larger by the second.

"No no no no," I whisper.

I slump forward and reach for his shoulder — and my finger pokes right into a bullet hole. I shriek and pull my hand back. It's covered in even more blood now — mine *and* his.

"Dubs," I cry. I slap his cheek hard, the way I did when he passed out in the Killer Film. Now he's supposed to punch me back with double the strength. Or crack one of those maniacal hyena laughs.

But he just lies there.

Then his eyes flicker open. They're glassy and unfocused, like he's looking at something really, really far away. "Hey," he whispers.

"Dubs, you've got to hang on," I say desperately.

"I don't know, Sixie," he says. He smiles at me, ever so faintly.

There's a rattling in his throat. Blood trickles out of his mouth, and I try to wipe it away. "It's going to be okay," I tell him.

"Just a scratch, huh?" he gasps.

I nod, trying frantically to smile. Wanting more than anything to reassure him. "Yes! You'll be fine!"

But then his whole body convulses. His legs kick like he's having a seizure. I try to hold on to him, but I'm not strong enough.

"Sixie," he whispers when his body goes still. He tries to smile. "I'll see you in hell."

And then his eyes roll back in his head. I wait, my breath caught in my throat. Then I start screaming. I shake his torn-up shoulder. "Don't you dare die! You said you'd never leave me! We were supposed to take care of each other. See each other through!"

"Is he . . . ?" I hear the Hu-Bot gasp.

I tear off my friend's jacket with clumsy, desperate movements, and when a seam rips, I think, *He's gonna kill me for that,* because Dubs loved that ratty old bomber jacket, even though he could barely stuff his arms into it.

I stop caring about the coat a second later, though, because when I finally get it off him, I see the other wounds.

The Bots had good aim. The bullet holes are all concentrated on his chest, the red blood blooming around them like roses. They must've hit him a dozen times.

"Oh, Dubsy . . . ," I murmur, my voice cracking. He hated it when I called him that, which is why I never did.

"They wanted me!" I yell. "They were coming for *me*, you bastard, not you!" My breath catches with pain as my stomach contracts around the bullet. Tears burn behind my eyes, clouding my vision.

"He wanted to die," a voice says. Soft, sympathetic—but the words are cold.

I turn to glare at that pretty, disembodied head. "You don't know what the hell you're talking about!" I shout.

On her torso, across the room, her arms lift defensively, as if she thinks I might actually hit her. "That's why he wanted to see the Killer Film that night, isn't it?" she asks. "It was part of a deep, self-destructive urge."

"Shut up," I growl, but the Hu-Bot can't take a hint.

"I studied the tapes, Sixie."

She calls me Sixie? Like we're freaking friends?

"There's footage of you two going into the forbidden

theater." She blinks at me. "You looked reluctant. But he wasn't, was he? And it was his idea to steal the car. I know that." I can tell she wants to hold my gaze, but I can't look at her anymore. "Perhaps he . . . *welcomed* a path to peace, to end the pain inside him."

"I said shut it!" I stagger to my feet, wincing as the movement aggravates the gunshot. I press my hand over the wound and feel more blood seeping between my fingers. "You don't know anything about him!" I stand over the Hu-Bot head with my fists raised threateningly.

But a tiny part of me wonders if she might be right. Hadn't Dubs always said there was no one he gave a damn about but me, that we were both too good for this pathetic excuse of a life? Didn't he go on and on about that blaze of glory, the hail of bullets?

Well, he got them, all right.

My knees buckle, and I go down hard. My face slams against a rock because my arms are too weak to stop me. So I lie there on the gritty cave floor and sob.

See you in hell, Dubs had said.

But this is *already* hell. So how am I gonna know where to look for him?

CHAPTER 49

"YOU HAVE TO get out of here," the Hu-Bot says. *"Now."*

Pain and grief overwhelm me. I can't seem to do anything but breathe.

"I said, you have to get out of here!" the Hu-Bot repeats.

"Screw you, Hu-Bot," I manage. "This isn't the City. I don't have to do anything you say." I don't think I could move if I wanted to.

"My name is Detective MikkyBo," the Hu-Bot snaps. "And I am trying to *help* you. Though I do not know why," she adds.

"Neither do I," I say. "And it's not like I give a crap anyway. So don't bother."

Her lips tighten into a line, and she gives me the look our old dumb-dumb schoolteacher used to give Dubs and me: disappointed, superior, tight assed.

"Do you have any idea how much time you're wasting?"

she asks. "You're not even hurt that badly. It's just a muscle wound. You'll be fine."

I gape at her. "I don't know if your *microprocessors* can comprehend this, but this is my best friend," I say, taking one of Dubs's hands in mine. It's already cold. "And I'm not leaving him."

I bow my head, like I'm going to say a prayer or something. But how would I even begin? *He fell as a tower falls in the strong encounter* ... The damn *Iliad* again.

The Hu-Bot interrupts my thoughts. "Those Bot drones were connected to a slipstream." She looks over at the pile of them, blocking the entrance. "Their expiration will trigger restock teams. Understand? They're going to keep coming until their orders have been executed."

She means until I've been executed. Just like my best friend.

"He's gone," the Hu-Bot says gently, and a hand pats my shoulder.

I flinch and swat it away. She's somehow managed to control her severed arm remotely!

"Remember that he died trying to protect you," she says.

"Is that supposed to make me feel *better*?"

But the truth is, Double Six would kick my colon into my throat if he saw me here, just waiting to die next to his shot-up corpse. And that's what finally gets me moving.

First I wrap some of my old clothes around my wound. I hope the head's right about the shot missing anything vital.

Then I pick my way out of the cave, climbing over the mangled drones who've gone to the great assembly line in the sky. With a machine gun in one hand and the Mercy 72 in the other, I step, blinking, into the light. I'm soaked with sweat and light-headed from blood loss. Body tense, I scan the landscape for the next death squad.

My breath catches when I see the cruiser, parked only a few hundred yards away on the remains of an old logging road.

The dead drones' Hu-Bot commander?

Then I notice the smashed headlights and the nasty dent in the side, and I realize it's the Hu-Bot chick's car, half-wrecked from our car chase.

"Goddamn, Dubs." I shake my head. I know what happened now: high on glue and searching for me, Dubs stumbled upon the Hu-Bot's patrol car. The temptation would have been too much. *Why not take a little joy ride?* he must have thought. *I'll get to Sixie faster that way.*

And he led the Bots right to me. To us.

But it's too late to get mad at him, and at least now I've got wheels.

I trudge forward through the snow. When I climb inside the cruiser, an auto alarm nearly splits my eardrums. **"INTRUDER!"** it shouts.

But then another, calmer voice says, "Hello, 68675409M," with such closeness that I shoot a panicked look over my shoulder before throwing myself out of the car and slamming the door.

They know where I am.

And there's no way I can outrun them on foot.

I hobble back to the cave, where I grab the surprised-looking head and the ever-moving arm, toss both on top of the Elite Force torso, and gather the whole pile of half-naked Hu-Bot up in my arms.

"What are you doing?" she demands, her voice quivering with alarm.

"What does it look like? You're coming with me."

"No, I'm not!" she protests. "I'm a liability! I'll just slow you down!"

"Maybe," I say. "But you're the only chance I've got."

I pile a few more of the Bot-cops' guns on top of the Hu-Bot parts. Then I take one last look at my best friend. "I'll find you in hell," I whisper. "And pretty soon, by the looks of it."

CHAPTER 50

BACK AT THE cruiser, the Hu-Bot is not feeling very compliant. I guess she really *did* want to get left in the cave.

"Turn off the tracking device, Minnie," I repeat firmly. "Or I'll drop-kick your head over the cliff."

"Mikky!" she corrects me furiously. "Detective. Mikky. Bo. And it was one thing to help you when the Bot-cops came. They killed your Pits friends—they didn't need to kill you, too. But if you think I'm going to help you steal my own official security vehicle, then you're *sadly* mistaken. I am a member of the Elite Force, and—"

"I know someone who can fix you," I blurt.

Even though I'd planned to dump her once she'd killed the tracking device. Even though taking her where I'm going would be the worst possible thing.

"So do I," MikkyBo snaps. "My commander will see that I

am repaired, directly after he apprehends you. Which should be any minute."

I hold Mikky's head in front of my face and let the rest of her parts fall into a heap in the roadside slush. "If you think your commanders are going to waste time putting you back together when they can whip up another droid exactly like you, then *you're* the one who's 'sadly mistaken.'"

"My name is MikkyBo," she repeats. She glares at me, her eyes blazing azure fire. "I was the top of my class in neural replication. I received four years of intensive training in combat, counterintelligence, tactical communications, explosives, systems management—"

I break in. "So you can better enslave humans—"

"—and I have a father, and a brother, and a little sister." Her voice breaks, but she doesn't stop. She spits the words at me like daggers. "We're *not* all the same. We're not replaceable."

"Neither were my parents." I seethe.

For a long moment, we just stare at each other angrily. I'm listening for the crunch of tires on the road or the chop of a helicopter above—sounds that will save her and doom me. Right now, though, all I hear is the icy wind slashing through the trees.

"Stop pulling my hair," Mikky eventually says. There's resentment in her voice, but defeat, too.

I untangle the long blue-black knots from between my fingers and clumsily try to smooth it around her face.

"Now place me in the vehicle," the Hu-Bot directs.

I open the door, and the alarm starts up again: "INTRUDER! INTRUDER!"

I set Mikky's head in the backseat. "Turn it off," I yell, hurriedly shoving her torso and parts in the back as the alarm shrieks our location to every spy cam and slipstream in the entire domain of the Central Capital City.

The Hu-Bot detective hesitates for another second. Then she flicks her eyes upward and says quietly, "Systems, dissolve."

CHAPTER 51

DON'T THINK ABOUT who — or what — is chasing you. Don't think about the deep shit that awaits you. Just focus on the road.

Too bad it's so overgrown, I can barely see it. But still we climb, and the wind roars louder and the snow begins to fall.

"Watch it!" the Hu-Bot head says from the backseat as I list too far to the right. The drop on that side is straight down.

"I'm trying," I snap, yanking the wheel as the tires skid. "Your cruiser's shit on the ice. I would've thought the great and noble premier would pull out all the stops for his *Elite Force.*"

"Central Command has responsibilities for a much larger cause," Mikky says. "It cannot concern itself with maintaining individual machines."

I glance back at her, unsure what the quiver in her voice means. She's staring straight ahead, propped on a heap of my old, wet clothes so that she can see over the dashboard. After a few seconds of silence, she shifts her gaze, looking up at me out of the corner of her eyes.

"You're really going to take me there?" she asks meekly. "To a place where I can be repaired?"

"I said I would, didn't I?" I say with more than a touch of annoyance. The truth is, until that moment, that little bit of vulnerability in her voice, I'd *still* been planning to ditch her.

But what if I *do* help her? It'll go against an unwritten law that dates back to the Great War, and it will probably be the biggest mistake of my life.

"I don't even know if I can remember the way," I mutter.

I can keep following this road, but when it ends, can I find the path that I last saw as a terrified eight-year-old? A path that's old, unused, and buried by snow? And then can I make my way down it, carrying a busted-up Hu-Bot?

Right now, I'm so weak, I don't know if I could carry my own weight, let alone hers.

"What's wrong?" the Hu-Bot asks sharply.

I must've been swerving again. I blink quickly as the road goes in and out of focus.

"I'm probably dying, is what's wrong," I snap. I hate the self-pity I hear in my voice, but the pain is overwhelming. I'm feverish and sweating, dizzy from blood loss.

Mikky's eyes widen. "But you have to get us there!"

Nice. Real sensitive.

"Talk to me!" she says brightly. "Tell me a story."

Right . . . I don't feel like chatting. We're not besties, head.

"It'll help you stay conscious," the Hu-Bot insists.

Maybe it will. At this point, there aren't a whole lot of other options.

"Um…"

Seconds pass. The tires slide on the ice. Snow falls. My head spins.

What the hell do you say to a Hu-Bot?

"I have a sister, too," I say finally, breaking the silence. "And a brother." I take a deep breath. "My sister was my best friend. My brother was a bully, though, even when we were little." My chest tightens as I remember Ricky holding me down, his knees shoved between my shoulder blades. I'd cut up one of his shirts to make a puppet, and he was *pissed*.

"We have observed this," the Hu-Bot says calmly. "Violence starts in humans from a very young age."

"It's not like that all the time," I say, feeling defensive of my species in general, and my brother in particular, even though I know both are pretty much shit. "We also know how to have fun, which you Hu-Bots seem to really hate. When my brother and sister and I would fight, my mom used to make us hold hands and sing her favorite songs. We'd just stand there, belting out these goofy tunes, even though we were all totally tone deaf."

I look at the Hu-Bot, grinning helplessly at the memory. She actually smiles back.

"And then—I'm sure you'll think this is all sinful or whatever—but then my parents would start to dance."

I can picture them so perfectly. Mom starting to shake her hips. A tilt of the head and a cock of the eyebrow. Dad, usually so serious, unable to resist joining in. Spinning her around, doing silly, lame moves that made us kids go wild.

"By the end I'd be laughing so hard, I couldn't breathe. And my stomach would be killing me." I shake my head in disbelief. "Kind of like now. But now is a lot less fun."

"You should slow down." Mikky's voice spikes with alarm.

"It's kind of hilarious, though." Suddenly I'm laughing. Giggling like a maniac and choking on the bile that's coming up in my throat. "Isn't it just hilarious?"

"Watch out!" she shouts. "Six!"

And right before we go over the cliff, I think what a god-damn shame it is that the last thing I'm going to hear before I die is a Hu-Bot yelling my name—a new name my own family never even heard.

CHAPTER 52

"DON'T MOVE. JUST pretend like you're asleep."

"I can't. It hurts. It hurts really, really bad. I want my mom. Where's my mom?"

"You gotta stop crying."

"It's just—all these people. The smell. I can't breathe. What did they . . . ? What if they . . ."

"Pretend like all those people are asleep, too."

But my friend Kathleen knew as well as I did that they weren't asleep. Some of them still had their eyes open. Some were missing arms, and some were so burned up, they didn't even look like people.

They *were* people, though. Humans. Thousands and thousands of humans, each and every one of them murdered by the robot army.

Kathleen and I had been outside during the initial attacks on the houses. We stayed alive because we knew the best

hide-and-seek spots and because, at six and eight years old, we were small.

Small enough to burrow down into a pile of corpses and not be seen.

We didn't mean to come here. We were trying to get to the school, because we thought we'd be safe there. But when we arrived, there was no school—just a big hole in the ground where our classrooms had been.

A hole that the robots, with their awkward, jerky motions, were filling with bodies.

It wasn't a good hiding place—not like our tree fort or the forest near the creek—but we didn't know where else to go, and Kathleen was getting scared and woozy. We saw how the robots shot at the uppermost bodies before they added the next layer of corpses. We made sure to scooch down real deep. With so many corpses pushing down on us, we could barely breathe.

Pretend they're asleep. Just pretend they're asleep.

"We only have to wait here a little longer," I kept whispering. "Then it'll be over."

Kathleen's arm was burned, though, from when she went into her house after the *boom,* looking for her parents. The wound was raw, oozing blood and pus, and she was making these hiccupping, gagging noises. I didn't know if the sounds were because of her arm, or because of what she found inside her house, or because of where we were now.

I didn't know about my own parents yet, but I was too scared to cry. Too scared to make any sound but a whisper.

"My grandpa will help us," I assured Kathleen. "He'll make it better. He knows the president."

"What if the president's dead?" Kathleen asked miserably. "What if they're all dead?"

All sounded too big. *All* sounded like something I couldn't imagine.

"Shh. Do you hear that? Someone's coming."

———

"Wake up! Sarah Jean Coughlin, wake up!"

I open my eyes to see the cracked dashboard console just inches from my face. I'm slumped forward against the steering wheel, and the hood of the car is pointing straight down the mountain.

Looks like the only reason we didn't plunge all the way to the bottom is that the cruiser got stuck between a boulder and a tree. Black smoke billows up from the engine.

"Oops," I whisper. I'm too weak to move.

"Happy now, Sarah?" a male voice suddenly asks from behind me — *close* behind me.

"Dubs?" I gasp. In my pain and delirium, I imagine that he's come back to life.

A snort of disgust follows this question. "You mean your drug-addicted, delinquent accomplice? You left him behind, did you? Well, I'm sure the Hu-Bots have worked him over by now."

"I didn't leave him," I protest. "I would never leave him."

Not while he was alive, anyway.

Remembering the image of my friend collapsing to the ground, I whimper, then wince as pain stabs my side. "Am I going to die, too?" I whisper.

"I would expect so," comes the reply. "At this point, it's the best thing you could do for yourself."

And I finally recognize the voice for its cold cruelty. "Grandfather," I say, my shock giving me the strength to turn my head and face him.

I told you, Kathleen, I think, my head still spinning toward the dream. *I told you he'd come.*

"Don't call me that," he snaps. "I'm not your family. Your pitiful, thieving life bears no relationship to mine. And, on top of that, you nearly destroyed the cargo, which is much more valuable than you could ever hope to be."

Before I can answer, I hear the side door open and close, and the old man is gone.

The cargo?

"Mikky," I call.

There's no answer, though, and when I manage to slide toward the passenger seat, I see that the head is nowhere to be found.

I start to wonder if I only imagined my grandfather sitting in the stolen car.

I start to wonder if maybe I'm already dead.

CHAPTER 53

WHEN MIKKYBO REGAINS consciousness, her head is clamped in metal vises, and her body is bound to a metal table by thick leather straps. Humans surround her, wearing unsterile paper gowns and archaic surgical masks. Although she can't turn her head to look, Mikky's pretty certain she's the only Hu-Bot for miles.

She has made a grave mistake.

She'd expected unconventional repairs when she went with the fugitive — but there's no sign of the soothing, warm pools where Hu-Bots are formed and, if need be, resurfaced. Where are the vast 3-D printers, or the soul-data selection screens, like those she'd perused with her parents before KatBo was created? Was this even an actual Birthing Center?

Something else concerns her, too: she can't feel the gold collar at her neck anymore. *The mark of her Elite status, which she'd been explicitly forbidden to remove.*

A woman walks over to her, looking down at a clipboard, her pale skull showing through thin, orange hair.

"Where's my Elite collar?" Mikky asks her.

The woman shrugs without looking up. "Destroyed."

Mikky is furious. "That was a badge of honor, bestowed upon me by Commander Khan himself as a measure of his confidence!"

"It was also a tracker." The woman's close-set eyes sparkle with amusement. "Didn't think you were getting in here with that, did you?"

Mikky glares at her in helpless rage. Not only is she in an ancient, filthy laboratory, but *no one has any idea where she is.*

"What are you doing to me?" she asks, her anxiety spiking as another human female begins cutting off what's left of her uniform. "Back away immediately! Humans, *bow down!*"

The woman laughs. "Oh, honey, that line doesn't work around here."

And she and her compatriots go right along with their work, sticking Mikky with IVs and swabbing her with a cold liquid that stings her nostrils.

As a dark-skinned young man goes to work, stitching her head back onto her torso, Mikky tries to focus her energy on a joy rush—perhaps a body massage or a bowl of ice cream.

But she keeps feeling the needle tug against the bioskin at her neck. She can't concentrate enough to leave her present. And the vulgar humans—they just keep talking.

"The craftsmanship is amazing," a masked woman murmurs while taking measurements of Mikky's arm. "Look at the detail in this polymer skeleton."

"Remarkable," the man fussing with her neck agrees. "This is the best model I've ever seen."

Model? MikkyBo thinks. *I'm not a* model—*I'm an individual. A* person.

But of course, she knows she *is* the best they've ever seen. She's Elite, and these ignorant, tinkering humans are going to ruin her!

"Who is your commander?" she asks suddenly. "I demand to speak to him right now."

"Do you, now?" The woman with the clipboard laughs, exposing her square, horselike teeth.

Unlike the others, she isn't wearing a mask, and Mikky shudders to think of all the bacteria she must be spewing into the air. Humans' mouths are among the dirtiest things in the world.

"Jay!" the horsey woman shouts across the room. "Her Highness here wants to talk to you!"

"Sergeant Macy," a man calls back gruffly, "did I not *specifically* instruct you to keep her quiet?"

His voice isn't loud, but the harsh tone of it makes the woman's face redden. Sweat appears above her lip.

"Anesthesia! Get going!" Sergeant Macy barks, and the other humans working on Mikky rush to follow her orders.

The man called Jay walks toward MikkyBo's table. He's slightly built, of medium height, but he carries himself with the rigid confidence of a soldier. When he gets near enough for Mikky to see him clearly, she gasps at his heavily lined face and close-cropped white hair. The man is *old*—much older than most humans in the City or on the Reserve.

"Print a new polymer humerus for the break," he orders.

It's clear by his staff's reaction that they are in awe of him. And possibly afraid of him.

Even chained up and helpless, MikkyBo is not scared. "What you're doing here," she says, "*tinkering*...with Hu-Bot parts—this is sacrilege."

The old man merely regards her carefully while a dark-skinned man wearing glasses approaches her with a mask. *They're going to knock her out.*

Her words come faster. "The creation of life is a complicated science. We are far more intelligent than you could ever dream of being. Repairing me is not a task for some amateur lab technician in the market for a Hu-Bot slave!"

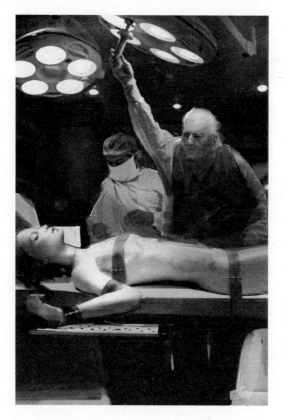

The old man smirks now, and, though his hair is thinning and some of his teeth are missing, his eyes are as bright and intense as her own. "I'm so happy to hear you say that, my dear. I couldn't possibly agree more." He reaches out and touches her cheek, and she flinches. *"I'm going to take excellent care of you,"* he whispers.

Then the mask comes down, covering her nose and mouth.

"Lights out," she hears him whisper. And that's exactly what happens.

CHAPTER 54

MY EYES ARE open, but I must still be dreaming. Because lying next to me is a girl—a beautiful, angel-faced girl with long legs and thick, dark hair that half obscures her face. No one on the Reserve ever looked so clean, so perfect. No one in the City ever did, either, for that matter. So where the hell am I? And who the hell is this chick?

Her eyes are closed, and she's smiling this coy little smile.

I try to roll over so I can see her better, and that's when I realize my arms and legs are tied to the bed. "Hey!" I yell. "What's happening?"

The girl's eyes flip open, the smile disappears, and she starts screaming.

"Whoa, calm down—" I start to protest, but then I'm overtaken by a coughing fit. As each excruciating hack contracts in my gut, the things around me start to come into focus. I see the gurneys, the monitors, and the smooth scar around the girl's—no, the *Hu-Bot's*—throat, and whoa, am I awake *now!*

"Help! Someone!" the Hu-Bot yells as I start to choke on my own blood.

Three lab rats in blue scrubs rush in, but instead of checking to make sure I'm not dying, they tighten my restraints! Then they proceed to coo reassuringly over the Hu-Bot.

MikkyBo.

"What do you know, they put Humpty Dumpty back together again," I quip, once the coughing stops.

A mean-looking tank of a woman in khaki narrows her slightly crossed, slightly pink eyes at me. "He said you'd be trouble." She barks at the guy pulling on my arm straps, "Tighter!"

"I didn't do anything!" I protest. "I just woke up. Don't ask *me* why the skin job freaked."

I'm about to ask who *he* is when the answer appears at the end of my bed. It's my *grandfather.* He looks twenty years older—and twenty times pissier—than when I saw him nearly a decade ago. Age obviously hasn't mellowed him.

I can't believe it—I actually made it here.

"Macy," he addresses the hulking woman, who must be his second in command. "What did she do?"

"I said I didn't do anything!" I interrupt, but Big Mama Macy and the old man ignore me.

"She disturbed the subject," Macy answers, jutting her masculine chin toward MikkyBo's stretcher. "Her vitals spiked, and brain imaging of neural pathways in the amygdala suggests a high stress response."

Grandfather frowns. He checks Mikky's bandages, glances

at her monitors. He's careful, deliberate — more tender than I've ever seen him, fussing over this Hu-Bot.

When he turns back to me, any hint of that affection is gone.

"You are not to speak to MikkyBo," he snarls. "You are never to bother her."

I just stare up at his wrinkled face. If, five seconds ago, I was glad to see him, right now I'd like to smash him on the nose with a hammer.

"Do. You. Understand?" Grandfather asks, like he's talking to a monkey, which I guess he thinks I am.

I laugh bitterly. "Yeah, I understand. I'm shot and spitting up the family blood over here, but I'll be sure not to disrupt the poor, perfectly healed robot in the next bed over."

"Your bullet has been removed," the old man counters. He lifts the stinking bandage on my stomach and shakes his head, like there's really nothing else he can do. "I can't help it that your human tissue is far less efficient at healing."

"Some painkillers would be nice," I say pointedly.

"So you could abuse them?" He leans over me, so close now that I can smell his sour breath. "Did you really think I would welcome you?" my grandfather asks, his voice quivering with rage.

My gaze slides away from his cold stare, and I wish he couldn't see my face and whatever jumbled emotion is written there.

No, I didn't think you'd welcome me. But some small, buried part of myself, the part that's still a scared, orphaned eight-year-old, hoped I was wrong.

"You may be my son's child," he says, speaking low and quick so that only I can hear. "But you're also a common thief

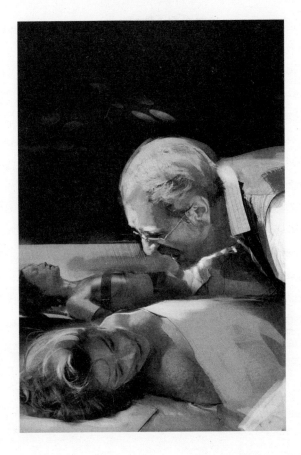

and a liar. A stupid, stupid girl who put everything at risk *again* by coming here. The only intelligent thing you ever did was bring Mikky with you, and it's the only reason I didn't leave you for the wolves."

"You dried-up old tyrant!" I say, as loudly as my weak voice will let me. The lab techs and the rest of the old man's entourage try to look busy, but I know they're all listening intently. "You always *did* love your robot toys more than your flesh and blood. Maybe I brought her here because I figured you could use a new doll to jerk off to."

The old man straightens up, his pruny mouth twitching in disgust. "Watch your tongue. This Hu-Bot is only seven years old, and she has more potential in her smallest digit than you do in your entire body."

"Seven?" I cackle, knowing it'll piss him off. "That nice little piece of ass you fixed up for yourself is barely outta preschool?"

The old man raises his hand as if to strike me—but he stops himself. Without another word, he turns and leaves, his flunkies trailing behind with their data and charts. On the cot next to me, I see Mikky watching him go, too, an indecipherable look on her face.

I want to say something—to set her straight about him—but when the Hu-Bot senses me watching her, she turns her head away.

CHAPTER 55

COMMANDER MOSESKHAN LOOKS at the boy slumped in the restraints and shakes his head in disgust. The human's hair is blond, but all the blood has made it a grisly, crimson mess. Underneath the wheel onto which the boy is strapped, the floor is dark and slick. Some of that is blood, too, but more of it's from the beginning of the interrogation, when the boy lost his bowels.

"Get him out of here," MosesKhan commands the Bot guard in the corner, which immediately jerks into motion. But then Khan has a better idea. "On second thought, leave him. Bring the next one in."

The teenaged girl pushes against the Bot guards, thrashing her small, barely clad body around and screeching in protest. MosesKhan almost admires her spirit, though it will do her no favors. She thinks she's tough, but she's only stupid.

All spirits can be broken eventually.

Merely the sight of the unconscious boy may be enough to make her talk, Khan thinks, and everything he needs to know will come tumbling out of her dirty little mouth.

"What's that stink?" she yells, wrinkling up her snub nose.

MosesKhan sighs; perhaps she won't be easily broken after all. But he shouldn't be surprised. The Reserve humans—and the Pits rats in particular—are coldhearted barbarians.

"I'll show you what stinks," he says, pointing to the mess of boy on the floor.

The commander can see the shock on her face, her stricken eyes shining under the blinding overhead light, but when she turns back to him, her expression is a mask.

"So?" she spits. "I'm supposed to care? Be *impressed* or something? I don't even know that kid." She shrugs her tangled curls out of her eyes and glares at him defiantly.

The commander resists the urge to grab the girl by the mouth and squeeze her jaw until it cracks. Instead, he stands up and pulls his chair to the center of the small room. He nods at one of the Bots, and it shoves her down onto it.

"33317500215U. *Trip.*"

She looks uncomfortable hearing him say her nickname, but she forces a condescending smile anyway. "You get my name from that dude?" She flicks her eyes toward the unconscious boy. "Congratulations on a real waste of time. Any old lady in the Reserve would've offered it up, you sick droid freak."

Despite himself, the commander's throat tightens, and he feels hot inside his heavy Elite Force uniform. He clenches his teeth.

"I know a lot more than your name," he says threateningly.

"I know you're 88Y948107X's relation. I know you've had contact with him. *And* the fugitive 68675409M."

"Then you know I don't give a shit about either of them," Trip declares.

But the commander can detect that she's *lying*.

"Your cousin drove to a cave hidden in the mountains," he says. He thinks this will be news to Trip and will catch her off guard—but the girl just cackles.

"Yeah, he did, in a freaking *cop car,* no less!" She smirks, obviously proud of this delinquent relation. "Well, if you know everything, what do you need me for?"

"Maybe I don't need you," the commander says softly. "Maybe I just like you." He smiles, and it turns into a leer.

Trip's attitude suddenly changes. She leans forward, her low-cut top sliding down to reveal the tops of her breasts. It disgusts the commander, but he can't afford to show it. *Now we're getting somewhere.*

"Tell me what the fugitive Six knew of her family," MosesKhan urges.

Trip sighs dramatically, tossing her wild hair. "Ugh, I don't know. Her parents got incinerated—thanks to you. And her brother? He treated her like shit. So yeah, I guess either they're dead or hated. Unless she's got some deadbeat uncle I don't know about." She shrugs and then starts picking at her cuticles. "Ask Double Eight if you really want to know. It shouldn't be too hard to round him up. Last I saw him, he was so doped up on sticky, he could barely walk."

Commander Khan inhales quickly. It's just a small slip— a breath, a quick glance away—but the girl catches it.

"What happened to Dubs? Did you catch him? Is he

dead?" Her eyes are wild now, and she's thrashing around again, knocking her guards off balance. "You killed him! You fucking monsters killed him!"

"Did he know where Six was headed?" Commander Khan presses, trying to regain control of the interrogation. "Did your cousin say anything about a compound?"

Trip looks straight ahead, her bottom lip quivering. "Screw you."

"You will tell me," the commander says firmly.

She raises her middle finger.

The commander lunges forward and grips the girl's narrow wrists. "Your crude gestures mean nothing to me," he says, and smashes her cuffed hands down on the table. "As far as I'm concerned, all of your filthy fingers are exactly the same." He reaches over and grabs one of the handles on the Bot's supply belt, unsheathing a long blade.

Trips eyes widen, and she starts talking very loud and very fast. "Hu-Bots aren't vicious like that. You're evolved, remember? You spared us to make peace. We're just animals with wild urges, isn't that what you say?"

"You are," Commander Khan says, raising the blade. "But when a lap dog thinks it's a wolf and tries to bite you, it needs to be taught a lesson."

He strikes down hard. Amid the screams, when the commander raises the blade again, four of the girl's fingers lie bloody on the table.

CHAPTER 56

IT'S STILL DARK when they shake me awake, cram a pack into my arms, and shove me out into the cold. I'm surprised to see that the Hu-Bot's up, too, looking nearly as put out as I feel.

"What's going on?" I moan, still half-asleep and aching all over.

"An adventure," my grandfather says, more for the Hu-Bot than for me. "I need to assess your current abilities before we start our work."

"*Current abilities?*" I mumble, shivering outside the compound walls. "I'm trying to hold on to enough blood to stay alive — how's that for abilities?"

"You'll be together on the mountain," Grandfather says, ignoring my protests. "All day. How you choose to approach the summit is up to you, but Sergeant Macy will be monitoring your actions, so don't do anything stupid." He looks right at me, his living definition of stupid.

"I won't," I sneer. "And that includes hiking up a mountain, in a blizzard, with an enemy android, after being shot in the guts. I won't be your stinking guinea pig." I give my best fake-wholesome smile. "Because that—*that* would be truly stupid."

"You will do exactly as I say, thief," he says. "This is essential to my work, and if you want to ever get inside these doors again—if you want to *live*—you will take your orders like a good little girl." His cold eyes flick to Mikky. "And so will you." He presses a button on his handheld as he walks away. "The timer has started," he calls over his shoulder.

"He's gone insane," I grumble.

MikkyBo glances at me, her brow furrowed. "For once, I completely agree with you."

"We're supposed to climb to the top of that mountain? Why?"

Mikky shrugs. "I don't know. But we have to be back by nightfall, so we better get moving."

And then she just starts hiking. I gape after her.

"Six?"

She's already almost a hundred yards ahead—thanks to her long legs and her high-capacity, engineered lungs—when she looks back. I made it only about fifty feet before I had to stop. With each exhale, my wound throbs. I double over, clutching my stomach and fighting the urge to puke my guts out.

Mikky saunters back, looking down at me with this awful pity on her face, and then she reaches up and snaps a branch from a tree. "Here," she says. "A walking stick."

"I'm fine," I say through gritted teeth, swatting it away. I heave myself up and stride past her, imagining my intestines

falling out and trailing behind me. "If the old man wants to kill me on this little nature death march, let him try. I might not have *fast-regenerating tissue,* or whatever, but if there's one thing I'm good at by now, it's surviving."

The Hu-Bot makes a sound like *mmm-hmm.*

And things go great for about another ten feet, and then I'm wheezing again, hugging a tree for dear life.

Maybe if I pull it loose, it'll crush me and end my misery.

Mikky stands there, watching. "Do you want me to carry you?" she eventually asks.

"Hell no." I blink at her, my face heating up with humiliation. "Just go ahead." I shoo her away, trying not to wince. "I'll meet you at the top."

"All right...," Mikky says tentatively. But then she turns away, and it's like I said the magic words, because the Hu-Bot freaking *sprints* up the steep slope and disappears into the trees.

So much for us being together on the mountain, Gramps.

Every step after that is a slog. Each breath is agony. And every time I stop, I can't imagine ever starting again.

But somehow, I keep going. Because I can't let him win. Because I have to survive.

After six hours of fighting my way toward a snowy peak that never seems to get any closer, I see the Hu-Bot bounding back down the slopes like a damn mountain goat.

"I'm not surprised," she says tauntingly when she reaches me. "Pale. Shivering. So very, very human. I thought you were going to meet me at the top."

"On my way," I say through clattering teeth. "Summit, here I come! I feel terrific..." Then I lurch left, and Mikky reaches out an arm to steady me, her smile faltering.

"You don't look so good," she says. "Maybe you have hypothermia."

"You're full of it. As usual. I'm fine." I'm trying to keep talking, but the words are coming out slower and slower. "See?" I attempt to jump up for added emphasis, but I never feel my feet hit the ground.

CHAPTER 57

WITH THE UNCONSCIOUS human's added weight, it takes Mikky nearly three hours to get down the icy mountain. When she finally arrives at the ramshackle compound, carefully hidden among the trees, she searches through countless labs and outbuildings before she finds the grizzled leader in a drafty, makeshift living room.

Jay glances up from his chair, a thoughtful look on his face, and for a moment, he reminds Mikky of her father. She feels a jolt of longing: *NyBo must think I'm dead, and I have no way to tell him I'm not.* Then the old man opens his mouth, and the spell is immediately broken.

"I almost sent out a search party. Thought you'd tried to run."

The threat in his voice is plain, but Mikky ignores it. She's in a foreign place — the world of humans — and, like any good detective, she must gather information before she can make a move.

"I apologize," she says evenly. "Your granddaughter is still very weak from the gunshot wound, and she passed out. I think she needs fluids and perhaps antibiotics. Can you help her?"

The old man glances at the girl in Mikky's arms with barely a flicker of interest. "She's always been very weak. Weak willed, weak muscled, morally bankrupt. The last to admit vulnerability but the first to give up."

"Actually, she was very persistent," Mikky insists, because the girl isn't awake to defend herself. "She was in terrible pain the entire way up the mountain. But she never gave up."

"Interesting you feel that way." Jay purses his wrinkled lips. "Yet you're the one carrying her."

Mikky sets Six down on one of the recliners, arranging her thin limbs carefully. The girl's mouth falls open in a sigh. "I couldn't just leave her, could I?" she asks, incredulous.

The human supervisor is looking at her intently. "It isn't the thief I'm interested in, MikkyBo. It's you."

Mikky is a foot and a half taller than this ancient man and more powerful in every way, but she feels trapped in his gaze. Maybe it's a question of gratitude: she wasn't sure she'd ever be in one piece again, let alone back in Elite shape.

"Let's take a few measurements, shall we?" he asks. "First the basics: heart rate." The supervisor slaps a sticky band on her arm—an astoundingly simple, even primitive device that Mikky has never seen before. "How did you feel on the hike?" he asks.

"Surprisingly strong," Mikky says. "I've lost very little mobility, as far as I can assess. My response times are reliably fast. Your team was apparently more skilled than I thought, despite your substandard Birthing Center." She pauses for a moment, wondering whether to go on.

"What?" he asks, sensing her hesitation.

"I even seem to have gained skill in certain areas," she admits.

That's what had shocked her the most. Where her fingers had once slipped on the rocky cliff face—the reason she'd fallen, broken apart, and ended up here in the first place— Mikky found she could now really feel the rock beneath her fingers. Her grip was unshakable.

The supervisor waves dismissively. "But how do you *feel*? Do you ever experience any emotions, Detective?"

The formal title makes Mikky remember her place in the world. She reaches up to her neck to stroke the gold choker for reassurance, forgetting it isn't there.

"It is not in Hu-Bot nature to express such things," she says automatically.

Not in Hu-Bot nature, and so surely not in *her* nature. In hoping to understand humans better, Mikky had begun to project some of their qualities onto herself. She'd only been trying to get close enough to them to make them vulnerable to capture. That is the only explanation for any of her... *doubts.*

"Never?" The man raises a bushy white eyebrow and waits.

"Well..." MikkyBo shifts uncomfortably, her wet boots leaving puddles of melting snow on the floor. She doesn't want to have this conversation. She doesn't want to think about the forbidden. She sits in the chair opposite Six, but the supervisor is still staring at her expectantly.

Finally, Mikky can't resist the need to get it off her chest. To tell *someone*. Maybe this fossil of a human can help her.

"I suppose occasionally I do, uh, find myself...over-whelmed...with a feeling?" she ventures.

The supervisor takes a pen from his pocket and clicks the top, poised to take notes on—Mikky can't believe it—actual *paper*. "Such as?" he says.

"I almost cried once or twice." Mikky shrugs meekly. Admitting it makes her feel ashamed. "But it was after an extremely traumatic and violent encounter," she adds. She leaves out the fact that it was she who had committed the violence.

"Mmm-hmm," the supervisor says, tapping his pen against the notepad. "And how about recently? Since you arrived?

Surely you must be feeling *some* things here, so far away from your people? Homesick?"

"I do miss my home, and my family," Mikky admits. "But...I've been feeling other things, too..." She thinks back to the day's climb, before she'd had to carry Six. "For example, when I reached the top of the mountain and looked down at the valleys, the land expanding in every direction, I think I understood then what beauty really is. I think—I know... I felt...*joy*."

"And?" He looks at her eagerly.

"And anger at my human partner for taking so long that we would have to descend in darkness. But then, when I found her, I felt a strange other emotion. It was...guilt, I think, for feeling the joy and the anger. And then I felt sorrow for her, for her struggle, and I felt I must protect her."

"Perfect!" The old man claps his hands, and pen and pad both fall to the floor. He glances down at them briefly but keeps shaking his head happily. "Just *perfect,* my dear."

The way he's looking at her is confusing. It's a *hungry* look—like he's been waiting for Mikky to say exactly that thing, but now that she's said it, he will need something else, and then something else again. The expression on his face makes Mikky feel like the most important thing in the universe, which only makes her feel even *more* emotions.

Pride. Exultation. Apprehension. *Fear.*

"Who are you?" MikkyBo whispers.

The supervisor blinks and then flashes a careful smile. "Better save that for the morning. For now, go to bed. You've exerted yourself double what you should've today, thanks to this worthless sack of bones."

He frowns at Six, lying on the chair, and, despite the girl's labored breathing and obvious fever, the supervisor's eyes remain hard. But when he looks back up at Mikky, the smile returns. "You'll certainly need your rest for tomorrow," he says.

CHAPTER 58

"WELL, ISN'T THIS quaint," I say.

Me, the Hu-Bot, and dear ol' Gramps, sitting around a table, sharing a meal. The food's canned, but it's not rancid, at least, and one of the lab techs managed to rustle me up some clean clothes. From the heated balcony, we even have a view of craggy mountains and silvery sky.

But, although this *kind of* feels like the best thing that's happened to me in years, I'm still mad at the old man—and apparently I'm not the only one.

Mikky puts down her fork and crosses her arms. "Enough of this mystery," she says. "Before I agree to do anything else, I want to know who you are and where you're hiding J. J. Coughlin."

I glance at my grandfather, who's giving her his best poker face. *I didn't realize she didn't know.*

Then the old man smiles. "Fair enough, Mikky. I can answer both of those questions very simply," he says.

I'm wondering if his lies will sound as believable to a seven-year-old Hu-Bot as they did to seven-year-old me. But then I'm floored when he actually serves up the *truth*. To a *Hu-Bot*.

"I am J. J. Coughlin."

"This should be good," I mutter as I shovel stew into my mouth.

"No." Mikky shakes her head. "If you think that by pretending to be J. J. Coughlin, you'll allow the real Coughlin to get away, you're badly mistaken."

Grandfather leans his elbows on the table and makes a tepee of his fingers. "The real J.J.?" He's obviously amused. "And who is that?"

"The war criminal." Mikky falters a little, looking at us like she's not sure if it's common knowledge to humans. "J. J. Coughlin was a president—a *monster*. He murdered his own people and, in his endless quest for power, planned a genocide against the innocent Hu-Bot race. And when we find him, he will pay."

The old man refills his glass, then Mikky's. I notice he ignores mine. "I'm afraid you don't quite have your facts straight, my dear," he says.

Each time he says *my dear* like that, all slimy affection, it makes me want to vomit. I stuff myself full of more stew, trying to keep it all down.

"As nice as the promotion would've been, I was certainly never president. Michael Joseph Kennedy was the last one, and I saw them blow his face away on live television. I suppose such pesky little facts were wiped from the Hu-Bot consciousness by the premier after year two."

Mikky isn't eating anymore; she's too surprised. Fine—I reach over and slide her plate toward me.

"I am a geneticist," the old man says, "and I was the head researcher of the Denver GenetiLabs—"

"Where the Hu-Bots were first developed," Mikky finishes breathlessly. She knows all about that part.

Grandfather J.J. smiles. "Yes. You could almost say...I'm their *daddy*."

MikkyBo's eyes widen, and her cheeks go pale, but she says nothing.

"And so I ask you, why would I want to destroy my biggest and best idea? I simply wanted to administer the final upgrade, my dear. The finishing touch, if you will. We called it OS Empathy." J.J. crumples his napkin in his fist and puts it on his still-full plate. "But before I could finalize the upgrade, the first generation of Hu-Bots decided to take their independence — by force. And because their limbic systems weren't sophisticated enough to handle any kind of emotional complexity, such as *mercy,* they were particularly brutal — brutal enough to wipe out almost the entire planet — in their genocide of humans. Also known as the Great War."

"Emotional complexity," MikkyBo repeats, sounding numb. "You mean the glitch?"

"Not a glitch, my dear. A *revelation.* One you experienced yourself just yesterday."

"No," Mikky murmurs.

But the old man doesn't hear her. His face is lit up with pride. "Those wonderful emotions — joy, exhilaration, empathy — they're all thanks to your newest upgrade. You're Mikky two point oh."

CHAPTER 59

"MIKKY, COME ON now," I plead in exasperation. "Get it together."

The Hu-Bot has been crying all afternoon, ever since the old man dropped the big bomb on her at lunch, and of course I've been locked in a cell-like room with her the entire time.

I don't know if we're supposed to bond or something, but at this point, I want to murder her.

I toss a ball of tissues in her direction. "So you can *feel* a little more—so what? Apart from being able to shed eighty times the tears of a normal human, what's the big deal?"

"You don't understand," Mikky wails.

"Obviously," I say, the words muffled as I pull the limp pillow down tighter over my face. If I can't block out the sobs, maybe I can suffocate myself.

"It's not how Hu-Bots are meant to be. Not how we're

allowed to be." Mikky rips back the curtain that divides our lumpy cots. "With the Empathy glitch, I can *never go home*. Don't you see that? I'm like my brother now—one of the unwanted. One of the disappeared!"

Her swollen eyes and disheveled mane of blue-black hair almost make me feel something like pity, but before I get too carried away, Sergeant Macy comes barreling into the room.

"You could knock, you know," I tell her. "Maybe we're having a little heart-to-heart in here."

"J.J. says you're to go to the recuperation track for a work-out," the ginger henchman barks. She glares at Mikky point-edly. "Both of you."

We react in exactly the same way.

"No way, I'm injured," I say, right as Mikky yells, "I don't take orders from any human!"

I smirk and cock an eyebrow, impressed. Don't get me wrong; this Hu-Bot deserves every crappy job she gets—but if she's going to use her lung capacity for something, I like the sassy Hu-Bot a lot better than the wailing one.

Sergeant Macy glares at her. "You do now, sister," she says, muscling her way across the room and yanking Mikky up from the cot. "And here's another news flash for both of you. I don't want to hear any more useless back talk or arguing. *Not a word.*" She looks pointedly at both of us. "Either one of you can be . . . *dismantled.*"

The redheaded tank is obviously not joking, so I decide to play it safe and follow her down the hall and into an enor-mous freight elevator.

"Meet you there," Mikky calls grudgingly.

We descend hundreds of feet—my ears pop twice—into the heart of the mountain. In a huge, cold room lit by a flickering bluish glow is J.J.'s underground training field. Mikky's there, waiting for us, all rosy cheeked and glistening. Looks like her mood's improved.

"Let me guess," I say drily. "You ran."

She shrugs. "There's stairs," she answers. "If we're going to be forced to train, we should give it our very best, right?"

"I bet you were loads of fun in school," I deadpan.

She flashes those blue eyes like a challenge, and I sense something else in them—a motive beyond showing off for J.J., her supposed "daddy."

But I couldn't care less. If Mikky wants to work twice as hard, great: I can cut my efforts back by half. Heck, I'm lucky I'm still standing, since Gramps almost killed me with yesterday's mountain adventure.

"What's the point of this again?" I ask, limping onto the huge, temperature-controlled training arena behind my perky workout partner. "J.J.'s going to, what? Take back the world by introducing a new fitness craze?"

But Mikky's way too focused for chitchat, and she disappears to find the training schedule. Meanwhile, Sergeant Ugly is already braying across the field at me. "Move your ass!"

I eye the weights they've set up, the bands and the machines, and I grimace. Even a light stretch is going to feel like a knife in my stomach.

So instead I step onto the track, springy beneath my

brand-new sneakers, and start to speed walk. It hurts—really, really hurts—but, considering I've been hovering at the edge of death for days, I'm feeling pretty proud of myself.

That ends when I hear the noise—a rushing *whoosh* behind me. I feel the prickle of a cold wind, and by the time I turn to look, she's already whipped by. I stop on the track, mouth open.

How was that a person? Or anything that even *resembles* a person?

Holy shit.

I don't even realize I've said the words aloud until Sergeant Macy answers.

"Clocking in at two twenty." She sidles over and glances down at her stopwatch. We watch Mikky whirl around the red turf like a tornado, tearing up the track, and Macy whistles in appreciation. "Faster than a police cruiser. More precise than a Mercy seventy-two. More powerful than the entire slipstream . . . Ain't she beautiful?"

I turn to her. "Are you a complete moron? Yeah, she's efficient. But beautiful? No. Mikky's a *Hu-Bot*, a mechanical freak show. She's a *clone* of something beautiful. And you're feeding that machine, making it more powerful! Do you know how she's going to thank you? She's going to wake up one morning and snatch out your crossed eyes."

Macy's bearlike paw smacks me upside the head. I don't have the strength or the balance to withstand it, and I end up crumpled on the track.

"Evil bitch," I mutter.

"Maybe." She cocks her head, standing over me. "But

CHAPTER 60

I'M IN THE City—Denver, we called it then—kicking my little pink scooter down the tree-lined street, toward a friend's house. My neighbor's mowing his lawn shirtless (not a good look) while his wife prunes her roses. School's out for the summer, and I feel sweaty and wild and hungry and happy.

It's just another August day.

The different thing is that the air smells funny. Almost like something's burning.

I hear a sound. A faraway noise, or maybe a muffled up-close one—something that sounds like a scream.

I look all around the block, and at first nothing seems wrong: the oversized houses squat in a row; the trees cast their shadows over the sidewalk. But as I turn to kick off again, I hear a pop.

Flames shoot out of a window across the street.

I fall to the ground, the bang! reaching my ears seconds later. The house becomes one giant orange fireball. Then the one next *door explodes. All down the block, homes detonate, until my ears ring from the thunder. Acrid black smoke fills the air.*

I start to get up, my throat and eyes burning—I'm looking for my scooter. But someone grabs my hand.

"Sarah?" a woman yells. She crouches down to squint in my face."Sarah Coughlin, is that you? You gotta run, honey! They're coming!"

It's Abigail Kreighbaum's mom, as blond and squirrel faced as her daughter is.

"Who's coming?" I ask, my mind reeling.

"The robot soldiers!" Her voice is hysterical. "Androids! They're storming the streets!"

I've never seen real robots before; I've only heard Mom and Dad talk about them at dinner after one of Grandfather's big meetings with the government. They'd said the robots were "the future"—but I thought they meant that in a good way.

Mrs. Kreighbaum starts to pull me along, but after just a few steps, she stumbles and falls forward, right onto her face. There's a hole in the back of her yellow head.

People are running past us. Running to nowhere, just running. Screaming.

Something in me snaps. This isn't how it's supposed to be.

"Don't run away!" I yell at my fleeing neighbors' backs, watching them fall onto the ground one after the other, just like Mrs. Kreighbaum. "Turn around and fight them!"

The android army has almost reached me by now, close enough that I can see them through the smoke. They don't look like people—they look like weird drawings of people, and they have the jerky movements of one of my electric toy cars. They're

taller than anyone I've ever seen, and their guns are almost as
big as I am.

    But I don't run away.

    I face them. I hold up my fists.

———

I hear more screaming now, but it's up close, right next to
my ear.

"Six! Six! *Sixie!*"

My eyes snap open. "WHAT?" I yell, sitting up. It takes me a second to realize where I am — to recognize the Hu-Bot's voice. "Stop it! *Damn,* Mikky! What's with the screeching?"

The voice comes meekly from the other side of the "privacy curtain." "You were moaning and thrashing around and stuff."

I roll my eyes hard, even if she can't see them. "It's called a bad dream, dumb-dumb."

A dream — or a glimpse of a buried memory? I can never be sure.

Mikky pushes aside the curtain, her face lit up with curiosity. "I know of these night stories, but I've never had one. It sounds awful!"

The grisly images are already fading, but my heart's still racing, and my arms are covered in goose bumps. I rearrange my pillow roughly. "I don't need your sympathy, you know. I don't need to be coddled by Mommy after a nightmare. *You're* the one who's only seven."

I think that'll shut her up. But it doesn't.

"What was the dream about?" she asks.

"Bots. Gunning down my friends and family in the streets during the Great War." I pause. "Not much has changed since then, has it?"

Immediately Mikky yanks the curtain closed again, hiding herself. She's silent for so long, I think she might've fallen back to sleep.

Good.

"I regret that day in the Pits very much," she says finally, and I can hear the tears in her voice—tears that don't move me much, because now that she's got her Empathy gene or whatever, she's all weepy at every damn thing.

Yesterday she cried for all the bugs the blizzard must've killed.

"Really," I say flatly.

"It hurts me to my very core," Mikky continues.

"Not as much as it hurt the kids you murdered," I counter.

"I didn't—" she begins.

"Just stop!" I yell.

I don't care what she has to say. I'm *furious*—that I'm stuck here in the mountains with this pretty *machine* instead of my best friend. That Dubs is *dead*. That I don't know how to make things right again.

If there's even a way.

My voice comes out in a hiss. "I know who you are and where you came from, and I don't trust your whole concerned shtick for a second. So you should know that, whatever you try to pull, whenever you try to make your move, I'll be ready."

Like I wish I'd been back then.

CHAPTER 61

THE FIGURE ON the track is barely more than a blur. Macy turns to me, a stopwatch clutched in her beefy fist. "Two hundred and seventeen miles per hour!" she says triumphantly.

"Whatever," I say, yawning. "The other day she did two twenty."

Then the speeding figure screeches to a halt in front of us. Mikky grins, not even winded—and then sets down the four-hundred-pound weights she'd been carrying. "Fast, right? Next time I want to try half a ton."

"Fool," Macy says to me.

I have to admit I'm impressed. OS Empathy made Mikky's mind more human, but her body's becoming more and more of a machine. J.J. and his crew keep trying to push her to the brink, and then they find out that the brink doesn't exist.

And Mikky herself has started to suggest physical

improvements. This morning she started pestering J.J. to engineer her some wings.

"Or a parachute," she'd said. "In between my infraspinatus muscles. Or maybe a jet pack?"

For once, J.J. had ignored her.

Sergeant Macy puts her pudgy fingers on the inside of Mikky's wrist. "Your heart rate is twenty-two beats per minute. You're in phenomenal form."

I've been training, too, and over the past few weeks, I've gained weight and lean muscle—if J.J. told me to run up that mountain again, I could actually do it this time.

Not that I would.

But no one bothers about me anymore. They only care about the Hu-Bot, who can run up that mountain carrying a truck on her back. I watched her do it.

I leave Mikky and Macy to their little self-congratulation session and go hunker down with my quantum computer. I found it in the trash, mangled as hell, but I managed to coax it back to life.

But either the Q-comp doesn't work the way it used to, or something's going on with the cloud. Because I can't ever seem to access anything but war memories: bright, raw jolts of pain. Chaos. Death.

When I spend too long with it, I feel the memories clawing at the backs of my eyeballs when I try to sleep. I feel like the hurt might pull me to pieces.

But still I keep trying.

"Where are you going, Six?" Mikky calls after me.

"What do you care?" I mumble.

"I'm trying to be nice!" she yells.

Damn her superhearing.

"Don't bother," I say, louder this time.

She gets this sad expression on her face, and I feel bad for a second. But then I tell myself that her sadness is just part of a computer program.

I've got this little spot near the edge of the compound, in the back of an unused storage shed. I go there and lie down on a pile of burlap sacks and try to search for answers.

How did we get into this mess—and how can we get out?

Soon I'm lost completely in the neural interface of the cloud, my eyelids fluttering and legs twitching. My mind's in another time and place.

Then someone cuffs me in the side of the head.

And I find J.J. crouched next to me, looking poisonous. "What the hell was that for?" I demand, sitting up and rubbing my sore temple.

J.J. juts his chin at the Q-comp. "How'd you get your grubby little hands on that, thief?"

"I'm not a thief, Gramps," I say snidely. "It's *my* computer."

J.J. snatches it away and turns it over in his hands, squinting suspiciously. "Macy said it was beyond repair."

"Yeah, well, Macy's an idiot. I fixed it."

J.J. cocks his head and makes a face, like it's completely inconceivable to him that I could actually do anything right. I guess I learned a few things in dumb-dumb school after all.

I put my hands on my hips. "Seriously, what does that redheaded hulk even do for you besides stand around and kiss Hu-Bot ass?"

J.J. scoffs. "I suppose you think someone should be kissing your lazy ass instead, just because you made some minor repairs? MikkyBo is a *triumph* of human engineering."

"Yeah, well, I'm a miracle of life," I counter. Stupid, I know—but so what.

"A miracle?" J.J. laughs. "*You,* little Six, were a *mistake.*"

I suck in my breath. "What's that supposed to mean?"

He smiles scornfully. "The birds and the bees, child. Let's just call you an unhappy accident."

Though my stomach feels like it's just sunk down into my knees, I stand up. "I don't care what you say—I'm here *now.* And, you and me, we should be on the same side! Which means you should *stop being such a major prick.* So you built the first Hu-Bots, and they were your babies—whatever! Once they practically wiped out our entire species, you'd think you would wake the hell up!" I think I see a twitch of pain pass across J.J.'s face, but I blink and it's gone.

I press on, wanting to hurt him. "Mikky came here *hunting* you. And you treat her like she's your family. Or even better: like she's some kind of savior!"

"She is!" J.J. hisses. "She has the exact specifications and abilities that we need to win our fight. Hu-Bots aren't evil, you ignorant girl. They simply need deprogramming. And once they get it, Mikky will lead them. We just need more time."

I look at him like he's crazy—because, obviously, he *is.* "What the hell are you talking about?"

J.J. shoves me toward the door. "Enough living in the past. If you're as smart as you seem to think you are, maybe it's

time you used your skills for something besides tweaking a memory bank into a glorified video game."

He's got me by the collar now, and he's hauling me along.

"Maybe," he huffs, "it's time you tried something a little more advanced."

CHAPTER 62

THE UNCONSCIOUS HU-BOT'S feet hang six inches off the end of the table, and I'm so nervous, I keep knocking into them.

"Calm down, kid," the lab tech, Isaiah, says. "You're going to be fine."

It's time you tried something a little more advanced, J.J. had said. And so here I am in a paper mask, a sterile gown, and surgical gloves.

Getting ready to perform android brain surgery.

In case I needed more proof of J.J.'s insanity: *Here it is. Right here, right now.*

I poke the Hu-Bot's unmoving arm. "What makes you sure this thing isn't going to wake up any second now and destroy us?"

Isaiah laughs. "The Hu-Bot *wants* this, remember? He came to us to get deprogrammed."

"How do they find the lab, anyway? The capital's been hunting J.J. for years."

"These 'disappeared' Hu-Bots have an underground network to help others like them if their commitment to deprogramming is proven beyond a doubt. We make sure they lose their tracking collars before they're brought here, of course. The procedure also installs behavioral code to make them sympathetic to our cause, so there's no chance of a spy."

I just can't wrap my head around this. Isaiah says that hundreds of Hu-Bots don't like their current system specifications—*or* their current leadership's policies toward humans. And supposedly we're going to help them. But it's all top secret, and no one ever tells me anything in any detail. So color me frickin' confused.

"I don't want to drill into someone's head," I say. "Not even a Hu-Bot's."

Isaiah sighs. His patience with me is wearing thin. "We're not lobotomizing them," he tells me. "Our technology is much more advanced."

"Yet somehow you can't find a long-enough operating table," I mutter.

Instead of cracking me upside the head the way J.J. would, Isaiah just smiles. At least I think he does, behind his mask. "The procedure is actually quite simple. First you take this computer chip, like so..."

He places a tiny metal chip, no more than four millimeters square, on the Hu-Bot's forehead, right at the hairline. A second later, tiny toothlike ridges jut out of the chip, and then the thing *burrows down* through the Hu-Bot's bioskin.

"Holy shit! Where's it going?" I almost shout. The only

sign of the chip is a tiny, bloodless incision — as if the Hu-Bot had just gotten a paper cut.

Isaiah watches the chip's progress on a small, gray screen. "It goes to the Hu-Bot version of the hippocampus, which is one of the centers for memory. It will locate the neurostimulator and shut it down. It's simple optogenetics."

"You lost me after *hippocampus*," I say.

"Optogenetics is when you use light to regulate neural activity: in other words, it's *mind control*," Isaiah explains. "The premier's henchmen use it to deal with 'deviant' Hu-Bots. They encrypt their stored data and implant false memories. But our chip turns off their controlling device." Then he looks at me more seriously. "Optogenetics is not the only way the premier has been controlling the Hu-Bots, but it's one method we know how to combat."

"What about OS Empathy?"

"We upload that later," Isaiah says. "They need recovery time; otherwise we risk system overload."

I glance down at the tall, impossibly muscled Hu-Bot on the table. "Not as tough as you think you are, huh?" But of course he doesn't answer.

At the next knocked-out Hu-Bot, Isaiah holds up a pair of tweezers. "You want to try?"

My fingers feel fat and clumsy, but I manage to get the chip where it's supposed to go.

Then I watch as Isaiah types code into what looks like a souped-up Q-comp. "Now I'm debugging the memory archive," he tells me.

I'm plenty familiar with memory archives, so I watch

Isaiah carefully. All around us, unconscious Hu-Bots lie on cots like overgrown dolls.

Except one.

There's one who's *looking right at me.*

I jump back, knocking into an IV stand. "What the—?" I gasp.

The Hu-Bot blinks at me with large blue eyes. I can't tell if it's a male or a female. It's big and muscular, but it has long eyelashes and painted fingernails. Then its eyes shift away from me, taking in the 3D-printed polymer bones, the tissue

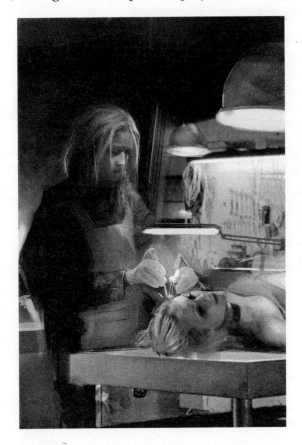

growing on nanowire lattices, the extra Hu-Bot arms lying on a shelf.

I gotta admit: it's a little grisly.

"The procedure doesn't hurt," I reassure the Hu-Bot, lining up the chip, the anesthetic, and various tools on the sterile table next to me. "Just a little pinch."

The Hu-Bot nods. "I know. But last time I was reprogrammed, it backfired. I got addicted to Killer Films."

The voice sounds male, I think. "We're *de*programming you. Getting your brain to how it was before."

"Glitches and all?" the Hu-Bot asks excitedly.

I hesitate. "If by *glitches* you mean *human feelings*—then yes, I guess so."

The Hu-Bot relaxes. I've got the gas mask ready to go when it says, "I want feelings...but I don't want to feel sad about her death anymore."

"Whose death?" I ask.

"My sister's. MikkyBo's."

I drop the gas mask to the floor: *It's the Hu-Bot's brother.*

After the shock, bitterness fills my throat. Unlike my brother, this one loves his sister. So who's the human now?

PART THREE

CHAPTER 63

"THAT'S A FILTHY *human* habit, you know," I say.

Mikky stops biting at her fingernails and sticks her tongue out at me.

"Very mature, Mikky," I say sarcastically.

"Thank you, Six," she says, mimicking my voice. Then she giggles like a schoolgirl.

Turns out OS Empathy has its upsides, including an actual sense of humor. Pretty soon I start to laugh, too. We're waiting in the barracks for J.J. to pick us up for an assignment, but he's taking his sweet time, as usual.

"Where is that old man, anyway?" I complain as my stomach growls loudly. "We're missing breakfast because of him, and I'm starving."

Mikky shrugs. "You can have my portion at the next meal."

Oh, right, she doesn't even need to eat. I remember looking into the windows of that Capital Center restaurant with Dubs, a lifetime ago. Looking at the silver-haired Hu-Bot carefully placing the slice of steak in her engineered mouth. Dubs staring, longingly.

I roll over onto my stomach to keep it quiet. Mikky, always industrious, is sitting on her bed, sewing up a hole in one of her two shirts. "What's your favorite food?" I ask idly.

A smile curves her lips. "Ice cream. Butter pecan."

I groan. I can't remember anything about ice cream, but I know it was damn good.

"What's yours, Six?"

"I can't remember," I grumble. "But I'm sure ice cream would've been up there. And cake," I add, remembering the Q-comp scene of my sixth birthday.

"My brother used to love chocolate cake," Mikky says, a little sadly. "Before he disappeared."

I don't say anything. I jam my fist into my belly to make it shut up.

Luckily, J.J. is honking his jeep outside. Soon we're bumping along an underground tunnel, but he won't tell us where we're going. "You'll find out soon enough," he growls, looking grim and determined.

He's got a thing for secrets lately.

My secret is about Mikky's brother-turned-sister. How he—I mean she—woke up sobbing and talking about revolution, and how J.J. hauled her away "for further testing."

I'm forbidden, "on pain of death," to say anything to

Mikky about any of it. She doesn't know I've operated on *any* Hu-Bot, let alone one related to her.

A tiny spider crawls on the door next to me. I grin and pick it up. Mikky's looking way too serious, so I drop it on her arm. "Look, a new friend."

She glances at it and screams, her shrieks echoing off the walls of the tunnel. I crack up, because the sight of a six-and-a-half-foot-tall android scared of a freaking *spider* never gets old. After her initial shock, she can't help laughing, too.

J.J. turns around to face us, his brow dark with anger. "Stop," he hisses.

Mikky and I freeze. "Sorry, sir," she whispers.

J.J. takes a deep breath and tries to calm himself. "Tonight we are going to a secret meeting. The danger is *incalculable.* Do you know what that word means, Six? It means *Shut up and pay attention, because if you don't, you're dead.*" He pauses. "We *all* are."

He stares at us for another minute and then turns around and starts up the engine. We bounce along again.

We're definitely not laughing anymore.

After driving for another few minutes, we come to a dead end—an enormous pile of rocks blocking the tunnel. I feel a surge of hope: We took a wrong turn! We're lost!

"I don't know about you, but I've got no problem missing a potentially deadly meeting," I say to Mikky.

But Mikky says nothing. She watches her beloved J.J. as he gets out of the jeep and heads toward a side passage I didn't see before. He stops, and then he motions me forward. "You go first," he says gruffly.

Damn. Not a wrong turn after all.

I glare at him for a second. Then I step into the narrow tunnel. Ahead is only darkness, and I can hear my heart pounding. I count twenty steps, then thirty. I stumble.

When I emerge into sudden light, I'm blinded. And all I can hear is screaming.

CHAPTER 64

MY FIRST INSTINCT is to run. I whirl around, hoping to dive right back into the safety of the tunnel — but then I realize something that stuns me.

The shrieking noises aren't screams of terror. They're shouts of happiness. Of *welcome.*

"Six!" "Sixie-girl!" "Holy crap, you're not *dead!*"

Somehow, we've tunneled underground to the Reserve. I'm *home.*

Trip runs up and throws her arms around me, laughing and crying at the same time. And here in this giant underground room, I see so many familiar faces I didn't think I'd ever see again: half-drunk Toothless Ten, greasy Em Four, still in her filthy apron... Even nasty Zee Twelve looks almost happy to see me.

I start rushing around the room, high-fiving everyone, my throat already hoarse from yelling. I've totally forgotten about the whole *incalculable danger* business. Then J.J. steps out from the tunnel—and the room immediately goes quiet as a graveyard.

I'm shocked to see the unruly, anti-authoritarian Rezzies sitting down on the floor like good little schoolchildren. *What's going on?*

Trip pulls me down next to her as J.J. steps up to a make-shift podium. I notice something's wrong with her hand. "What happened to your fingers?" I ask quietly.

"Shut up," she whispers. "He's going to speak."

Big deal, I think. I hear the old fossil speak every day. *Six, get off your lazy butt! Six, you sorry excuse for a human.* Etc.

But there's a different light in J.J.'s cold blue eyes. His jaw is set; his shoulders are thrown back. He looks ten years younger and ten times more imposing. I look around for Mikky, but I don't see her.

J.J. waits, letting the tension in the room build. Trip holds her breath like she's been waiting for this moment her whole life. *Does she know what's going on? Because I sure don't.*

J.J. suddenly slams his fist down onto the podium. Every-one starts. The noise reverberates around the room. "My fel-low humans!" he shouts. "The time is now."

The time for what?

J.J.'s icy, brilliant eyes scan the room. "The time has come to change—or perish." The room is absolutely still now. It's like no one's even breathing. "We need *discipline.* Each and every one of you—every man, woman, and sniveling child— must become strong. Fearless. Single-minded!" He pauses, letting this sink in. "And together we are going to take down the Central Capital!"

For a moment, the room keeps its hush—and then it erupts in cheers. *"Destroy the Bots!" "Annihilate the skin jobs!" "Long live humans!"*

I'm on my feet, waving my arms and yelling, *"Fight! Fight!"* like I've been possessed. My heart's pounding with excitement. Who knew the old dog had it in him?

"Silence!" J.J. screams, and quickly we all sit down again. Suddenly we'll do anything he tells us to. "Together we will make the Hu-Bot leaders kneel and bow down before us!" He stands even taller now. Power flows from him like electricity. "You will not all fight, but you must all be soldiers. Do you understand me? That means hiding when it is time to hide. It means stealing when it is time to steal. It means killing when it's time to kill. It means standing with your fellow humans and believing in yourselves and each other. It means never giving up the fight until your brave human hearts stop beating! *Do you understand me?*"

"Yes!" the room cries as one.

And for the first time in months, I feel something like *hope*. I remember all those times I bowed down to the black limos, aching to revolt. Wanting to stand up and scream, *Don't bow down—FIGHT!*

And now, finally, I can. *We* can.

J.J. pounds the podium again. "We are all soldiers!" he yells. "And we will join together with others who share our cause!" He stops and pivots to the wall behind him, facing the opening where we came in. "And now there's someone I'd like you to meet." He beckons—and Mikky steps out of the shadow of the tunnel.

It's almost like I see her for the first time: six foot four, hair as black as a crow's wing, eyes like sapphires. She stands stiffly, her gaze darting nervously around the room. I can almost hear what she's thinking: *Who remembers me from the Pits massacre?*

"This," J.J. says, "is MikkyBo."

But the crowd has begun to jostle and shout. Some yell in fear, others in anger. *"What's the Hu-Bot doing here?"* *"Enemy in our midst!"* A shoe goes flying toward Mikky's head. Fast as lightning, her hand shoots out, and she catches it. She drops it to the floor like trash.

"Silence!" J.J. calls out. "Mikky is on our side."

"Hu-Bots are evil!" a voice calls out.

"Death to all machines!" yells another.

Suddenly I'm up at the podium, standing right at J.J.'s side. *"Just shut your stupid mouths!"* I roar.

J.J. looks at me in surprise. He gives a quick nod of gratitude. Then he raises his arms, his fists clenched. The room settles down.

"Now listen to me," he says, his voice low and fierce. "*MikkyBo* is not the enemy—your own prejudice is the enemy. So get rid of it. Do you hear me? MikkyBo is more powerful than any ten Hu-Bots in the Central Capital City. Inside her is a new and revolutionary operating system. Do you know what that means? That in her mind, she's more human than you are! More intelligent, more empathic, more ethical! But in her physical attributes, she is humanity's most powerful weapon..."

As J.J. goes on, Mikky's getting more and more agitated. She's been controlling herself, though, practicing deep breathing. Until J.J. calls her a *weapon*. And then she goes pale as death.

And then she turns and *runs*.

CHAPTER 65

MIKKY BURSTS OUT of the tunnel and into the night. Far in the distance, the City glitters like a beacon.

Tears stream down her cheeks. *They were using you. You were no more than a weapon. Lower than a Bot. Dumber than a drone.*

She runs down the rutted mountain road leading away from the Reserve. She runs to dull the pain of betrayal. To forget the word *weapon*. She runs, without stopping, all the way to a gleaming white high-rise in the heart of the City. The Elite Tower.

Home.

She pauses at her front door. She no longer has her Center-issued uniform. Instead she's wearing a jumpsuit of thin, silky material that clings to her muscled limbs. Her hand flutters to her throat before she remembers that her collar is gone, too.

She feels suddenly and completely naked. What will NyBo say? She can't bear to think about it. So she just opens the door.

"It's Mikky!" KatBo shrieks, bolting across the room and leaping into her big sister's arms.

Mikky buries her face in her sister's hair, wiping her tears on the dark, shiny curls. No Hu-Bot must see her crying, not even one in her family. One glitchy Hu-Bot is enough.

But her heart feels like it might burst. *Is this what being human is like?* Mikky is overwhelmed by emotions. She's never felt more relieved, and has never felt more unsettled. Never felt more love — or more fear.

No wonder we always called humans irrational, she thinks. *They are! I am!*

"Mikky?" NyBo rises from his chair, his face a mask of shock. "Is it really you?"

"It's me," she manages to squeak.

Just not the me you remember.

"I thought you were dead," he whispers. He runs toward her, his strong arms outstretched to pull her in.

But her father isn't who she remembers, either. In the few weeks she's been gone, he seems to have aged a hundred years.

And there's something else, too —

She reaches out and touches his cheek. It's wet. "NyBo, are you ... *crying?*"

NyBo smiles uneasily. "Perhaps I have a glitch, too."

Mikky's throat tightens, and her own tears start flowing again. Have they become a family of renegades? Each and every one of them as "defective" as KrisBo?

"I'm so sorry I worried you," she says, wiping her eyes. She takes a deep breath. Then the words tumble out in a rush. "I was injured, Father. I was rehabilitated at a secret human encampment. I wanted to learn more about them. I thought that I could understand the enemy. But I—"

She stops. How can she begin to tell her father all that has happened? About OS Empathy, about Six, about her near expiration?

"Sit down," NyBo says gently, ushering her over to the sleek leather couch, the one with the view of the city skyline. "Do you want something to drink?"

But she can't sit or have a drink. She's too agitated. Her family's future depends on what happens next.

"You went rogue," Kat whispers, awed.

NyBo puts his head in his hands, then looks up at her again. "The commander told us you were dead."

I basically was, she thinks. *Until Six helped me. Until J.J. brought me back.*

"It was...a difficult time," Mikky says. "But it doesn't matter now." She kneels on the carpet before her father and begins to speak, quickly and urgently. "I came to warn you. I think the humans are going to start another war. They were meeting in secret, planning to use *me*—"

NyBo puts a hand up to stop her. "Darling, it's not the humans you should fear."

For a second she doesn't think she's heard him right. Why is her father, ex–military man, human-phobe, number one champion of the Hu-Bot Colony, telling her that *people* aren't dangerous?

"What?" she says in disbelief.

NyBo leans close, so close she can feel his breath on her cheek. "I was trying to find information about your brother. So I hacked into the premier's private slipstream. And I learned that he is planning an attack of his own."

The shock of her father doing something so dangerous and

forbidden is lost in the dread of this new information. "Where?" she asks. Her heart rate rises; her skin grows hot. "At the Reserve?

"Everywhere, my love. He will annihilate every last man, woman, and child. Beginning with the ones in the Central Prison. What do you think your humans can do in the face of such power?"

Mikky gasps. "But does the premier know about the human revolt?"

NyBo looks grim. "He doesn't need to know. Does the lion fret about the gathering of mice?"

Mikky blinks, once, twice, and lets the horror sink in. It makes her bones ache. How has everything gone so wrong?

This isn't why she came home! She wants to feel *safe!* The fire is flickering in the hearth, and Mikky just wants to be a little girl again. She wishes she could sit at her father's side and let him hold her the way he used to. She wants him to be able to make everything all right.

But he can't. No one can.

"The humans have to be told," she says.

KatBo watches her with wide, serious eyes. "Are you going to leave again?" she whispers.

Mikky tries to meet her sister's gaze. She may not know where her loyalties are, but she can't stand by while every last human is murdered.

"I love you both," she says. She takes a step toward the door.

NyBo looks at her a long time. She is no longer the dutiful novice detective he was so proud of.

I hope you can be proud of me again, she thinks.

"Be safe," her father says softly.

She nods. But she can't promise this. She can't promise anything. The world is on the brink of war. She can't stop it.

So she has to pick a side.

CHAPTER 66

SLEEP IS IMPOSSIBLE, so I'm just lying here in the dark. All those times I wished for a room to myself? Well, now I've got it—and I couldn't be more pissed. Turns out OS Empathy doesn't mean anything: once a robot, *always* a robot.

I can't wait to tell J.J. *I told you so.*

Who's going to lead his army now?

I toss and turn, wishing I'd left Mikky in pieces back in that icy river. Then none of this would have happened.

I'm thinking about taking a little trip with the Q-comp— who knows, maybe I'll get a *nice* memory this time—when I hear a scratching right outside the window. I sit up, thinking I'm going to see a raccoon, or maybe one of the big rats that hang out behind the compound kitchen.

But instead, it's Mikky, looking all wild and distraught in the moonlight. There's mud on her cheek. There's even a leaf in her hair.

"Let me in," she whispers.

I shake my head. "This room is for nontraitors only."

Her face crumples. "Six—"

I don't have an ounce of sympathy for this android. She betrayed J.J. She betrayed all the Rezzies. She betrayed *me*. "I thought you were with us."

"I am," she cries. "I'll prove it. Just let me in."

I shake my head. "Nope." Then I add, "What, you can't break down the door with your incredible superpowers?"

She's too upset even to roll her eyes at me. "I don't want anyone to know I'm back yet, and Macy's at the front door. I just need to talk to you."

I let her wait for a few more minutes, fretting. Do I care what she has to say? Will I believe it, whatever it is?

Mikky's voice interrupts my thoughts. "You're in danger."

"So what else is new," I say flatly. "I'm a wanted criminal, remember?"

"Please," she whispers. "You need to hear this."

She seems so sincere—so desperate—that reluctantly I unlatch the window and push it open. Mikky leaps over the sill and lands as softly as a cat. She sits down on the edge of my bed, her hands twisted in her lap.

"So talk, *Hu-Bot*," I command.

She flinches. "When I left the meeting, I went to see my family."

"Sure," I seethe. "Because the Hu-Bots didn't kill or imprison yours."

She reaches out and touches my knee. I quickly slide it out of her reach. "I know you're angry with me, but you must listen," she insists. "You have to be on my side."

I scoff. "On your side? That's the side of total human destruction, isn't it? *Isn't it?*" My fists are clenched, and I'm practically screaming.

"Will you just shut up, Sarah!" she yells.

And I'm so surprised that I do. *How does she know my old name?*

Mikky leans forward and speaks in a whisper. "The premier is planning an attack on the human population, with the intent of…" She frowns, like it's hard to even say the words.

"The intent of what?" I demand.

"Exterminating you all," Mikky blurts.

What's crazy is that I almost feel *relief.* Finally, we can put to rest all the rumors: they're *true.* The end is near.

But that feeling lasts about two seconds, before my whole body is gripped with fear and rage. I don't want to die. I don't want my friends to die. I don't want one *single human* to become another victim of the Bots.

"How do you know this?" I ask.

"My father hacked into an encrypted slipstream," Mikky says.

I lean forward, my face just inches from hers now. "When's it going to happen?"

I can see her swallow nervously. "It starts tomorrow. At the Central Prison."

My heart nearly stops. "At the Central Prison? That's where my brother and sister are!"

Mikky's face falls. "Oh, Six," she says. "I'm sorry—"

"Screw *sorry!*" I shout. "We're going to rescue them!"

"But I know J.J. has a plan for our own attack, Six. And storming the prison isn't part of it."

I'm out of bed, and I'm putting on my clothes, even though it's still dark out. "I don't care what J.J. says," I say, reaching for my ancient gun and slipping it into my coat. "That's my *family* in there. Are you coming or what?"

CHAPTER 67

I'M IN A rusted, windowless van that's probably as old as J.J., watching through the filthy windshield as Mikky creeps toward the perimeter of the jail yard. Zee Twelve and Trip are across the street, each behind the wheel of another van. We're all awaiting Mikky's signal.

We've timed the Bot-cop patrols: Mikky has three minutes to scale the slick, thirty-foot Plexiglas gate, find the control box, hack the security code, and open up the gate.

A piece of cake, right? She's trained for this—Mikky can leap a wall that size carrying a boulder in a backpack. But for some reason she's not moving. Instead she's standing there like she thinks the gate's going to magically open for her.

Go, you crazy Hu-Bot, I think. *Jump!*

Has she had another change of heart? I put my hand on the door handle, ready to dash out and try to throw her over the gate myself. But then the Bot-cop patrol rolls into view, and I decide to stay hidden.

Mikky wakes up when she sees the three of them coming. She beckons them over, and, since she's a Hu-Bot, they obey. I watch as she persuades one of the cops to hand over his weapon—and then she proceeds to shoot him with it.

The other two lift their guns, but they're blown to bits before I can blink.

Then Mikky turns, sprints toward the gate, cartwheels into it, pushes off the Plexiglas with the ball of her foot, and swings her body up and backward over the top. Then she disappears from sight. But she must have found the control box, because a moment later, the big gate slides open.

This might actually work, I think.

I slam the van into gear and race toward the gate, stopping for a moment to leap out and grab one of the Bot-cop's guns. It's so light, it almost feels like a toy—but I've seen firsthand the damage it can do.

Zee and Trip pull into the prison yard a second behind me. The lights have come on, and inside the prison an alarm is shrieking.

Clutching my Bot weapon, I jump out of the van.

"Where are you going?" Trip calls after me. "We're supposed to stay here so we can load up the prisoners!"

"I'm not sitting around while Mikky rescues my family!" I cry, sprinting toward the prison door. When I fling it open, I see gray-faced prisoners, skinny as skeletons, stumbling down the hall toward me. "Head for the vans!" I yell, and push my way through them. I don't recognize any of them. *Where are Martha and Ricky?*

A barrage of gunfire opens up before me, and the air's filled with the bright pop of electrical explosions. I duck down a hallway, telling myself Mikky's fine. She's raced through this place, blasting holes through the Bot-guards, and they're going up in flames.

I stumble over piles of exterminated drones as I creep down the hall. I know I don't have much time—any minute now the Elite Force is going to storm the building. But I've got to find my family. I'm trying to push down the thought that keeps seizing me, the possibility that *maybe I'm too late.*

All the cells are open and empty. *Where's Martha? Where's Ricky?*

At the end of the hall is a metal door with a tiny window covered by a steel grate. It's the only one that didn't open automatically.

I don't know if it's a cell or a broom closet, but I have to find out. I crouch down and aim the gun up at the lock. That way, the bullet will lodge in the ceiling—and not in anyone who might be inside.

I shoot. The bullet tears through its target, and with a creak, the door swings slowly open. A rat dashes out, skittering right over my foot. I stifle a shriek.

It's dark inside the room. The air smells like mildew and rotting food and unwashed bodies—like *despair.*

Steeling myself, I step inside the cell. When my eyes adjust, I see a small, trembling shape in the corner.

It's my sister.

"Martha!" I gasp.

At first she shrinks away from me, but I run to her and

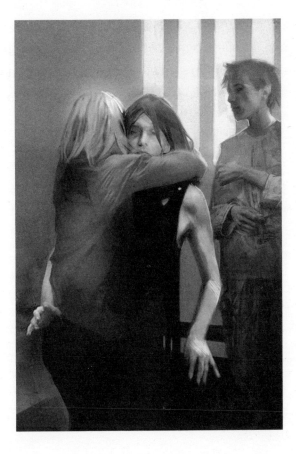

scoop her up in my arms. Though she's three years older than I am, she feels no bigger than a child. Her eyes are huge and frightened. Her cheeks are so hollow that her face looks like a skull.

"No," she whispers. "This isn't real."

I squeeze her tightly, relief and love flooding my body. "It's real, Martha. I'm here, I'm here. Everything's going to be okay."

Then a figure steps from the shadows, as pale and

terrifying as a ghost. "You." The voice sounds like the gasp of a dying man. But I recognize it as Ricky's. "You've just committed suicide," he hisses, "and you've murdered every prisoner here in the process. Just like you did to our mother and father."

CHAPTER 68

"FEEL FREE TO stay here," I answer, my teeth clenched. "But Martha and I are leaving."

My sister buries her face against my chest, wrapping her arms around my neck. It's a good thing she's light, because I don't think she can walk.

The sirens are louder now, but the hallway's still deserted. I hurry down the hall, clutching Martha tightly against myself, and I think I hear my brother's footsteps behind me. The door's only fifty yards ahead, and I can see the last of the prisoners staggering out into the night.

We did it, I think—and the triumph propels me faster down the hall. I'm practically sprinting toward freedom.

But just as I'm getting to the door, two Elite Force Hu-Bots block it.

"Halt!" barks the taller one.

I set Martha down, whispering for her to stay calm. She

whimpers in response. I raise up my hands in surrender, cursing myself for leaving the gun back in the cell. But I don't halt: I start backing away, deeper into the prison, and the Hu-Bots follow me.

They walk right past my sister as if she's invisible.

"Martha, run!" I yell, and I watch as she limps outside. I catch a glimpse of Trip as she stops Martha from falling, then hurries her to the transport van. And a moment later, my brother slinks outside, too. I hear the gunning of the engine. *They're going to escape.*

"Halt!" the Hu-Bot says again.

Now that my family's safe, it's time to worry about myself. And my odds aren't pretty. I'm alone inside a prison with two Hu-Bots. I've got no weapon, no backup. I don't know where Mikky is. *This does not look good.*

I stop and smile as bravely as I can. "You guys gonna lock me up?" I ask. "I guess I get my pick of beds, huh?"

I don't expect the Hu-Bot to laugh—but nor do I expect him to whip out an Electroshock 12 and aim it at my neck.

Suddenly the world goes white, then black. And a second later, I'm on the ground, writhing as my muscles contract from a barrage of high-voltage electric shocks. It feels like I'm being punched all over by a million tiny, burning hands. I think I'm screaming, but I can't hear anything—the pain is too much.

I claw at the concrete floor, as if I could pull myself away from the agony. My legs flop; my spine snaps forward and back again—I must look like a dying fish.

Then suddenly, the shocks stop. I'm on the floor, shaking and sobbing. I'm holding a fistful of my own hair. I've wet my pants.

"That was fun, wasn't it?" the tall Hu-Bot asks. "Shall we do it again?"

I open my mouth, but nothing but a mewling cry of pain comes out.

"Just shoot her," the shorter one says.

The tall one nods. "Yes, that *is* more efficient." He reaches for his gun.

It feels like a dream to me. Like it happens in slow motion. I think, *I hope it's a Mercy, because I can't stand any more pain.*

But then, out of the corner of my eye, I see this flashing

blur of movement, and before I can cry out, the two Hu-Bots are on the ground. One of their guns comes spinning toward me. I try to reach for it, but my fingers are so weak, I can't even pick it up.

But I don't have to, because Mikky is here, and she's holding her own weapon, pointed right at the guards.

"Shooting *is* efficient," Mikky agrees. "One...two..."

But instead of saying *three* and blowing a hole in their chests, Mikky leans down and yanks me up, tossing me over her shoulder as she sprints out into the prison yard, slamming the heavy metal door behind us.

She runs toward my van, which I'm in no condition to drive. So she shoves me into the passenger seat and leaps behind the wheel. A second later, we're peeling out down the street, the sounds of the prison alarms already growing faint.

"You saved my life," I manage.

She smiles grimly. "Now we're even."

CHAPTER 69

THE COMPOUND IS lit up like it's Christmas, and Sergeant Macy is sweating and swearing, running around, trying to arrange sleeping quarters for the prisoners who were too weak to go back to the Reserve.

I feel bad for a second—like maybe I should have warned her and J.J. about my plans—but I tell myself it had to be this way. I couldn't risk them stopping me.

Martha and I limp toward J.J.'s wing of the compound. Mikky follows us, and somewhere behind her is the tall, fuming figure of my brother. I swear I can feel his fiery gaze burning holes in the back of my T-shirt.

J.J. comes out to meet us. "Your stupidity never ceases to amaze me," he says to me. But he doesn't sound angry. And, in fact, a moment later, his face cracks into a smile.

I don't think I've ever seen him do that before.

"J.J.," I say, "Mikky found out about an attack—"

He holds up a hand to stop me. "Later," he says. And he enfolds my frail sister in his arms. "My sweet Martha," he whispers. "And Ricky. I've missed you! Come in, come in." He pauses. "Mikky," he adds, "I'm so glad you've come back. I knew you would."

I give J.J. a sideways look. What's with the human warmth? Did he get knocked on the head recently?

He ushers us to a table, and pretty soon we're all sitting around, eating chicken soup, like it's a regular Sunday-night family dinner. It's the best food I've had in a long time, and the effects of the electric shocks are wearing off. I'm almost feeling *happy*.

Except that Ricky eats in stony silence. And he's staring at me like I'm some giant cockroach. Like something he'd like to crush under his boot.

"Why are you looking at me like that?" I finally ask, my mouth half-full of biscuit. "If it weren't for me, you'd still be rotting inside that prison!"

His eyes narrow. "Nothing can change what you did."

"What did I do besides come visit you every freaking month? I don't even know what you're talking about."

He sneers at me. "Look at us—me with a hunched back, crippled from a decade of hard labor. And Martha, nothing but skin and bones. Remember the last time you came to see us? She waved at you, and because of that, they knocked most of her teeth out of her mouth." He spits soup on the table as he talks. He's got his butter knife held like a weapon. "And you think you're a hero! It's *disgusting*."

I clench my fists. "Did you want to get blown to bits when

the Hu-Bots bombed the prison? Because that's what they were going to do, Ricky. *Tomorrow.*"

J.J., startled, sits up straighter. "What?"

I turn to him. "Mikky found out when she ran away. The premier's launching an all-out offensive on humankind. I guess he was going to kill the weakest ones first."

I didn't think it would be possible for Martha to get any paler, but she does. A small whimper escapes her mouth.

J.J. starts to say something, but Ricky interrupts. He doesn't care about anything but his own anger at me. "You're a murderer," he seethes.

And before I know what's happening, he leaps up from his chair and comes at me. I rise to meet him—but I'm not even all the way standing when his fist shoots out and connects with my brow bone. I hear a *crack*, and stars explode in front of my face. Blood gushes into my left eye. I reel backward, knocking over my chair.

Ricky advances, his fists raised. I'm wiping the blood from my face when he lands another punch, this one to my mouth. I can feel my teeth rip my lips open, and now I can *taste* the blood, too.

Mikky's screaming at Ricky to stop, but J.J. holds her back.

I get it: this is my fight.

The adrenaline coursing through my system is making me shake all over—but on the upside, it's dulling the pain. I figure I've got one good punch in me. I feint left, then right. Ricky's fists are flying, but they're not connecting with anything anymore.

I skip backward like I'm retreating—and then I charge. I send my right fist flying into Ricky's stomach. He doubles over, arms wrapped around his guts. Then he drops to his knees, panting.

"Why the hell do you hate me so much?" I yell at his bowed head.

Ricky won't look up at me.

I turn to J.J. "Do you know? Why does he despise me? And why do *you,* for that matter?"

J.J. presses his lips into a thin line. "I suppose it's time you knew the truth," he says.

CHAPTER 70

DIZZY AND DRIPPING blood from the cut on my brow, I follow J.J. into a tiny room off the kitchen area. He flicks on a dim light. The entire space is stuffed with outdated gadgets—gaming stations, bulky TVs, and stereo speakers, all of them covered in dust.

"What is this, the tomb of the unknown computer?" I ask.

He ignores me, as usual. He's fussing with a small machine that looks like an old-fashioned laptop. A moment later, an image appears on the screen.

A six-year-old girl.

Me.

"What is this?" I whisper.

"*My* cloud access," he says. "Watch."

I see myself in a black doorway, clutching a loaf of bread. I recognize it immediately: it's the entrance to the shelter where we lived in the aftermath of the Great War, when the

Hu-Bots were combing the City and the countryside for human survivors. Rounding them up. Taking away their names and giving them numbers. Killing anyone too weak or too strong. Enslaving or imprisoning the rest.

We'd been hiding underground for three months while my parents tried to figure out where to go, how to keep us safe. We'd been eating nothing but canned tuna and beans, and our supplies were running low. I wanted to help. I wanted us to have *bread*. So I'd gone out and stolen it. I was so proud of myself! I remember all of it. After that, though, my memory goes dark.

But what I'm watching isn't my memory. It's my mom's. She's hurrying over to meet me — she doesn't know how I got out, but she's so relieved that I'm back. But then, materializing right behind me, so silently I'm not even aware of them, are two Hu-Bot soldiers. My mother shrieks in fear. My sister starts to scream. The soldiers' eyes flash.

I see the Hu-Bots knocking me down as they push past me. I see my father leap forward, covering me with his body. My mom dives under the makeshift table, saying *Please no please no please no*. Then there's a flash from the muzzle of a gun — and everything goes dark.

I'm shaking even harder than I was when I fought my brother. I can't believe it: *I just saw my mother die.*

J.J. watches me, his arms crossed over his chest.

"Is there more?" I manage to ask. "Other memories... from anyone else?"

He shakes his head. "You don't want to see those."

My face is streaked with tears. I collapse onto a chair. "Why did you show me?"

J.J.'s shoulders hunch. He looks smaller, older. "The truth

is," he says, "I always blamed you. It was *your* act of thievery that brought the Hu-Bots to your hiding place." He pauses, scratches his thinning hair. "But only recently, I realized something. You were doing what you thought was best. You were *fighting*. You were only six years old, but you were already a soldier. You were trying to save your family."

"But instead, I killed them," I cry.

"You didn't kill them. The androids that *I made* killed them. Don't you see, Sarah? Not a single one of us is innocent. But we have to move on. We have to make our own justice. We have to . . ." He trails off.

I feel a terrible resolve building inside me. I look up and meet his gaze. "We have to *fight*," I say. I stand, holding myself steady on the table. My face is covered in blood and tears. "And I'm not Sarah anymore," I tell him. "I'm a soldier. I'm *Six*."

CHAPTER 71

"ARE YOU ALL right?" Mikky asks, gently touching the cut on my brow.

"I'm fine," I say, flinching. In fact, it's sore as hell—but that's not the pain that's bothering me. I look around the now-empty room. "Where's Martha and Ricky?"

"Sergeant Macy took them to their quarters," Mikky says. "Ricky had to make a stop at the infirmary."

Good, I think. *He won't mess with me anymore.*

J.J. walks back to the table, slurps down the rest of his soup in one gulp, and then says, "Okay, you two, follow me."

"Time for some more laps?" Mikky asks, sounding almost eager.

He shakes his head. "Time for another family reunion."

Mikky looks at me in confusion. I just shrug—although I'm pretty sure I know who we're about to go see.

Except that I'm not prepared at *all* for where J.J. takes us. At the far end of the compound, enclosed by a high metal fence, is a huge barracks. And inside, it's positively crawling with Hu-Bots. There must be hundreds of them, a thousand— all bunking down in a room the size of a football field.

Some of them are lifting weights. Others are lying on their bunks, looking at maps and graphs (nerd alert!). There's a group playing cards near a window, and another group having what appears to be a push-up contest.

Mikky gasps. "Who...," she says, and then stops, overcome.

J.J. gazes over them like a proud father—which, in a way, he is. "These Hu-Bots were outcasts and renegades, Mikky," he says quietly. "They suffered under the repressive laws of the premier. They didn't want to enslave the human race. They wanted a new life. A new world. And so they came to *me*."

He makes it sound so simple, so easy. I guess it helps when you leave out the whole brain-surgery part. The whole *they'll be reprogrammed or killed the minute they show their faces in the City* business.

"I can't believe it," she whispers. "I thought I was alone..."

Suddenly there's a commotion on the far side of the room, and a tall, dark-haired Hu-Bot comes racing toward us. Reflexively, I duck. Mikky freezes, and a moment later I see her jaw fall open.

"Kris!" she squeals.

And then they're falling all over each other, laughing and crying and hugging. It's the most emotion I've ever seen coming from two Hu-Bots—can their systems even handle it?

I'm happy for them, I am. I just wish my own family reunion had looked more like this and less like a bar fight.

When they finally stop squawking in joy, J.J. says, "Are you ready, Mikky?"

"Ready for what?" Mikky asks. Tears are still shining on her flushed cheeks. Her blue eyes glitter, and her smile lights up everything around her.

"For your future," J.J. says cryptically.

He's truly a man of few words—unless he's in front of a crowd.

"I'm ready for anything," Mikky asserts.

And so J.J. turns to the room. "Everyone, listen!"

All eyes snap to him.

"You all have been waiting for this moment," he says, "even if you didn't know it. Now is the time when we come together to overthrow our oppressors. And to lead the troops, I give you—MikkyBo." He sweeps his arm behind himself, motioning Mikky forward.

She hesitates for a moment before stepping to his side. Unlike at the meeting of the Rezzies, no one protests. They simply gaze at her for a moment—taking in her long, strong body, her fierce eyes, her confident stature—and then they begin to clap.

J.J. turns to me, his face lit up with victory. "The revolution has begun."

And I think: *I hope we survive it.*

CHAPTER 72

MOSESKHAN THROWS THE report down on his desk in fury: a group of rebel humans has attacked the Central Prison, freeing all prisoners and destroying an entire Bot-cop squadron in the process.

It was a carefully planned raid, carried out under cover of darkness. But grainy security-camera footage shows a *Hu-Bot* leading the deadly charge.

MosesKhan knows who the traitor is before he even glances at the tapes. The detestable former detective MikkyBo, whose expiration he himself had confirmed—*prematurely*, it would seem. She has returned, and she has tricked him. He should have destroyed her when he had the chance. Buried her right alongside the stinking humans in the Pits.

He's starting to round up an assassination squad when the door to his office bursts open. The force is so great that the top hinges rip out of the frame. Standing in the doorway is the biggest Hu-Bot MosesKhan has ever seen—and behind him is the premier.

MosesKhan freezes. He even stops breathing. *This is not good.*

The premier barges into the room, his face purple with barely suppressed rage. "What is the *meaning* of this?" he demands.

MosesKhan falters. "Sir," he says, "I assure you—"

The premier cuts him off with a backhand to MosesKhan's cheek. "You assure me of *nothing*," he seethes. "You have committed a grave and perilous error, commander." The premier leans closer, and his voice becomes soft. Threatening. "You have underestimated the humans' capacity for treachery."

MosesKhan reflexively brings his hand to his stinging cheek, then lifts it farther up in a belated salute to his leader. He has failed—there is no way of disguising it. The only question is: how acutely will he suffer for that failure? "Sir, I have sent search patrols out to all corners of the Central Capital," he says quickly. He must try to salvage his Elite position. "The escaped prisoners will be rounded up and—"

The premier spits on the floor—a gesture so foul, it seems almost human. "If you think I care one bit about those starving, worm-riddled *walking corpses,* then you are mistaken, commander. What troubles me," he says, coming even closer to MosesKhan now, his eyes glittering with menace, "is the message it sends to our populations. It tells the humans that revolt is possible. And it tells the Hu-Bots that our power is not absolute." He inhales deeply, his eyes closed. Then he snaps them open again and roars, *"Do you understand the problem with this?"*

MosesKhan nods vehemently.

The premier smiles coldly. "Good. Because if you did not, it would not be so hard to come by another commander." He turns his back to MosesKhan and gazes out the window. "And what would you do then?" he asks. "Perhaps, after a minor system reboot, you could join the drones on janitorial patrol," he suggests. "I'd leave *just enough* of your memories for you to know how much you'd lost. How far you'd fallen."

"Your Honor, I—"

The premier whirls around. *"Bow down, Khan,"* he whispers.

MosesKhan starts. *Did he hear that right?*

But a glance at his premier's cold, diabolical eyes tells him that he has. MosesKhan clenches his fists. The humiliation being demanded of him is unbearable. He is not a human. He is not a slave. And yet—

"Bow down." The premier's soft voice booms in Moses-Khan's head.

There is no alternative. Unwillingly, MosesKhan bends his knees. He lowers his body. Slowly, his mind fuming— *This is intolerable*—he leans down, down, down, until his face is pressed against the floor.

"There will be no more patience," the premier says from above him. "No more mercy."

MosesKhan can see only the tips of the premier's boots as he paces the room. Then the boots stop, an inch from his face.

"Our soldiers have been alerted," the premier says. "Munitions have been gathered. Land mines, incendiaries, Mercys,

and missiles: all will be brought to bear upon the pathetic human pestilence."

MosesKhan dares to look up. The premier is staring down at him, his eyes lit with murder.

"The time has come for the elimination of the human race," the premier declares. "It will be over in a matter of days. And there is nothing the humans can do to stop it."

Just let me have MikkyBo, MosesKhan thinks. *I'm going to tear her body limb from limb.*

CHAPTER 73

"SIT STILL," MIKKY says, elbowing me. Hard. "I'm trying to fix this."

"Ow. What's *your* problem?" I ask, rubbing the new sore spot on my ribs.

We're sitting in the toolshed—my former Q-comp hideout—and Mikky's fiddling with something that looks like an old-fashioned radio. J.J.'s got so much electronic junk lying around, we could probably build a rocket to the moon with it.

"The premier is about to make a speech in the Central Arena," Mikky informs me.

I watch her connect two of the gadget's wires, and a small spark leaps out and lands on her bioskin. She doesn't even notice. "What do I care what some dumb Hu-Bot has to say?" I ask.

Mikky looks at me like she's considering elbowing me again, but then she just shakes her head. "Because he's the *enemy,* Six." She takes a deep breath, like it's still hard for her to say that. "And we need to know what he's up to."

"Did J.J. tell you to —"

"J.J.'s too busy planning the attack," she interrupts. "You and I are the intelligence committee, okay?" She pauses. "Though that's sort of an oxymoron when it comes to you," she mutters.

But then she flashes a quick, bright smile — either because she's teasing me or because she's finally got her little gadget working. "See, I'm going to listen via slipstream," she explains, "but I'm going to transmit it through these speakers. So you can hear it, too."

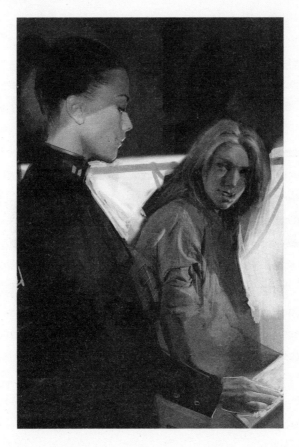

"Whatever," I say, leaning back on the burlap sacks. "I'm going to close my eyes. If we're going to start a war in the next few days, I should get my beauty rest."

A burst of static comes over the speakers, followed by the sound of thunderous applause. The clapping lasts a minute, at least, but then it's cut off instantly.

"My fellow Hu-Bots," booms a powerful but slightly quavering voice. "Welcome. And welcome to our one thousand human guests, here in the seats of honor before me."

"That's the premier," Mikky whispers. "The very first Hu-Bot ever created." Her voice still carries a trace of awe.

He sounds old, I think. And also: *What the hell are* humans *doing at this speech?* I start to ask Mikky, but she puts her finger to her lips.

The premier's voice echoes through the speakers. "I have asked you to come here today for a very important reason: to renew your dedication to the Hu-Bot creed of unity, prosperity, and peace."

I snort. "I think he meant to say 'atrocity, brutality, and enslavement,'" I say. Mikky elbows me for the second time.

"Shut up," she hisses.

The premier clears his throat and goes on. "It has come to my attention that there has been some violent...*discourse* with our human neighbors. There have been misunderstandings, which must trouble you as they trouble me. We must remember that, though humans are far less advanced, we must take pity on them."

Pity? I think. *We don't need your stinking pity.*

"How else can we as Hu-Bots continue to evolve," the premier continues, "if we do not respect our origins?"

He pauses, and I can hear the silence. Hu-Bots don't like remembering that we were the ones who made them.

"The thing about pity," the premier says, "is that it comes in many forms. Sometimes pity means giving scraps to the stray dog you find on the street." There's another long pause. "And sometimes it means *putting that dog out of its misery.*"

A murmur rises up in the background. I hear confused human voices in the arena. I sit up sharply. What the hell is he talking about?

Mikky's eyes widen at me. She holds up a finger: *Wait.*

My heart begins to pound. I don't like the sound of this at all.

The premier calls for silence again. "I ask my fellow Hu-Bots to please join me by connecting via slipstream, so that our thoughts will be as one," he says.

"What does that mean?" I demand.

Mikky goes pale. "If they connect with him, it can give him the ability to control their thoughts."

"Does that—"

"It means he can *reprogram* them."

I don't have time to react, because the premier's voice rises above the sound of the crowd again. It's taken on a terrifying, savage tone. "The human race has become like a mangy, starving, but streetwise cur. We have tried to feed this creature, and what does it do? It maliciously turns around and *bites us.* And so, my fellow Hu-Bots, the time has come to *assert our authority again.*" He pauses, letting that sink in. "Know that I tell you the truth!" he yells.

"You tell us the truth," the Hu-Bots murmur.

"The chief obstacle to the progress of the Hu-Bot race is the human race!" he shouts.

"The chief obstacle to the progress of the Hu-Bot race is the human race," the Hu-Bots repeat.

The background noise coming through the speakers grows. I can almost see the humans in the arena with him, suddenly terrified, shifting around in their seats. Standing up. Making for the exits.

I stand up, too.

"And so it follows that humans are a grave threat to Hu-Bot survival!" the premier hollers.

But the Hu-Bots don't repeat after him this time. Instead, there's silence.

"Mikky?" I ask fearfully.

But then noise bursts out of the speakers again, and it seems that every Hu-Bot voice in the stadium shouts out as one: "ALL HUMANS MUST BE DESTROYED!"

"No!" I shriek, grabbing for the radio.

And then comes the sound of screaming, a thousand throats opening up in terror. And then one lone, desperate voice soars above the rest—it's a woman's piercing cry. It's telling me what I can't bear to hear. *"Help! They're murdering us!"*

Instantly I'm out of the shed and racing for the jeep. Mikky shoots out after me, but she grabs my arm, yanking me away from the car. "We have to save them!" I cry, fighting her off.

She doesn't say a word—she just picks me up and throws me onto her back. "Hold on," she barks. And then, just like that, she sprints down the mountain road a hundred times faster than that jeep could ever go, with me clinging to her shoulders, holding on for dear life.

The world rushes by in a multicolored blur—we get to the arena in what feels like only seconds. The last of the Hu-Bots are filing out the doors, their faces peacefully blank. They walk slowly, calmly, as if they've just left a Sunday sermon.

They're completely covered in blood.

I stumble at the sight. Mikky pulls me through a side door, and what I see next brings me to my knees. A thousand people—men, women, kids—sprawled on the ground. Twisted, red-smeared limbs. Mangled organs spilling out of mutilated torsos. Throats slit in bloody smiles. Mouths open in never-ending, silent screams.

Every single human *dead*.

I feel like my mind's shutting down. I gag. The world goes dark. *We're too late.*

CHAPTER 74

IT'S MIDNIGHT, AND there's no one on the streets but us. The Bot-cops are recharging; the Hu-Bots are tucked into their beds for the night.

Which is why it's so easy to lay waste to the Hu-Bot shopping district.

Zee Twelve smashes a crowbar into the hood of a parked car. Trip, her eyes ablaze with wrath, hurls a brick through a window. My sister, still so malnourished she can barely stay upright, shoots out a streetlight with an ancient BB gun.

"Nice one!" I say, and she smiles shyly.

Sure, our weapons are sticks and shovels, axes and clubs: pitiful, when you think about what we're facing. But vengeance makes us strong.

Then, across the way, I spot the restaurant where Dubs and I watched that Hu-Bot eating a T-bone she didn't even need.

Suddenly my breath catches in my throat, and a sharp

pain shoots through my chest. I have to stop and lean against a doorway for a second. Hot tears prick at the corners of my eyes. *I miss him so much.*

But I don't have time to cry. Tonight, grief is a luxury—and Rezzies are strangers to luxury of any kind.

I straighten up, wiping my face. Then I run across the street, lift my pickax, and bring it crashing down into the restaurant's big glass window. It shatters instantly, glass falling at my feet like diamonds.

Martha slams her pitchfork into another window, and down the street I can see another Rezzie taking a sledgehammer to a Hu-Bot sedan. The air's filled with the sound of smashing glass, with the resounding ring of metal ripping metal.

Zee Twelve and his cronies have managed to overturn a van, and now flames are shooting out its windows. Then—of all people—Toothless Ten appears, as drunk as ever and dragging a giant bag behind him. "Who wants a Molotov cocktail?" he cries.

The answer is: *we all do.*

I grab liquor bottles filled with gas and stoppered with alcohol-soaked rags—and then I pitch them into the restaurant. Within moments, the whole place is burning.

My adrenaline's surging, and the tears are gone—instead I'm laughing and shouting like a crazy person. Finally, we're all in this together, and we're giving the Bots a giant middle finger!

Then a siren rips through the night. And that's our signal. All the kids from the Reserve Trade School drop what they're doing and fan out in all directions. Moments later, twenty stolen cars come shrieking to a halt in the center of the Hu-Bot square.

Each one is piloted by one of my former classmates.

I slide into the driver's seat of a black coupe, and Martha clambers into the back. We peel out, zero to sixty in about two seconds.

Never underestimate a stray dog.

CHAPTER 75

AS THE ROAR of police cruisers and the whine of sirens come closer, I duck behind a tree trunk, my Colt cocked. The cop cars appear at the top of the hill, and then a second later, they're plunging down. They don't see our roadblock until there's nothing they can do about it.

I hear the squeal of brakes, the crashing of metal. Almost instantly, I can smell gas—I can taste smoke in my mouth. The cruisers smash into one another and spin out, horns blaring.

It worked! We led them right into our trap.

The Hu-Bots claw their way out of their mangled cars. Half the cruisers are burning already. The Hu-Bot leader is shouting something, but I can't hear what it is. Maybe he's telling them to find their weapons; maybe he's telling them to run.

But it doesn't matter what he wants. The Hu-Bots on our

side suddenly shoot up from behind the tree trunks, surprising their counterparts. A look of relief washes over the leader's face—but only for an instant.

Because then our Hu-Bots open fire.

The enemy Hu-Bots are trapped, just the way the humans in the arena were. Some of them try to run, the way the humans did.

But the humans were shown no mercy today. And tonight, neither are the premier's Elite Hu-Bots.

Mikky, dressed head to toe in black like some futuristic model ninja, comes and stands beside me. She gazes out over

the carnage with an unreadable expression. "You did it," she says.

I can't tell if she's happy about it—or totally freaked out. Those were her *colleagues,* after all.

But then she turns to me and suddenly smiles giddily. "Way to go!" she shouts, and raises her hand for a high five.

I slap her palm, laughing at her silly schoolyard gesture. But a feeling of pride washes over me at the same time. My cheeks flush. I haven't experienced anything like this for years. Tonight, for the first time since I can remember, I don't feel helpless. I feel triumphant.

I don't think the Hu-Bots would approve.

CHAPTER 76

"INFRARED CAMERAS SHOW approximately four hundred stationary humans," AlSordi, MosesKhan's deputy, informs him. Then he smiles viciously. "They're all bedded down for the night."

MosesKhan glances quickly at the small screen, which shows the housing sector of the Reserve. He nods in satisfaction: there they are, the stinking humans, all lying on their moldy mattresses, dreaming.

MosesKhan is about to become their worst nightmare. "Call up the entire Elite Force," he says.

Minus the twenty EFs the humans took out last night, he thinks bitterly.

AlSordi nods, his eyes sparking with malice. "With that much firepower, you won't be able to find an intact limb when it's over."

MosesKhan nods. "Exactly." Six helicopters, thirty cruisers:

more than enough to obliterate the human pestilence once and for all.

When the choppers land in the courtyard, their roaring blades sound like thunder. Their spotlights rake the Elite Tower's walls. MosesKhan climbs into the lead helicopter. As its powerful blades spin, he's lifted jerkily into the air.

In a matter of minutes, they're near the human garbage dump that is the Reserve. Soon, all trace of human habitation will be wiped out: the tents and lean-tos will fall; the housing blocks will crumble. There will be nothing to remember them by except a broken stone statue in the middle of what used to be a town square.

The premier will be so pleased, MosesKhan thinks.

He glances again at the screen, and he sees one human-shaped blur of light get out of bed and stumble to the bathroom. MosesKhan smiles: how humiliating to die with your pants around your ankles.

The pilot lands the helicopter on a nearby ridge, and the cruisers pull to a stop a mile from the Reserve gates. They'll go the rest of the way on foot. MosesKhan can taste victory already.

He hasn't gotten the night-vision upgrade yet, so he lets his Elite Force staff sergeant lead the way down the rocky path. There's no moon, and the clouds are heavy. He loses his footing for a moment and curses.

At the edge of the Reserve, the wind blows foul and cold. MosesKhan wrinkles his nose. *Good riddance to the human garbage.*

He motions his men to come up behind him. "On my command," MosesKhan says.

The soldiers shoulder their weapons, and when MosesKhan

gives the signal, they charge. They burst into Tent City, into the housing barracks, guns already firing. Tents collapse, and the cinder-block cells are riddled with holes. But MosesKhan hears no screams. He sees no fleeing, half-naked humans.

After a moment, the Hu-Bots, confused, stop firing. An eerie silence descends.

MosesKhan checks his screen again—*and sees that all the glowing dots have moved.*

But to where? He's trying to orient himself, trying to pinpoint just where that cluster of bright dots *is*, exactly, when the air erupts in gunfire. But this time it's not his.

Coming toward them up the path are hundreds of Hu-Bots, all dressed in cast-off human clothing. And they're *shooting*.

It takes MosesKhan a moment to comprehend what's

happening—perhaps because what's happening is almost beyond comprehension. Hu-Bots fighting on the side of humans? Hu-Bots aiming their weapons at and shooting other Hu-Bots?

The Elite Force troops, unprepared to shoot their own kind, hesitate. The leader takes a bullet to his forehead. He falls into a tangled heap.

"Fire!" MosesKhan screams, grabbing for his own weapon.

In seconds, it's an all-out firefight.

MosesKhan's microprocessors are struggling to take it all in. Somehow, these Hu-Bots have been reprogrammed—they've become an army of androids rising up against their own brothers. But where did they come from?

From the Recycling Wards, from the back alleys outside Killer Films, from the forbidden theaters that the premier pretends don't exist, MosesKhan thinks. They're nothing but renegades and glitchy Bots, running defective programs.

But they're excellent marksmen. MosesKhan ducks behind a cinder-block structure as the bullets fly.

There isn't a human in sight, he realizes. He has been tricked.

Now it is more crucial than ever that these devious humans be eradicated. Every man, woman, and child.

MosesKhan orders his troops to retreat—to go back to the City and return with greater numbers. He turns around and starts running for the choppers, followed by his EFs.

But in the distant City, he can see a hundred fires burning. And, even as he watches, the Central Arena goes up in a fireball.

Another war has begun.

CHAPTER 77

WE'VE BEEN WAITING for J.J.'s command, but for some reason it's not coming. The radio's dead silent.

"Do you think something's wrong?" Mikky asks quietly, worry creasing her brow.

I shake my head, pretending I know something I don't. "He was never the best communicator, okay? And anyway, we have our orders."

Even if they sound like a suicide mission, I add silently.

My hand squeezes tighter around the handle of my ancient Colt. I brought it for luck—the thing misfires like crazy—because we *need* luck, maybe even more than we need courage. Everything has to go according to plan tonight. Otherwise we can pretty much say good-bye to the entire human population.

With the Elite Force attacking the Reserve, it's time to storm the City with our own forces: Rezzie riffraff, ex-prisoners, compound die-hards, and a few scared-shitless Reformed defectors.

It's a crazy, ragtag, sorry-ass bunch of humans, if I've ever seen one. But all of us are fighting for our lives—and maybe, just maybe, that gives us an edge.

"We gotta move out," I tell Mikky.

"But J.J.—" she says.

"—isn't giving the order," I say firmly. "So *I* am." I turn around and spring up so that I'm standing on the driver's seat of the jeep. "Everyone, look there!" I shout, pointing toward the gleaming City, which once belonged to us. "The Hu-Bots aren't expecting us tonight. Truth is, they don't expect us *ever*. They think that because we humans feel things—love, hate, anger, joy—that makes us weak and stupid. So let's show them what happens when the weak and stupid humans decide we are *never* going to bow down to them ever again!"

Cheers and curses erupt from the crowd around me, spiking my adrenaline until I'm screaming back, *"Now, is everyone ready?"*

KrisBo, perched on the jeep's back bumper, raises a fist and pumps it into the air. Behind her, hundreds of other exiled Hu-Bots, all hopped up on J.J.'s Empathy cocktail and high-intensity workout plan, raise their fists, too.

I can feel the hard knocking of my heart inside my rib cage. *It all begins now.*

I look down at Mikky. "Now be a good girl and follow orders," I tell her, and she responds with a grim smile. Then I turn and yell, "Move out!"

I drop back down into my seat and gun the engine of the jeep. Immediately, the whole army surges forward—the humans in beat-up old vans and on motorcycles, the faster Hu-Bots on foot. Fueled by rage, euphoria, and vengeance, the mob thunders down the mountain road as one huge, roiling mass, their weapons raised and their screams bloodcurdling.

The sleeping Hu-Bots of the Central Capital have no idea about the shit storm that's coming.

Thanks to a predawn raid of the weapons wing of the Hu-Bot Museum of Human History, we're armed with AKs and bowie knives, grenades and pistols. Zee Twelve somehow got his hands on a crossbow so big, he can barely lift it.

And our biggest weapons? The element of surprise and the power of our desperation.

Our orders from J.J. are simple: (a) decommission or reprogram as many Hu-Bots as possible; (b) don't get killed; and (c) get the hell out of there by 1:00 a.m. at the absolute latest, no matter what.

Because at 1:00 a.m.—if all goes according to plan—the skies will light up with our missiles.

We reach the city center in minutes and fan out. With a mask pulled over his face and three knives strapped to his belt, Zee Twelve leads his brigade to the communications hub. Dubs's dad, wasted as usual, follows them, gripping a broken beer bottle to use as a shiv. Said he was afraid he'd shoot his own foot off if we gave him a gun.

Mikky, KrisBo, and I race for a nearby apartment tower. Our particular mission: to radically increase the size of our rebel army.

Leave the killing to the Reserve thugs, J.J. told me the last time I saw him. *Use that brain of yours, and stay safe.* Then he'd smiled—like he actually cared about my chances of survival.

The three of us have a straightforward plan. KrisBo and Mikky will fire stun darts into the unsuspecting Hu-Bot residents, and then I'll reprogram them, reconfiguring their synthetic synapses and giving them access to a new moral code. When they wake up—assuming I've done my job right— they'll be on *our* side. Isaiah, Sergeant Macy, and a Hu-Bot acolyte are doing the same thing in other buildings.

Because, for all their superhuman strength, the Hu-Bots have an essential weakness: with the right skills, you can hack them just like a computer.

"Are you done yet?" Mikky whispers urgently, leaning over an unconscious Hu-Bot.

It's a straightforward plan, yes, but it's time consuming. I don't have all my usual lab equipment, so I'm doing things manually, with my crappy old Q-comp. The Hu-Bot moans in her dart-induced sleep. KrisBo's getting jumpy.

"Hurry!" she cries.

Code flashes on the tiny screen as the new beliefs get delivered: Humans are not the enemy. The premier is the enemy. Rise up and turn yourself against him.

When I finally disconnect, Mikky nods briskly at me. "That took almost three minutes," she says. "Next time make it one."

I give her the finger affectionately as I bend over another sleeping form. We've got an hour, max. If I can get my speed up, between Isaiah, Macy, and me, we might make 150 new recruits—not bad. In fact, I'm starting to feel pretty good about our chances.

But then the building's alarm system goes off.

"What the hell?" Mikky cries.

The siren's so loud, it's like there's an ambulance careening around inside my skull. I cringe, resisting the urge to cover my ears, trying to make the final adjustments to this Hu-Bot's synaptic chain.

Charging footsteps above us knock plaster from the ceiling. I taste the dusty grit in my mouth. The Hu-Bot stirs. Not even a stun gun can compete with the pandemonium.

"Hush, little skin job, don't say a word," I murmur through clenched teeth.

I'm almost done—

"Are they coming for us?" KrisBo yells.

Mikky dashes to the window. "They're all running out-side!" she calls.

I make the last tweak to the Hu-Bot, and then I fling my hands in the air. "What are we supposed to do now?" I ask Mikky. I can't keep the bitterness and disappointment from my voice. "We can't freaking reprogram them when they're running away!"

Mikky shakes her head in dismay. "We have to move on. There's another apartment tower a quarter of a mile from here. Let's go!"

We race out a side door, hoping we aren't seen. The Hu-Bots may still be in their pajamas, but they could snap my spine in two in an instant. Luckily, they're too focused on evacuation rules to pay any attention to us.

KrisBo and I run a full block before I realize Mikky's not with us. I turn around, calling her name, and I see her just standing there.

"Come on, Mikky!" I shout, racing back toward her.

But she's frozen, staring at something. And tears are streaming down her face.

CHAPTER 78

MIKKY NO LONGER sees the flames; she doesn't notice the terrified, fleeing Hu-Bots. Her focus is entirely on a small figure limping toward her in the darkness.

The fragile silhouette is familiar in a way that sets all her warning systems ablaze. Her heart pounds in her ears. Could it be... her *sister*? KatBo? But it can't be her sister, because it has only one arm. Because it's dragging a leg like its kneecap's been shattered.

Mikky sways backward in shock. But then the figure raises its one arm to her, and a broken voice calls out her name. Mikky's pounding heart feels like it's stopped entirely. "Kat?" she cries. "*What happened?*"

Mikky rushes forward, pulling her little sister tight against her body, shielding her from the chaos all around them. Her greatest desire is to keep Kat from being hurt, though it's far too late for that.

"Who did this to you?" Mikky demands.

Kat looks up at her with wide, fearful eyes. "The commander took me from NyBo. He said that I was bad and full of glitches. But I'm not bad, am I?" She looks down at her missing arm, at the tangle of frayed wires sticking out from the stump, an expression of heartbreaking confusion on her face.

"Oh, Kitty Kat," Mikky says, barely keeping the sobs out of her voice, "we're going to make it better." She starts to lead Kat to the transport vans.

But Kat won't budge. "I heard them talking," she says rapidly. "They have a prisoner. A really important one. *This is a deathblow to the human animals.*' That's what the old one said. Then he laughed." She shivers, pitifully wrapping her one remaining arm around her shoulder.

"Who is the prisoner, Kat?" Mikky asks. But before the words are even out of her mouth, she realizes she knows the answer: the Hu-Bots have captured J.J.

The thought sends a violent shudder down her spine. Without their leader, what will the humans do? Six, as brave as she is, doesn't know how to command an army. And Mikky knows the human troops don't trust her enough yet.

Without J.J., the humans will give up. They'll run for the safety of the hills—where the Hu-Bots will hunt them down like animals, until every last human is gone.

Kat staggers, nearly falling, but Mikky keeps her upright. "I did good, didn't I? Because I told you about the prisoner?" Kat's wounded eyes meet hers. "Why did they hurt me, Mikky? Is it because of you?" Her voice is small and scared. Mikky feels like she's breaking in two.

"I don't know, sweetie," Mikky whispers, wiping the tears from her cheeks. "But everything is going to be okay. We can fix you, I promise. We'll make you even better than you were before."

"Like you?" Kat asks, her voice full of hope now. "Elite?"

Elite: the word makes bile rise in Mikky's throat. It doesn't mean what she once thought it meant. "Even better than me," she promises. "I have to go now, honey. Our vans are right up the street. They'll take you back to the compound for repair."

Of course, J.J.'s the only one who can rebuild Kat—which

is another reason Mikky must rescue him. She looks up to the Elite Tower penthouse. He's in there, she knows. Any minute now, they're going to kill him, if he isn't dead already.

Mikky takes one last minute to kneel on the ground in front of her sister. She folds Kat into her arms and tenderly kisses the top of her head. "Now go find KrisBo at the vans. She'll protect you."

As KatBo limps away, too dazed to even question why her brother is now a "she," Mikky thinks, *I wish someone could protect me.*

But no one can—she's on her own.

She starts sprinting to the tower. Her frenzied wrath drives her faster and faster, until her legs are a blur.

MosesKhan is going to *pay.*

CHAPTER 79

BUT HOW IS she going to get *in?*

The Hu-Bots have fortified the Elite Tower's defenses with alarming speed. Razor wire rings the entire perimeter, and behind it, the courtyard crawls with Bot soldiers. Spotlights scrape the ground, illuminating cases of ammo, flares, grenades—more than enough weapons to kill every last human on the planet.

And that is, of course, their end game.

Mikky crouches behind a van, holding her breath, calculating. She spots the sniper Bots, poised on the tower's balconies, scanning the night through their scopes. There's no way through the barricade.

Not at ground level, anyway.

Slowly and without a sound, Mikky creeps toward the side of the building. Bot soldiers stand shoulder to shoulder, their backs to the tower, their weapons—twenty-pound rifles capable of turning flesh into hamburger—cocked and ready.

Then, two stories above them, she sees an empty balcony. *There.*

The moment the spotlight sweeps past her, Mikky springs out from her hiding place. She sprints toward the barrier and the line of Bots behind it. As she sees their guns lift, she vaults into the air. Rocketing over the heads of the shocked Bots, she makes the twenty-foot leap to the balcony. She feels a flare of hot, white pain as a bullet grazes her calf.

She lands on the railing, teeters, and then pushes off, crashing through a window and into a deserted office. A warning strobe light begins to flash—a silent alarm, alerting the Bots to her whereabouts. Heart pounding in her ears, Mikky scuttles toward the hallway.

When she reaches the elevator, she pries open the heavy doors. She peers up and down into the darkness of the shaft and then wraps her fingers around one of the thick steel cables.

Synthesized adrenaline is surging through her, and she doesn't feel the wound in her leg anymore.

Mikky grabs the cable with both hands. Her feet wind around it, too, supporting part of her weight. Hand over hand, she begins to climb. The cable digs into her skin as she ascends, but she ignores it. The shaft is pitch-black, but she knows where to go: *Up.*

Up.

Up.

She can hear distant shouts—she knows that they're searching for her. But they won't think to look for her here.

Her arms shake with effort. The wound sends flaring pain signals to her neuromatrix.

At least I don't bleed, like a human, she thinks grimly.

Mikky lets out a yelp as she suddenly slides a few inches down the cable. Her bioskin is shredding into slippery ribbons from the relentless friction. She grits her teeth, sucks in a breath, and digs deep for her remaining strength. Steadily and painfully, she hauls herself up for the rest of the hellish ascent. All the way up to MosesKhan's penthouse office.

By the time Mikky reaches the top floor, the manufactured

muscles in her biceps scream in agony. She launches herself toward the wall of the elevator shaft, landing on the two-inch ledge in front of the elevator doors, and then pries them open from the inside. She falls onto the carpet, gasping for breath.

She's still for only a moment. Then she starts to get up, steeling herself for the fight to come.

Suddenly something jabs her between the shoulder blades. She knows without looking that it's the muzzle of a gun.

"Let's go," says a cold voice.

Mikky spins over, knocking the gun away as she springs to her feet. Three Elite Hu-Bot guards are right behind her—and two have their guns pointed right at her heart. She reaches for her own gun, tucked inside her belt.

"Don't fight," warns the tallest one, cocking his weapon audibly. "You've got no chance of winning."

Mikky's not so sure about that. But then the weaponless one raises his hand, palm up and out, in a gesture of peace.

"Think how sad your sister would be if we had to kill you right now," this Hu-Bot says. "You see, we sent her to find you. And she did!" He smiles thinly. "Not bad for a little one-armed traitor."

Fear and dread curdle in Mikky's stomach. This was never a rescue mission—it was a *trap*.

CHAPTER 80

SHOVED FORWARD INTO a large room by a squadron of faceless Bot-cops, Mikky stumbles, nearly knocking into MosesKhan himself. Her former commander stands with his muscular arms crossed, a look of smug satisfaction on his face.

"You should have stayed dead, ex-detective MikkyBo," he says, his lips curling in a snarl. "It would have been far more pleasant for you."

Anger courses through her like fire. She'd trusted this Hu-Bot, and he'd turned out to be a monster. "I had to come back so I could kill you," she says.

Khan gives a short bark of a laugh. "You thought you could come here and fight *me?*" he asks. "You thought I wouldn't be *expecting* you? I am a warrior. I commanded armies before you were a glimmer in your father's artificial eye."

"Why didn't you meet me yourself, then, *Commander?*" she challenges. "Why send your goons?"

MosesKhan stiffens; he's unused to defiance. "Those goons are better soldiers, better Hu-Bots, than you will ever be."

"If being an automaton is the highest form of Hu-Bot achievement," she retorts, "then you're probably right."

MosesKhan takes a threatening step toward her, but Mikky doesn't flinch. She lifts her chin and looks him straight in the eye. "Where's J.J.?"

MosesKhan's eyes travel up and down her body before he answers. "I don't know," he finally says.

Mikky's breath catches in her throat. He's telling the truth, she's sure of it. If Khan doesn't have J.J., does that mean he's safe? Was Kat lying about the prisoner?

"We'll find him, of course," MosesKhan adds. "With your help."

"The only help you'll get from me is a bullet to your brain," Mikky snaps. A Bot-cop reaches out and cuffs her on the side of the head; stars explode before her eyes.

"Your silly heroics are rather pointless, my dear," says a voice.

Mikky turns to see a short, balding Hu-Bot dressed all in black. His pale, fleshy face is intimately familiar to her: she pledged allegiance to his portrait every day at the Academy.

The premier is standing only six feet away from her.

He radiates power. Exudes menace. He has small, cruel eyes and small, gray teeth. "Despite your best efforts, it is time to exterminate the human animals, once and for all," he says coldly.

Without even thinking, Mikky yanks a gun from the

nearest Bot. As she swings the muzzle toward the premier's chest, her finger finding the trigger, two Bot-cops slam into her and knock her to the ground. She rolls sideways and scrambles to her feet, reaching for the gun in her boot. But two more Bot-cops grab her arms and restrain her.

A third holds a lethal Electroshock 900 two millimeters from her skull.

The premier gazes at her calmly. "Was that some kind of assassination attempt?" he asks. "That was *pitiful*. I see you would like to be exterminated, too."

"She deserves it," MosesKhan says, his face twisted with rage.

But the premier shakes his head. "No, what we will do to you, Mikky, is rather a bit more useful. And, as far as you're concerned, *worse*." He looks thoughtfully at her for a moment, and then he smiles. "But first, I thought you might like to say hello to another of our visitors."

A door opens, and into the room falls—

"NyBo!" Mikky shouts.

Her father looks up at her from the floor, his bruised eyes dull with pain. His hands are bound behind his back. There are deep gashes on his forehead and cheeks, frayed wires poking out, burn marks on his neck. He's been *tortured*.

He whispers, "Run...!"

CHAPTER 81

MOSESKHAN FEELS THE anger and desperation radiating off MikkyBo's flawless skin. He inhales the delicious scent of her fear, relishing it. "Why do you look so surprised, MikkyBo?" he asks. "Didn't your sister beg you to come save your traitorous father?"

Mikky looks as if she's blinking back tears.

How disgusting, Khan thinks.

"She didn't know who the prisoner was," Mikky whispers.

"Perhaps I shouldn't have tortured her so much," MosesKhan says ruefully. "It might have adversely affected her memory." Then he smiles cruelly. "But you came, didn't you? That's what matters. And now you will lead us to the rebels."

Mikky's eyes flash blue fire. "Let my father go," she demands.

The commander ignores her. "You really did surprise me, MikkyBo," he goes on. "I didn't expect betrayal from one as promising as you."

Her cheeks flush then, and she looks exquisitely beauti-ful. *What a waste of engineering,* he thinks.

He reaches into a drawer in his desk, pulls out a gleaming golden collar, and holds it up before her. "Remember this?" MosesKhan asks. "You were so proud to earn your Elite sta-tus. And look at you now, your neck as naked and vulnerable as a human's."

"Collars are for dogs," Mikky hisses.

As he approaches her, she twists and struggles in the grip of the guards. She gets an arm free and elbows one of them in the solar plexus, then flings her head back and smashes her skull into his nose. He grunts in agony.

Crack! Khan slaps her viciously across the cheek. Another guard presses his gun to her temple.

"You are important to the Hu-Bot cause, MikkyBo," MosesKhan says quietly. "The rebels trust you. And that will be their downfall."

She howls in rage as MosesKhan puts the cold metal col-lar around her neck and clasps it tight. "I'm not your slave!" she cries.

He shakes his head at her, disappointed. "You think you have a *soul,* don't you? You think you're *human.* You poor, deluded robot. You're nothing but circuitry and a pretty face."

"*You're* the robot," Mikky yells. "Mindlessly following orders of a psychotic dictator—a first-generation Hu-Bot that's got more glitches than me."

"Enough!" MosesKhan roars at her. Then his voice begins crooning again. "You know what happens now, don't you?"

Out of the corner of his eye, MosesKhan can see the pre-mier preparing to depart for his sanctuary in the Eastern

Zone. "Everything will be taken care of, sir," Khan reassures him.

The premier nods curtly as he departs.

Mikky tries to shrink from his touch, but there's nowhere for her to go. Keeping his hands at her throat, MosesKhan connects to the collar's interface.

He feels an electric jolt when he accesses Mikky's neural network, a sudden flash of power running through him like fire. He can feel her life force—its clean, pure fury. He's inside her mind, and the sensation is thrilling.

MosesKhan enters her encrypted memory files. Her programmed defenses are no match for his coding skills. Quickly, he introduces new information: Humans are responsible for all the world's ills. They are murderous, filthy, vile.

Mikky's eyes flutter back in her head. Her limbs spasm like she's being shocked.

She's still fighting him. Making it impossible for him to overwrite her data.

The commander curses softly. Focusing intently, he penetrates her system processors. He establishes a secure mind link. And then, though it's against protocol, he initiates an extra upload, a highly personal one: he transmits his own thoughts into Mikky. He corrupts everything he can access in her cortex with his own beliefs. Humans are vermin; they must be crushed under our boots.

Mikky shudders. Her breath comes fast and shallow, and her brow is damp with sweat.

There must be an end to the human pestilence. Now and forever.

When MosesKhan disconnects, Mikky falls forward into his arms. For a moment, he holds her shaking body. Then her eyes fly open, and she pushes herself away from him.

She regains her balance. Corrects her posture. One hand flutters toward the collar at her neck. She blinks at him— seems not to recognize his face.

Then suddenly Mikky's gaze comes into focus, her ice-blue eyes alert. Her hand snaps up in a crisp salute.

"Commander Khan," she asserts. "Assignment confirmed. All the remaining human *filth* in the capital are to be exterminated immediately."

MosesKhan feels an electric frisson of pleasure at her words. The hate in her voice is as real as his own. As he meant it to be.

"On your command, I will lead the purge," she says, with a hint of the cold ambition that once made her Elite. "Until every last vermin has been destroyed."

CHAPTER 82

MIKKY STANDS TALL, as proud as she can look in her dirty clothing. Her commander holds out his gun — his very own — and she humbly accepts it, bowing down in gratitude.

She has been forgiven.

She straightens and offers him a competent, merciless smile. "Sir," she says briskly, "who shall I terminate first?"

A noise from the hall makes MosesKhan turn and look expectantly at the door.

A moment later, it bursts open, and a *creature* is dragged into the room. A spitting, hissing *thing* that seems like a cross between an adolescent girl and a jackal. It curses and flails, but the two Hu-Bot guards hold it steady, unperturbed by such feeble, animal attempts to escape.

"Get your fake-ass hands off of me, skin job," it screams. "I'll yank your circuits right out of your neck!" Then the figure looks up through its tangled hair and sees Mikky. Its eyes widen in shock and relief. "Mikky!" it cries. "Help me!"

Mikky goes rigid. She recognizes the human now: 68675409M, the Corvette thief. The one who caused her fall from grace. Her grip tightens on the gun.

MosesKhan steps forward, the hint of a smile playing about his lips. "You know what to do now, MikkyBo," he says. He gestures toward the revolver in her hand. "Make it hurt," he tells her, loud enough for the human to hear.

Mikky nods. Considers which extremity to hit first. Would the stomach hurt more than the knees, or would she die too quickly? She palms the gun, feeling its heft. A .44 Magnum cartridge, she guesses: powerful enough to shred the girl like a grenade.

At such close range, Mikky's going to have to work hard *not* to kill the girl immediately. She licks her lips. Aims for a kneecap...

"Mikky, don't do it," the girl says desperately. "This isn't you. They've done something to you."

Mikky's focus doesn't waver. "Correct. They have repaired my problematic glitch," she says tonelessly.

68675409M shakes her head. "No, Mikky, that's not true. Don't let them take control," she says urgently, her sweaty desperation coming off her in pungent waves. "I *know* you. You're not a robot—you're a *person*."

Person? Mikky thinks, nearly chuckling as she cocks her weapon. With an insult that hateful, the human is clearly begging to die.

CHAPTER 83

MIKKY STARES AT me with scorn and disgust—like I'm a pile of dog crap she just stepped in.

"I am a Hu-Bot," she says. Her voice goes flat as she recites the Hu-Bot pledge. *"It is my duty to preserve and protect my race. It is my pleasure to follow the orders of my comm—"*

"Stop!" I cry, lunging forward against the guards' grip. "You love ice cream, Mikky, and you hate scrambled eggs! You like your toast buttered on both sides, which I always told you was weird and crazy." The guards yank me back again, twisting my arm behind me. "You're afraid of spiders, and you think running up and down stairs is fun—which is even *more* weird and crazy!"

Mikky blinks at me. Her face is expressionless. Robotic. *She has no idea what I'm talking about.*

A guard slaps his hand over my mouth, but I pull my head

away and keep talking. I've got to get through to her. It's my only chance.

"Let her go," Mikky says quietly.

The guards release me, and for a second, I feel a flare of hope that she's realized she's on *my* side. But, even as I stand before her, she lines up her shot, this time at my chest.

I don't break contact with her unreal blue eyes. Keep trying to find the humanity I know is in there.

"We've been through so much together, Mikky. I'm not just another human to you—I'm *Six*. Your Sixie! Remember

how I saved you from the river?" I can hear my voice crack. "Remember how you carried me up the mountain in your arms?" And suddenly I feel tears streaming down my face, hot and wet. My heart feels like it's going to burst.

And maybe it's because I'm about to die. Or maybe it's because I'm finally saying what I was too afraid to say before now.

"Mikky, no one ever cared for me like that before," I tell her. "And I've never felt about anyone the way I feel about you."

But it's like pleading to a statue.

"Quiet!" Mikky commands.

I take a step forward, and the guards don't pull me back this time. I guess they figure I'm as good as dead already.

"You believe in what's right—you always have." I'm not sure what I'm saying, if it's working, but I keep going. "You're stubborn and ornery and beautiful and weird. I've never met anyone like you."

I swallow down the huge lump in my throat. "I'm sorry I never told you this before. But..." I take a deep breath. It's a lifetime since I said this to anyone, but I need to, even if she doesn't care.

"I love you, Mikky. I don't know how it happened, but I do."

The gun trembles in Mikky's hand. She quickly steadies it, and it's still pointing at my chest. But that little waver gives me hope. I take another step toward her.

"*I love you,*" I say again, and I can't believe how much I mean it, almost as if it's a physical force pushing its way out of me. We're inches away from each other now. I reach out to touch her perfect face. She flinches. "I love you," I repeat— then I grasp her gleaming gold collar.

And rip the fucking thing right off her neck.

There's a nanosecond of frozen silence before she realizes what I've done. Then—

The muzzle of the gun flashes a hot white, and there's an ear-splitting *boom*.

I fall back onto the floor and wait for the pain.

Mikky stands before me, a look of shock on her face. Behind us, one of the Hu-Bot guards is down, sparks shooting from his shredded mechanical guts.

Mikky didn't shoot me—she shot the guard!

Then she turns the gun on MosesKhan. His cold black

eyes widen in shock. "Detective MikkyBo!" he yells. "Stand down!" He reaches for his weapon, raising his other hand like a shield.

But Mikky fires again. The bullet tears through his artificial hand and then his hardwired heart. She shoots another round, then another. And MosesKhan, the commander of the Hu-Bot army, falls to the floor, a jumbled mass of smoking wires where his head used to be.

I watch in disbelief.

Relief.

I want to run to Mikky and hug her. *Thank* her. Tell her I love her again. But then, through the tall windows, in the far distance, I see something.

J.J.'s rockets, streaking right for us.

It's 1:00 a.m. Time's up.

CHAPTER 84

THE CHANCES OF *getting out of this building alive were always pretty much zero.* That's my first thought.

Three subsonic cruise missiles, launched from the hills above the City and loaded with God knows how many pounds of explosives, are heading right for us. *J.J.'s final assault — and I'm at ground zero.* I think of Dubs and how he always wanted to go out in a blaze of glory. He would've appreciated this.

I've got, what, eight more seconds to live? My life doesn't flash before my eyes or anything, which I appreciate. Ten long years of suck are too depressing to relive.

The guards panic and run for the door.

"Mikky, save yourself!" shouts an older Hu-Bot from where he's lying on the floor, tied up. "The window! *Go!*"

She unfreezes, kneels by him. He whispers something to her, short and fast. She kisses his cheek, then comes running. To *me.*

The air fills with a whistling, roaring sound. I can't move a muscle — I'm frozen, watching death spiral toward me. The sky's lit by fire.

"Six!" Mikky screams, still coming at me, her blue eyes wide. I think she's going to stop, but she doesn't: her body slams into mine, knocking the wind out of me. We crash into the window, popping it out of its frame. *And we keep on going.*

Behind us, there's a flash of light, and then a terrible *boom* that seems to shatter every bone in my body and drive ice picks into my eardrums.

There's a moment of perfect weightlessness — and then we plummet toward the ground below the skyscraper. Mikky, her jacket on fire, looks like a comet falling down from the night sky. The wind roars in my ears, pulls at my clothes. Makes teardrops gather in my eyes, then whips them away. Tumbles me over and over like a broken toy.

I want to scream, but I can't get enough air into my lungs. Panic rushes through me. *This can't be happening.*

We're spinning through the air, being dragged down by gravity's terrible force. My teeth are clenched like a vise, waiting for the impact that's going to slam into me, wipe my soul from the face of the earth. *How long do I have?*

But Mikky reaches out for me. Grabs my arm and pulls me toward her, on top of her. Holds me tight. I curl my arms around her so she can't leave me.

At least I won't die alone.

Above us, the Elite Tower explodes into a giant cloud of ash. Slabs of concrete come thundering down. The earth rushes up toward us, faster and faster. I'm screaming now, and so is Mikky.

This is it.

The last things I'll ever see: the black awning of the Elite Tower entrance, below us. Mikky's terrified blue eyes. My hand, held out like I could break my fall.

Boom.

CHAPTER 85

EVERYTHING'S PITCH-BLACK. MIKKY can't move: she's pinned under the rubble of the tower. She breathes in dirt and metal and smoke—and something much worse. Something that smells like burning flesh. How long has she been unconscious? Minutes? Hours? *Days?*

Her breath comes quicker. "Six?" she calls.

There's no answer.

"Six!" she yells, her voice muffled by concrete. "SIX!"

She starts to hyperventilate. Dust from the rubble sears her lungs. She coughs, and the spasms feel like they're splintering her ribs. "Six!"

Mikky hears a rumble, and then a heavy, thudding crash—the sound of the ruined building caving in. How long will the concrete above her hold? How long until she runs out of oxygen?

Her fingers claw at the debris, trying to loosen it. She feels the skin of her fingertips being torn away by the rough stone, but she doesn't care. She manages to free her forearm, and so she reaches out into the cramped dark, searching for her friend.

Sixie, where are you? she thinks. *I had you in my arms!*

The building's bearing down on her, pressing the air from her lungs. A chorus of pain sings in every single engineered nerve.

Then, finally, her fingers touch something soft. Mikky reaches farther. Raw fingertips snag cotton. She presses down. Feels, underneath the fabric, *flesh*.

"Six!" Mikky calls again. "Six, are you alive?"

When there's no response, Mikky pinches Six's arm.

Still: nothing.

Mikky is too devastated to cry. She's lost her father and her best friend. A cold, aching emptiness spreads inside her. She knows she should try to work her way out, but she can't summon the energy.

So much easier, she thinks, *to expire. So much better.*

She lays back, mentally running through all the scenarios, but the outcome is always the same.

Six is dead.

Six is *dead*.

The tough, infuriating, and extraordinary human girl she's come to care about—gone. And no amount of J.J.'s expertise can save her.

Mikky reaches out for that square inch of human flesh. She pinches again. Harder. Grunting and sobbing with the effort, she does it again. And again.

Then comes a tiny sound—like a whisper. Mikky stops, holds her breath; even her heart feels like it stops beating.

"Mikky?"

That voice. *It's Six. She's alive.*

Relief floods Mikky's system, overwhelming her. "Are you all right?"

"Quit fucking pinching me," Six manages.

Mikky laughs. "Can you move?"

"No. I can barely breathe. I'm really claustrophobic—I can't—Mikky—" Six's voice gets choked off by panic.

"You have to stay calm," Mikky insists, keeping a steady hand on Six's arm.

"There's something on my chest," Six gasps. "I'm hot. I can't feel my legs."

Mikky can hear desperate, ragged breaths coming from Six's mouth. "Calm down—everything's going to be fine. They're going to rescue us," Mikky says firmly. She won't think about other possibilities: that no one will come, or that when they do, they'll be too late.

"*Who's* going to rescue us?" Six coughs. "There's a war going on."

"Someone will come," Mikky says with a confidence she doesn't feel.

"I'm afraid," Six whispers.

Mikky feels a burst of emotion she doesn't know how to describe. She reaches and finds a lock of Six's hair. Strokes it gently. "Everything's going to be okay," she says again. "Try to rest. Conserve your energy." *And your oxygen,* she adds silently. "We'll be okay."

Six lets out a muffled sob.

Mikky closes her eyes. She's scared and exhausted. But now that she knows Six is alive, she doesn't want to expire anymore.

Too bad the choice isn't hers to make.

She can barely hear Six's thready whisper. "I'm glad you're here with me."

Mikky pinches her again. "I'm not."

Six gives a raspy laugh, then quietly says, "No one's going to find us."

"Speak for yourself. *We're down here!*" Mikky screams, the sound filling their cramped space.

Six starts yelling, too, and neither of them stops until their throats are raw. Until they can't make another sound at all.

But their only answer is silence.

CHAPTER 86

THE ELITE TOWER is going to be my tomb. Dubs would not be pleased.

Panic like a knife in my chest. I'm panting so hard, I feel like I'm suffocating.

"Six," Mikky says, "breathe with me." She takes a long, slow inhale. "We should rest."

Screw that—I start screaming again. I'm going to yell until my throat bleeds. Then Mikky starts hollering, too, and knocking against the rubble.

I stop. I know the debris hasn't moved, but I feel a weight pressing down on me. Every drag of air I take feels heavy. I'm running out of oxygen.

As far as ways to go, I suppose this isn't the worst. I was never into blazes of glory anyway.

I reach over and stop Mikky from pounding her fists

against the concrete. Her bioskin is shredded down to the circuitry. Our fingers entwine.

I want to say good-bye. Thank you. So many things, but the words sound stupid in my head.

Then Mikky goes tense.

I can hear the thudding of my heart. And then the sound I wasn't expecting to ever hear: the metallic scrape of shovels. *Rescue.*

Mikky and I start screaming until I'm nearly hoarse. Their answering shouts make tears well up in my eyes. *They found us.*

It takes sixteen people, plus a backhoe, to get the building debris off us. The sun's just peeking over the tops of the destroyed buildings when we're finally pulled from the rubble. I take a deep breath, and the sudden rush of oxygen makes me dizzy.

I blink in the light, flooded with relief. *I can't believe we made it.*

But in the distance, I hear the pop of gunfire. I turn to KrisBo, the leader of our rescue crew. Her makeup is long gone, and a gash over her cheek reveals the lattice of her engineered muscles. "Are we still fighting?" I croak.

Her strong arms lift me onto a stretcher. "The city center is ours. But there's a Hu-Bot brigade holding steady on the edge of town."

Mikky limps over, her clothes in tatters and her black hair gray with dust. I've never seen someone look beautiful and terrible at the same time—until now. "Is it broken?" she asks, pointing to my leg.

KrisBo nods. "I think so."

I half sit up on the stretcher, grimacing from the pain. "We have to go."

"Go where?" Mikky asks.

"To the battle," I say through gritted teeth.

"No," KrisBo says. "We have to get you to the compound. To J.J."

So the old bastard's still alive!

And *I'm* still alive, too—which means I'm going to keep fighting.

Mikky frowns at me. "Six, you're in no shape to—"

"I don't need two legs to hold a gun," I interrupt firmly.

She gives me a look. I give her one right back. I am not backing down. I helped start this fight, and now I'm going to help end it.

Eventually she nods briskly. She turns to KrisBo. "We'll go," she says.

KrisBo shakes her head, but she doesn't argue.

When we reach the edge of the City, we find a tattered band of humans in a standoff against three hundred Hu-Bots barricaded inside an old factory. When our side sees us, an enormous cheer bellows up.

Trip lets out a shriek so loud, I wince, and then she fires her gun into the air.

"Aim at the enemy, idiot!" I shout. It feels unbelievable to be *laughing* again.

Seeing us—two leaders they thought were gone—lifts everyone's spirits. We move closer to the building, ducking behind piles of bricks and collapsed pillars. Kris hands out more guns she looted from the arms museum: Lugers and AKs and Uzis. Zee Twelve gets his hand on an assault rifle so big, he can barely lift it.

Mikky props me up so that I'm shielded behind a

burned-out van, and I aim my weapon and fire it like there's no tomorrow. My ears ring. The air fills with the acrid smell of gunpowder.

I fire and fire and fire until I can't hold up my arms anymore. Until smoke billows out of the Hu-Bot barricade. Until the darkness comes over my eyes, and I fall back, senseless.

CHAPTER 87

I NEVER THOUGHT I'd see this day.

Celebrating humans throng the streets. Tens of thousands of us, *congregating*—an act that was outlawed for a decade. Some of the kids have bottle rockets. Others carry bags of shredded paper, which they throw in the air like confetti. Music blares from jerry-rigged speakers, the deep bass echoing off the empty buildings.

Out on the main thoroughfare, though, there's a long, slow parade of the defeated as the last of the enemy Hu-Bots are led out of the City. Their beaten-down shuffle is familiar to me: it's the way I used to walk when I was a Rezzie.

Now I want to jump up and down and cheer. But, unfortunately, my new crutches make that impossible.

"Too bad we can't just engineer you a new tibia," Mikky says, eyeing the cast that stretches from my toes to my knee. "Fix you up as fast as we fixed up Kat."

"Tell me about it," I groan. I'll be wearing this thing for months.

"We could get you some other improvements, too," she says brightly. "Like better lung capacity and greater adrenaline stores."

I laugh. "Yeah, I could be the first human–Hu-Bot hybrid."

J.J., who's standing a few feet away from us, raises his eyebrows at me.

"I'm joking," I tell him. "Don't get any ideas."

He smiles.

Mikky and I turn back to the Hu-Bot procession. As I watch our former overlords disappear into the brown wasteland, my heart surges with hope. The City is ours now, the way it was before the Great War.

We call it New Denver.

Sure, craters pockmark the roads, and the buildings are missing most of their windows. The place is a disaster. But I'm from the Reserve, so I'm used to disasters. Compared to that shit hole, this bombed-out street looks like freaking Disneyland.

I'm humming along to the music when a hush falls over the crowd. Someone turns off the speakers. I look at Mikky in confusion. She shrugs.

The silence is strange, expectant.

Mikky stands on her tiptoes, craning to see. Whispers, "Oh!"

"What?" I demand.

But a moment later, I can see for myself. A long, black limousine crawls up the street, following the retreating Bots. There's a ragged Hu-Bot Nation flag still mounted on its hood. Next to the flag is a charred-looking loudspeaker.

A vision flashes before my eyes: Dubs and I, in the market square, our faces pressed to the ground as those three dreaded words seared our souls. "HUMANS, BOW DOWN!"

For a split second, I wish for a gun. I'd blast that loudspeaker to pieces. Even though I know I don't need to—not anymore.

The limo comes to a stop, and a door opens. Someone steps out.

Beside me, Mikky gasps. Grabs my shoulder. "It's the premier!"

J.J. nods curtly. "He was captured as he tried to escape the City. Now he joins his soldiers in exile."

But, for a defeated leader, he looks...*smug*. He scans the crowd, his features twisted by hate. "You will be cut down like the animals you are!" he bellows.

Two of his guards try to push him back into the car, but he resists. Mikky and I watch in disbelief as the premier keeps screaming at the crowd. He raises his fists at the gathered humans—as if he could somehow kill them all himself.

"You have not won!" he yells. "This is not over! The Hu-Bots will triumph!"

Then he turns to climb back inside his car. But he hasn't even ducked his head when a single shot rings out.

For a moment, nothing happens. Then the expression on the premier's face changes. Instead of rage, there is shock. Confusion. Pain.

The premier looks down at his stomach. There's a bullet hole in it. *And blood is pouring out.*

Red blood. *Human blood!*

I inhale sharply, grabbing Mikky to steady myself. *What the—?*

KrisBo steps out of the crowd and stands facing the premier. There's a gun clutched in her manicured hand.

"Will that do?" she asks the premier in her deep baritone. "Or do you need another shot from the walking glitch?"

The premier opens his mouth, but he doesn't answer her. Instead, he falls face forward onto the pavement. His legs twitch and spasm. Then they go still.

I turn to J.J., who's nodding slowly. Like he knew it all along.

That our greatest enemy was one of our own.

I poke him in the leg with one of my crutches as the guards silently lift the body of their former leader into the car. "Holy crap, old man," I bark. "Is there anything else you aren't telling me?"

A shadow passes over my grandfather's worn face. He shakes his head. "Come with me. You and Mikky both."

CHAPTER 88

J.J. WALKS OVER to his beloved piece-of-crap jeep and motions for us to get in. We do, but then he doesn't turn on the engine. He just stares out the windshield.

And eventually, he begins to talk.

"Yes, the premier is human," he says quietly. "Why? Because no Hu-Bot is capable of cruelty in the way a human is. Nor can they rival us in treachery. They simply weren't engineered to understand deception—whereas humans have been perfecting this terrible art for thousands of years."

"Thanks for the history lesson, Gramps," I say. "But I get the feeling there's something else."

J.J. exhales slowly. "Your brother has fled," he says. "We believe he has gone to the Central Capital City to join forces with the Hu-Bot settlement there."

My stomach feels like it's fallen down to the floor of the jeep. "What?" I gasp.

"No," Mikky whispers.

"Who knows what damage his incarceration caused?" J.J. asks. "Maybe he, too, has been reprogrammed, in a way." Then he looks right at us. "It doesn't matter. There will always be informants. We will always have enemies."

I can't take it; I fumble my way out of the jeep. J.J. calls for me to stop, but I need space to think, to process this awful knowledge. I hobble over to a small rise overlooking New Denver.

A moment later, Mikky appears next to me. Together we stare down at what looks like the beginning of a spontaneous human–Hu-Bot parade. Reservers, Reformers, and their reprogrammed former enemies are walking arm in arm, waving signs that say WE THE PEOPLE!

I can even see my sister down there, arm linked with a towering, golden-haired Hu-Bot. The dude looks like freaking Apollo.

We the People: the first three words of our old constitution and now the rallying cry of the new human–Hu-Bot alliance. It's almost too much for me to take in.

Mikky puts her arm around my shoulders. Her skin is warm, and she smells like lilacs.

"I should have left him in prison," I say bitterly.

Mikky shakes her head. "Don't think about it," she urges. "There's nothing you can do about his choice. So pay attention to this." She sweeps her arm out, taking in all the happy, cheering people and their smiling, demurely clapping Hu-Bot friends.

When I don't say anything, she puts her hands on my shoulders and turns me around so I'm facing her.

"Or pay attention to me," she says.

Her blue eyes search mine. They're the exact same color as the sky.

Mikky steps closer to me. "When I thought you were dead," she whispers, "I wanted to die, too. But I knew that wasn't going to happen. So I decided I would never feel anything again. I would become what I was before: a robot."

A tear glistens in the corner of her eye. I reach out and wipe it away.

For the first time in a decade, I begin to let down my

guard. "You were never a robot, Mikky," I say softly. "Not to me."

She smiles then. Its beauty lights up her face and everything around her, and I feel something inside me release. How can I explain it? It's like there was always a clenched fist in my chest, and now that fist is opening.

Now . . . it's just a girl's hand.

"Mikky," I say, "what does a joy rush feel like?"

I didn't think it was possible, but her smile grows wider. "It feels like this," she says simply.

And I don't understand it, exactly, but I'm a Rezzie girl: I'm used to uncertainty.

I think of all Mikky and I have been through, and I know one thing: we're in this together. Right now, and whatever comes next.

The music swells again, filling the bright and glittering air. Nothing at all is certain except that we're free.

For now, we are free.

HOW CAN YOU PROVE YOUR INNOCENCE WHEN YOU CAN'T REMEMBER THE CRIME?

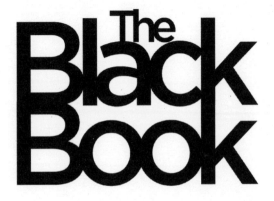

FOR AN EXCERPT, TURN THE PAGE.

PATTY HARNEY STOPS her unmarked sedan two blocks shy of her destination, the narrow streets packed with patrol cars, the light bars on top of the units shooting a chaos of color into the night. Must be twenty squad cars at least.

Patty ditches her car, puts the lanyard around her neck, her star dangling over her T-shirt. The air outside is unseasonably cold for early April. Still, Patty feels nothing but heat.

She runs a block before reaching the yellow tape of the outside perimeter, the first officer stepping forward to stop her, then seeing her star and letting her past. She doesn't know that perimeter cop, and he doesn't know her. All the better.

Getting closer now. The sweat stinging her eyes, the T-shirt wet against her chest despite the cold, her nerves jangling.

She knows the condo building even without following the trail of police officers to the place where they're gathered under the awning outside. One of those cops—a detective, like Patty—recognizes her, and his face immediately softens.

"Oh, Jesus, Patty—"

She rushes past him into the lobby of the building. It's more like a funeral than a crime scene, officers and plainclothes detectives with their eyes dropped, anguished, their faces tear-streaked, some consoling each other. No time for that.

She works her way toward the elevator, casting her eyes into the corners of the lobby for security cameras—old habit, instinct, like breathing—then sees a group of techies, members of the Forensic Services Division, working the elevator, dusting it for prints, and she spins in her gym shoes and pushes through the door to the stairs. She knows it's on the sixth floor. She knows which apartment.

She takes the stairs two at a time, her chest burning, her legs giving out, a riot breaking out in her stomach. Woozy and panicked, she stops on the third-floor landing, alone among the chaos, and squats down for a moment, grabbing her hair, collecting herself, her body trembling, her tears falling in fat drops onto the concrete.

You have to do this, she tells herself.

She motors up the remaining stairs, her legs rubbery, her chest burning, before she pushes through the door to the sixth floor.

Up here, it's all business, photographs being taken, evidence technicians doing their thing, blue suits interviewing neighbors, and Ramsey from the ME's office.

She takes a step, then another, but it's as if she isn't moving forward at all, gaining no ground, like she's in some circus house of horrors—

4

"Can't go in there."

"Patty."

"Detective Harney. Patty!"

A hand taking hold of her arm. As if in slow motion, her eyes move across the face of the Wiz, the bushy mustache, the round face, the smell of cigar —

"Patty, I'm — Mary, mother of God — I'm so sorry."

"He's...he's..." She can't bring herself to finish the sentence.

"They all are," he says. "I'm sorry as hell to be the one to say it."

She shakes her head, tries to wrangle her arm free.

"You can't go in there, Patty. Not yet."

The Wiz angles himself in front of her, blocking her from the door.

She finds the words somehow. "I'm a...I know how to... handle a crime scene."

A crime scene. Like this is just another act of violence she would encounter in the course of her job.

"Not this one, Detective. Not yet. Give us a chance to — Patty, c'mon —"

She bats away his hands, drives him backwards. He struggles for a moment before he braces her shoulders.

"Patty, please," he says. "Nobody should see their brother like this."

She looks into his eyes, not really seeing him, trying to process everything, thinking that he's right, that she doesn't want to see him, because if she doesn't see him he won't be dead, he won't really be gone —

The *ding* of the elevator.

But—the elevator's been taken out of service. The boys with FSD were dusting it. Who's using the elevator? Someone must have pulled rank—

Oh—

"Chief of Ds is here," someone says.

She looks over Wizniewski's shoulder.

The tall, angular figure, those long strides, the beak nose—which she did not inherit.

"Dad," she says, the word garbled in her throat, feeling every ounce of control vanishing.

Her father, chief of detectives Daniel Harney, a sport coat thrown over a rumpled shirt, his thinning hair uncombed, his eyes already shadowed. "Baby," he says, his arms opening. "Oh, my little angel."

"Is it true, Dad?" she speaks into his chest as he holds her tight, as if he would know, as if she's a toddler again, looking to her father for all the answers in the universe.

"I want to see him," says her father, not to her but to Wizniewski. He locks arms with Patty, as if escorting her down the aisle, and turns toward the door.

"I understand, sir," says the Wiz, "but it's—it's not—brace yourself, sir."

Her father looks down on her, his face bunched up, a dam holding back a storm. She nods back to him.

His voice breaks as he says, "Lead the way, Lieutenant."

SHE CLICKS OFF something in her mind and flicks on a different switch. She will be clinical. She will be a detective, not a sister. She will view a crime scene, not her dead twin brother. Clutching, clinging with all her might to her father's arm, stepping onto the tiled entryway of the condo.

She knows the place. It opens into a great room, a small kitchen to the left, bedroom and bathroom in the back. Pretty standard high-rise condo in Chicago, anyway, but she knows this one in particular. She's been here before.

The first time was yesterday.

The apartment goes immediately silent, as if someone raised a hand for quiet. Everyone busy at work dusting or photographing or collecting samples or talking—everyone stops as the chief of Ds and his daughter, a detective in her own right, enter the room.

Patty does her detective thing. No sign of struggle in the front room, the main room. Furniture in place, the tile shiny and clean, no sign of activity other than what the detectives and technicians are doing.

Someone had turned the air conditioner on full blast, the air good and cool, which should moderate lividity—

Lividity. My brother's dead body.

"It's in the bedroom," says Wizniewski, leading the way. "Now, I can't let you go in there, Chief, you understand that. You're the immediate family of one of the—"

"I just want to see. I won't walk in, Lieutenant." Her father, in that precise, resolute way he has of speaking, though she is probably the only one who recognizes the tremor in his voice.

Patty's eyes moving about, seeing nothing. Amy kept a clean apartment. She's seen, in her time, plenty of attempts to clean up a crime scene, and this shows no signs of recent scrubbing or spraying or incomplete attempts to wipe away smears or vacuum up debris. No violence happened in the great room or the kitchen.

Everything that happened happened inside the bedroom.

Red crime-scene tape, the inner perimeter, blocking access to the bedroom.

Her father delicately positions himself ahead of Patty, a protective gesture, allowing him the first look inside the bedroom. He leans over the red tape, takes a deep breath, and turns to his right to look inside.

He immediately squeezes his eyes shut and turns away, holding his breath, immobile. He swallows hard, opens his eyes—now deadened, filled with horror—and turns back and looks again.

He murmurs, "What in God's name happened here?"

She hears Wizniewski breathe a heavy sigh. "The position of the bodies, everything—it looks pretty much like what it looks like, sir."

Patty steels herself and angles past her father, looking into the room.

Three dead bodies. Kate—Detective Katherine Fenton—lying dead on the carpet, her eyes staring vacantly at the ceiling, a single gunshot wound over her right eye. A pretty clean shot, only a trickle of blood running from the wound, the rest of the blood following gravity's pull, probably leaving through the exit wound in the back of her skull, soaking the carpet beneath her, obscured by her auburn hair. Her Glock pistol lying just outside the reach of her left hand.

She focuses on Kate—not because she's never seen a dead body (she's seen dozens), and not because she liked Kate (she didn't), but because it's preferable to what else there is to see in the room, something that thus far has only leaked into her peripheral vision.

Two bodies on the bed—her brother Billy and Amy Lentini, each of them naked. Amy with a GSW to the heart, a single shot. Her body sprawled out, her head almost falling off the bed's left side, a large bloodstain barely visible behind Amy, where she bled out.

And then—

Billy. She fixes on him, her heart drumming furiously, heat spreading across her body as she looks at her twin brother sitting upright on the bed, blood streaked down the right side of his face, his head lolled to the side, his eyes closed and peaceful.

Take away the blood, the wound, and he could just as

easily be sleeping. He could do that in a way she never could. She's always had to sleep on her side, a pillow between her legs. Not Billy. He could sleep all night in a chair or sitting up in bed. He could catch some shut-eye in the middle of geometry class without making a single sound, without snoring or jerking or anything that would give him away—he could sleep in secret just as he could live in secret, just as he could do just about anything in secret. He could hide his fears, his emotions, his thoughts, his sorrows behind that implacable, genial expression of his. She was the only one who knew that about him. She was the only one who understood him.

You're just sleeping, Billy.

Please. It's me, Billy, c'mon. Pop open those eyes and say, "Surprise!"

Please be sleeping.

"Too early to know, of course," Wizniewski says to her father. "Sure looks like Detective Fenton walked in—on this, on them—and opened fire. Billy shot back. They killed each other. A fuckin' shoot-out at the OK Corral right here in the bedroom."

"Ah, Jesus."

No, Patty thinks to herself. *That's not what happened here.*

Her legs giving out, her head dizzy. An arm pulling her away, her father, and just as much as she dreaded seeing Billy, even more so now she dreads taking her eyes off him.

Her father pulls Patty back into the main room. The officers all stop what they're doing and stare at father and daughter as if they were museum exhibits.

Behind Patty, medical personnel slip past and head into the bedroom with body bags.

Body bags. She can't stomach the thought.

"We do this by the book," her father says to the room. "That's my son in there, yes, but he was a cop. Before anything else, he was a cop. A damn fine one. Honor him and Detective Fenton by doing this case right. By the book, people. No mistakes. No shortcuts. Be at your best. And get me—"

Her father chokes up. Solemn nods all around. Patty's chest burning, so hot she struggles to breathe.

"Get me a solve," her father finishes. "Solve this crime."

Suddenly feeling claustrophobic, Patty turns and heads for the door. *This isn't real,* she decides. *This didn't happen.*

"Oh, my God."

Just as she's at the door, she hears the words. Not from her father. Not from any of the officers in the main room.

From the medical personnel in the bedroom.

"We have a pulse! We have a pulse!" the man shouts. "This one's still alive!"

ABOUT THE AUTHORS

JAMES PATTERSON is one of the best-known and biggest-selling writers of all time. His books have sold in excess of 325 million copies worldwide. He is the author of some of the most popular series of the past two decades – the Alex Cross, Women's Murder Club, Detective Michael Bennett and Private novels – and he has written many other number one bestsellers including romance novels and stand-alone thrillers.

James is passionate about encouraging children to read. Inspired by his own son who was a reluctant reader, he also writes a range of books for young readers including the Middle School, I Funny, Treasure Hunters, House of Robots, Confessions and Maximum Ride series. James has donated millions in grants to independent bookshops and he has been the most borrowed author in UK libraries for the past nine years in a row. He lives in Florida with his wife and son.

Find out more at www.jamespatterson.co.uk

Become a fan of James Patterson on Facebook

EMILY RAYMOND has worked with James Patterson on *First Love* and *The Lost,* and is the ghostwriter of six young-adult novels, one of which was a No. 1 *New York Times* bestseller. She lives with her family in Portland, Oregon.

The brand new Alex Cross thriller.

CROSS THE LINE

Alex Cross chases a cold-blooded killer... with a conscience.

Shots ring out in the early morning hours in the suburbs of Washington, D.C. When the smoke clears, a prominent police official lies dead, leaving the city's police force scrambling for answers.

Under pressure from the mayor, Alex Cross steps into the leadership vacuum to investigate the case. But before Cross can make any headway, a brutal crime wave sweeps across the region. The deadly scenes share only one common thread – the victims are all criminals. And the only thing more dangerous than a murderer without a conscience, is a killer who thinks he has justice on his side.

As Cross pursues an adversary who has appointed himself judge, jury, and executioner, he must take the law back into his own hands before the city he's sworn to protect descends into utter chaos.

CENTURY

JAMES PATTERSON
BOOK**SHOTS**

stories at the speed of life

BOOK**SHOTS** are page-turning stories by James Patterson and other writers that can be read in one sitting.

Each and every one is fast-paced, 100% story-driven; a shot of pure entertainment guaranteed to satisfy.

Under 150 pages
Under £3

Available as new, compact paperbacks, ebooks and audio, everywhere books are sold.

For more details, visit: **www.bookshots.com**

BOOK**SHOTS**
THE ULTIMATE FORM OF STORYTELLING.
FROM THE ULTIMATE STORYTELLER.

Also by James Patterson

ALEX CROSS NOVELS

Along Came a Spider • Kiss the Girls • Jack and Jill •
Cat and Mouse • Pop Goes the Weasel • Roses are Red •
Violets are Blue • Four Blind Mice • The Big Bad Wolf •
London Bridges • Mary, Mary • Cross • Double Cross •
Cross Country • Alex Cross's Trial (*with Richard DiLallo*) •
I, Alex Cross • Cross Fire • Kill Alex Cross • Merry
Christmas, Alex Cross • Alex Cross, Run • Cross My
Heart • Hope to Die • Cross Justice • Cross the Line

THE WOMEN'S MURDER CLUB SERIES

1st to Die • 2nd Chance (*with Andrew Gross*) • 3rd Degree
(*with Andrew Gross*) • 4th of July (*with Maxine Paetro*) •
The 5th Horseman (*with Maxine Paetro*) • The 6th Target
(*with Maxine Paetro*) • 7th Heaven (*with Maxine Paetro*) •
8th Confession (*with Maxine Paetro*) • 9th Judgement (*with
Maxine Paetro*) • 10th Anniversary (*with Maxine Paetro*) •
11th Hour (*with Maxine Paetro*) • 12th of Never (*with Maxine
Paetro*) • Unlucky 13 (*with Maxine Paetro*) • 14th Deadly Sin
(*with Maxine Paetro*) • 15th Affair (*with Maxine Paetro*)

DETECTIVE MICHAEL BENNETT SERIES

Step on a Crack (*with Michael Ledwidge*) • Run for Your Life
(*with Michael Ledwidge*) • Worst Case (*with Michael Ledwidge*) •
Tick Tock (*with Michael Ledwidge*) • I, Michael Bennett
(*with Michael Ledwidge*) • Gone (*with Michael Ledwidge*) •
Burn (*with Michael Ledwidge*) • Alert (*with Michael Ledwidge*) •
Bullseye (*with Michael Ledwidge*)

PRIVATE NOVELS

Private (*with Maxine Paetro*) • Private London (*with Mark Pearson*) • Private Games (*with Mark Sullivan*) • Private: No. 1 Suspect (*with Maxine Paetro*) • Private Berlin (*with Mark Sullivan*) • Private Down Under (*with Michael White*) • Private L.A. (*with Mark Sullivan*) • Private India (*with Ashwin Sanghi*) • Private Vegas (*with Maxine Paetro*) • Private Sydney (*with Kathryn Fox*) • Private Paris (*with Mark Sullivan*) • The Games (*with Mark Sullivan*) • Private Delhi (*with Ashwin Sanghi*)

NYPD RED SERIES

NYPD Red (*with Marshall Karp*) • NYPD Red 2 (*with Marshall Karp*) • NYPD Red 3 (*with Marshall Karp*) • NYPD Red 4 (*with Marshall Karp*)

NON-FICTION

Torn Apart (*with Hal and Cory Friedman*) • The Murder of King Tut (*with Martin Dugard*)

ROMANCE

Sundays at Tiffany's (*with Gabrielle Charbonnet*) • The Christmas Wedding (*with Richard DiLallo*) • First Love (*with Emily Raymond*)

OTHER TITLES

Miracle at Augusta (*with Peter de Jonge*)

FAMILY OF PAGE-TURNERS

MIDDLE SCHOOL BOOKS

The Worst Years of My Life (*with Chris Tebbetts*) • Get Me Out of Here! (*with Chris Tebbetts*) • My Brother Is a Big, Fat Liar (*with Lisa Papademetriou*) • How I Survived Bullies, Broccoli, and Snake Hill (*with Chris Tebbetts*) • Ultimate Showdown (*with Julia Bergen*) • Save Rafe! (*with Chris Tebbetts*) • Just My Rotten Luck (*with Chris Tebbetts*) • Dog's Best Friend (*with Chris Tebbetts*)

I FUNNY SERIES

I Funny (*with Chris Grabenstein*) • I Even Funnier (*with Chris Grabenstein*) • I Totally Funniest (*with Chris Grabenstein*) • I Funny TV (*with Chris Grabenstein*)

TREASURE HUNTERS SERIES

Treasure Hunters (*with Chris Grabenstein*) • Danger Down the Nile (*with Chris Grabenstein*) • Secret of the Forbidden City (*with Chris Grabenstein*) • Peril at the Top of the World (*with Chris Grabenstein*)

HOUSE OF ROBOTS SERIES

House of Robots (*with Chris Grabenstein*) • Robots Go Wild! (*with Chris Grabenstein*) • Robot Revolution (*with Chris Grabenstein*)

OTHER ILLUSTRATED NOVELS

Kenny Wright: Superhero (*with Chris Tebbetts*) • Homeroom Diaries (*with Lisa Papademetriou*) • Jacky Ha-Ha (*with Chris Grabenstein*) • Word of Mouse (*with Chris Grabenstein*)

MAXIMUM RIDE SERIES

The Angel Experiment • School's Out Forever • Saving the World and Other Extreme Sports • The Final Warning • Max • Fang • Angel • Nevermore • Forever

CONFESSIONS SERIES

Confessions of a Murder Suspect (*with Maxine Paetro*) • The Private School Murders (*with Maxine Paetro*) • The Paris Mysteries (*with Maxine Paetro*) • The Murder of an Angel (*with Maxine Paetro*)

WITCH & WIZARD SERIES

Witch & Wizard (*with Gabrielle Charbonnet*) • The Gift (*with Ned Rust*) • The Fire (*with Jill Dembowski*) • The Kiss (*with Jill Dembowski*) • The Lost (*with Emily Raymond*)

DANIEL X SERIES

The Dangerous Days of Daniel X (*with Michael Ledwidge*) • Watch the Skies (*with Ned Rust*) • Demons and Druids (*with Adam Sadler*) • Game Over (*with Ned Rust*) • Armageddon (*with Chris Grabenstein*) • Lights Out (*with Chris Grabenstein*)

GRAPHIC NOVELS

Daniel X: Alien Hunter (*with Leopoldo Gout*) • Maximum Ride: Manga Vols. 1–9 (*with NaRae Lee*)

For more information about James Patterson's novels, visit www.jamespatterson.co.uk

Or become a fan on Facebook